THEN I'LL HAVE TO DECIDE WHETHER HE'S GOT 'EM OR NOT...

My heart races, escalating to jackhammer intensity as we glide through town, toward the house in which I hope to find my innocent and unsuspecting family—untouched.

The cabin stands nearly a mile past the edge of town, wedged behind several massive rocks and hidden from the road by tall evergreens. Sarah's car sits in the darkened, tree-covered driveway. I point it out to Eric. "They're here."

All the windows are dark. Straining to focus, I let my eyes adjust, but I can see only shadows.

Then, movement. A giant shadow, sliding catlike across the back of the kitchen, toward the bedrooms. A smaller shadow moves ahead of it and I bolt for the side door . . .

Eric's hand clamps my arm like a vise. "One chance," he whispers.

One chance. That's all I've got . . .

THE DEEP END

CHRIS CRUTCHER

ZEBRA BOOKS
KENSINGTON PUBLISHING CORP.

ZEBRA BOOKS are published by

Kensington Publishing Corp.
475 Park Avenue South
New York, NY 10016

Zebra and the Z logo Reg. U.S. Pat. & TM Off.

First Zebra Printing: January, 1994

Printed in the United States of America

To John and Candy,
but not necessarily John Candy

One

An Idaho mountain man from the start, I get to work early and pee in all the corners, as it were, establish myself as the lead wolf. That way if the day holds surprises, I'm waiting for them.

In my office I crank up the coffee machine and spread the morning *Review* across the pile of papers on my desk. I haven't seen its surface for more than five years. There are therapists here at the mental health center who could bowl on their desktops, or play shuffleboard, but I'm not one of them. At one point—maybe two years ago—I worked three weekends in a row, charted all my clients, terminated the deserters (some had stopped coming more than twenty-four months previously), and wrote every delinquent client report and letter to every state and private agency that had one coming. When all was said and done, a pile at least an inch and a half thick still covered the desk's surface: blurbs for upcoming trainings or new center procedural policies or enrollment information for noontime aerobics. My paper war obviously lost, I have never again tried to catch up.

I turn now to "Help Wanted" just as I have first thing every morning for the past five years. I'm forty-two and generally speaking I like my job, so it's not as if I want out of the mental health business, but knowing that I *can* get out allows me to stay longer, and probably to get in deeper.

Since the "Semi-skilled" section doesn't include a thirty-thousand-dollar-per-year position guarding some backyard wading pool on the South Hill, I turn to the sports and comics before working my way to the "Regional" section, where I can read which crimes occurring over the past twenty-four hours were committed by people I know. Domestic violence and drug-related crimes are staples in my business.

And there it is. Above the headline EASTSIDE CHILD MISSING—FEARED KIDNAPPED is Sabrina Parker. It's her school picture—Sabrina's a second grader—and her wide smile resembles a checkerboard for all the missing teeth. I linger on the photograph. *Damn.* Sabrina is Jerry Parker's older sister. The family is court-ordered into our therapy groups for victims and perpetrators of abuse and neglect. A year ago neighbors discovered Jerry, then age three, alone in his house. He had been there two days. His mother, Peggy, away on an alcoholic binge, claimed at the time she thought Jerry was with Sabrina at an uncle's.

The article goes on to describe a next-door neighbor telling police he heard something very late, around eleven-thirty or midnight, and looked out his bedroom window to see a man in an overcoat standing on Peggy's front porch. The man tried the door, then disappeared to the far side of the house. Peggy told police she heard nothing and had no idea what could have happened to her daughter. When she awoke yesterday morning, Sabrina was gone and Jerry was asleep in his room.

I know this family well. I know the neighborhood. I have a *bad* feeling, a feeling that Sabrina Parker is history, though it could be merely my general sunshiny outlook. God knows how Jerry will react to this.

The remainder of the article depicts community efforts to organize volunteer groups to aid in the search, and identifies gathering points. A shorter, accompanying article highlights the grieving mother, quoting Peggy on the difficulties of raising children alone and the danger that lurks everywhere today. My heart aches for her, deplores what she must be going through right now, but the nature of my job requires a certain hard edge of suspicion, and a small insistent voice in my head says there is more, and Peggy knows it. Much more. I have worked with Peggy Parker in both group and individual sessions and she is completely closed. She is a woman who presents her mental and emotional capacities far better than they really are, and it is not lost on me that she has pulled herself together for this interview as quickly as she has.

Whenever I encounter tragedy involving children, whether in the newspaper or through direct contact in my job, my mind races instantly to thoughts of my own kids. Are they safe? Can the bogeyman get to them? I know he can't, there are no mothers better than Sarah. But *I'm* not there. I was a competitive swimmer in high school and college and spent those summers as a lifeguard at a lake beach, and I was a *hawk*. Even during breaks I positioned myself to see the water. Something in me believed that as long as Wilson Corder stood watch, no one would drown. No one *could* drown. And in fact, the only drowning in the eight years I worked there, happened on my day off.

But I'm allowed to guard my own kids only every other weekend and on designated holidays, and though I know Sarah is every bit as caring and watchful as I am, still . . .

I fold the newspaper, glancing out the window at the 1100cc Honda Magna, which I hold responsible for my own mental health, and consider the swiftness with which things can change, the split second it takes to lose it all, to have your life's expectations crushed (a moment of inattention, one bad decision, one nighttime stranger allowed to prey upon your little girl), and I'm glad I own it. I laugh, thinking if we were still together, Sarah would have used just that argument *against* it, and she'd have been right.

I pick up the phone, dial her work number.

"Sarah Corder."

"Hi."

"Oh, hi, Wilson. Hold a sec, okay?"

I hold. Sarah is a manager in Women's Clothing at Blankenstein's, the largest and poshest department store in Three Forks. The Blankensteins are old Three Forks money and their store is famous statewide for service and taste. Major chains deal to buy them out almost yearly, but Stewart Blankenstein is a big duck in this pond of two hundred fifty thousand ducklings, and as loyal as his father before him. Women's Clothing is a big deal department in a big deal store, and Sarah is Top Gun. She's a very busy woman.

Several moments pass, then, "I'm back. What do you need?"

"Just checking in," I say, hoping to sound casual. "How the kids?"

"Just fine," she says. "You saw them two days ago. Did they look neglected?"

"God, was it just two days? Seems like longer."

"Nope. Just two days."

"They're okay, huh?"

"Wilson, what's wrong? I said they're fine." She pauses. "Oh. The girl in the paper. You know her?"

My chest surges and I force it back, waiting for my throat to clear, but Sarah knows me like a book—she

10

doesn't have to see my face to know what's on it. "Yeah," I say finally.

"She one of yours?"

"Yeah. And her brother. Her mom is in our adult group."

"I'm sorry, Wilson," she says. "I really am. It doesn't look good, does it? You think she's dead?"

In the first three years I worked here, we had one child death attributed to abuse in the county. This year alone we've had three and a near miss, and it's only late summer. For a while many of us in this business believed—or hoped—that the dramatic increase in abuse statistics was a result of greater public awareness. That was a nice thought, but when I want to know which way a trend is headed, I look to the cutting edge, and the cutting edge on violence toward women and children shows a frightening increase, not only in frequency but in ferocity and inventiveness. When I encounter a case I think can't be topped, I see three more like it and one that tops it. Children are being hurt in ways I couldn't have imagined ten years ago. And they're dying. It's as if there's a killing mood.

"Yeah," I say, "I think she's dead. Strangers in overcoats don't come in the dead of night to sell magazine subscriptions."

Sarah is quiet a moment, then softly, "Is there anything I can do?"

I laugh. "Just keep being the ferocious mother lion you are. Make sure my babies are safe."

"I always do."

Sarah doesn't take it personally anymore when I get nuts about work, which really isn't all that often considering my opportunities. She knows I don't really believe there's a problem with her supervision of the kids. In fact, it was *I* who pushed them to take risks, to leap from

11

the high dive and swim in the deep end before she thought they were ready, or go fast on their bikes or climb high rocks. It's just that I was *there*.

As I drop the receiver onto its cradle, Eric's snapshot, tacked just above my desk, catches my eye. A massive, hairy behemoth decked in dirty blue jeans and a black leather flight jacket cradles his two-year-old son in the crook of his elbow. The boy's eyes dance as he aims two fingers for Dad's nostrils, his spiked blond hair, studded earring, and sleeveless black T-shirt screaming out his father's rebellious message to the world. Eric and Little E—a true success story.

A knock on my office door.

"Come in."

Molly Comstock pushes the door open just wide enough for her head. Molly works the morning kids' group with me. She is a long, strong, dark-haired, earthy beauty with a cosmic edge who makes my life at the center hundreds of times better. "You about ready?"

"Just about." I look at my watch. "We've got five minutes." For someone who likes his work, I put it off as long as possible. We'll be in that room nearly three hours with fifteen kids between the ages of three and five, most poor, some underfed, many in foster care, and all hungry for their little piece of time with one of us to help find a safe path through their lives. Before the day is out we will work with an identical group of older kids and at least one group of parents. Our mental health center is the only game in the county for significantly abused and neglected kids whose parents have no resources for private help. I buy as many minutes as I can ahead of any given session to crank myself up.

Molly slides on in. "I think maybe we should take them in. It's pretty crazy in the waiting room."

12

"This is a mental health center," I say. "It's supposed to be crazy in the waiting room."

"Yeah, but this is crazy even for here. The place is buzzing with talk about Sabrina." She shakes her head. "Not a substantiated fact in the bunch, but the kids don't know that. I say we'll cut our work load later if we get the kids away from it now."

I'm up. *That* is good advice. "Did Peggy bring Jerry?"

Molly shakes her head again. "Huh-uh. But his cousin is here, and she looks a *mess*. Don't forget we're getting two new kids today, too. Twins. Supposed to be hell-raisers."

The race is on.

I leave the center around eight. Mondays, Tuesdays, and Wednesdays are killers. Along with the abuse groups I carry an individual client load of nearly fifteen adults and adolescents per week. As long as I'm willing to make my living in the arena of human pain, unemployment will never threaten me.

My bike stands waiting, like the true friend it has come to be. Carla, my supervisor, told me when I took this job I would need to make appointments with myself *for* myself, and that's what I'm doing now. I throw the saddlebags over the sissy bar and pull on my new impact-tested Bell helmet, wondering for a brief moment if they messed it up impact-testing it. I'm bothered sometimes thinking I might get the new car on which Inspector 6 performed twelve thousand test door slammings, visualizing a total structural collapse on the twelve thousand and first, like in cartoons.

Eight-thirty, and still the early August heat nearly stifles me as I climb onto the freeway, headed toward the flats out west of town, rather than toward the foothills of the Rockies. Three Forks is nestled in the hub of a smorgasbord of geography—a half hour one way to the base of majestic peaks, fifteen minutes another to lush farmland dotted with fruit orchards, forty-five minutes another to the rolling wheat fields of the Palouse.

It will be light until well after nine, and I take advantage of the bike's natural air conditioning, cranking it high. At eighty I unhook my chin strap and quickly jerk off the helmet, sliding it back over the sissy bar, before reaching into the saddlebags for my glasses. Shooting along in the far left lane, playing with a hundred, I rocket toward the setting sun. Traffic is light and I back off to glide across to the right-hand lane, then onto the Skyway Heights exit. Air Highway isn't a freeway, but at this time of day it's four lanes of nearly deserted roadway, recently widened and repaved to accommodate the air force and the farmers out west of town.

I float through the Heights—a small unincorporated area surrounding the air force base—within ten miles per hour of the limit, my right hand twitching on the throttle. A hundred and fifty yards outside the speed zone, I'm through all five gears, staring straight out at the narrow asphalt carpet stretching before me like an eternal runway. The hum of my tires soothes my heart, and with the low sun casting the eastern Washington scrubland in a golden blaze and the wind massaging my scalp like a heated lover, I open the throttle wide. I swear to God, at times like this I truly believe I can outrun what I know.

Two

"Hey, you guys." I can see my kids through the screen door, packing. Either a weekend's supply of entertainment takes up a lot more space than it used to, or I've become considerably less entertaining.

Emily looks up. She's fifteen now and sometimes it's hard to find the little girl in her. "Hi, Dad. You're early. That's good. You can help."

"Yeah, Dad," Trevor says. "You can help. Tell Em we're only gonna be there two days and she doesn't need to take her whole room over to your house." He points to her two athletic bags and the pile of clothes laid out over them. "One of us is gonna have to ride in the trunk." Trevor is ten and I have no trouble finding the little boy in him.

I smile. "You *are* going to have to change clothes a lot to wear all that in forty-eight hours," I say to her.

"I'm not going to wear it all, Einstein," she says to Trevor, though it's meant for me. "But I'm also not going to decide what to wear to the party tonight right this minute. Does that make any sense?"

"Makes sense to this Einstein," I say, "and if that other Einstein has a living brain cell left, it makes sense to him, too."

15

"That's right," Emily says with a quick warning look at Trevor. "It does."

"Let's go to Zips, okay?" Trevor says. "I'm hungry."

"Doesn't your mom feed you? It's nine-fifteen. I had breakfast two hours ago."

Sarah waltzes out of the bathroom in her robe. "I heard that. Why should I feed him? He only gets hungry again."

I say, "Hi."

"Hi." She walks over and touches my arm. Things are so much better than they were for the first two years following our separation, though nothing will completely repair the damage from that time. In some ways we may now be more intimate—though not physically—than we were when we were married, but that speaks more to our lack of intimacy then. Sarah couldn't tolerate my lifeguard mentality as it applied to her, but she also couldn't tolerate it as it applied to my clients or my colleagues when the cost was loss of family time. As I began drifting away, feeling unappreciated because the bullshit I had to offer was not the bullshit she wanted or needed, and being unable or unwilling to pass her constant tests of loyalty to home and family, I became *more* of a lifeguard with her, appearing to stroke close to save her when she wasn't drowning. In other words, if a little bit of dysfunction doesn't work, why not try a lot. It's embarrassing to me now that I look back at my actions, because they were empty, born of guilt—I would see it in a second in a marital session involving someone *else's* life— and I really don't do it much anymore, but Sarah had her part in it too and the truth is, we weren't much of a match. At least now that we understand it better, the "shoulds" are gone and our touches can mean what they mean. Her independence no longer means I'm a failure and my focus on my work no longer means I don't care

16

about my family—vicious myths put to rest. We have what I consider a relatively successful divorce. I feel remarkably fortunate to have come to this quieter place with her. She says, "Have any particular plans?"

"Thought I'd go home and take a nap. I have some old syringes they can play with."

"You're funny, Dad," Emily says. "You should go on TV. We could turn you off."

"You already turn *me* off," Trevor says to his sister. "Probably turn all the boys off pretty bad too."

"I may return with only one," I say to Sarah as I hoist both Emily's jock bags to my shoulder. "You have a preference?"

"Bring back the girl," Sarah says. "The boy needs a few years of freeze-drying, say maybe till he's thirty." She points her finger like a handgun at Trevor's head and looks at me. "It is not lost on me," she says, "that he has your exact sense of humor, such as it is."

"We had children too young," I say. "Remember that little dog we wanted? We should have settled."

"You *got* a dog when you got her," Trevor says, pointing at Emily, cackling at his own wonderful wit. "Got you with that one. Ooh, you're *burned.*"

"If you really burned me, you little four-eyed nose-wipe, you wouldn't have to point it out."

"And if he hadn't burned you," her mother says, "you wouldn't have to call him such a nasty name."

"Yeah," Trevor says, having been caught momentarily between the need to remain on the offensive and the urge to call foul on the slanderous remark about his glasses, and fold in a tearful heap. Sarah is a genius. If Trevor falls to his wounded stance, this could last forever, but she has given him a power boost. She isn't about to let something major erupt until the kids are safely in my care.

With Em and Trevor at the car, waiting, I drop the bags on the lawn. Sarah touches my arm again and asks if my week got any better.

I say not much. "You and Rob going somewhere for the weekend?"

"You kidding? No kids, a hundred degrees, and bright blue skies? We sure are going somewhere for the weekend. To a place where the sun always shines, no one skins their knees, and children don't bitch." She sends the last sentence to Trevor on a glare. Then back to me. "A friend of Rob's rented a houseboat over at Eisenhower Lake. We're leaving in about an hour. I plan to drink heavily."

"Have a good time," I say. "Tell Rob to keep his hands off my ex-wife."

"Too late," she says. "I've already told him to keep his hands on your ex-wife."

I nod, smiling, and say, "Either way," at the car, thinking now that most of the "ownership" issues are resolved, how much better I feel that Sarah is with someone with whom she can share her passion. When she believed she wasn't as important to me as a client in distress or a burned-out colleague fallen in a heap in my office two hours after quitting time, she began to lose her passion for me—said she couldn't be intimate with someone who didn't care as much as she—and I took mine elsewhere. For a while I thought I'd have to live with robbing her of it forever. It was hard at first, when she began seeing Rob. We hadn't been physical for more than a year, but the first time I called her house and he was there, I cheerfully cut the conversation short, lightly dropped the receiver onto its cradle, and sat in a dark room for more than two hours, stunned, watching head movies of a man I'd never seen gently caressing those tender areas that in thirty-seven years had been touched only by me. It felt exactly the same as the day after Christmas in 1951 when my mother made me let Bruce Landon play with my new truck. Even though I wasn't using it, I knew Bruce wouldn't treat it right and I stormed off to the bathroom and locked myself in.

The fight over the front seat has come to an abrupt and threatening end and Trevor sits pouting in the back declaring his sister's spot in Hell, when Sarah taps on the window, motioning me back to her.

"Trevor's having a tough time with this Sabrina Parker stuff," she says. "His scout troop went to help look for her last week. He slept with me the last two nights. You might leave a spot for him."

I close my eyes. I hate it when work and home come together.

"I think it was good for him," Sarah continues. "Mr. Woods told them the only way anyone would ever have to pay for this is if she's found. I think he feels a little less helpless, but all the kids in the neighborhood are scared to death."

I agree it's probably good that Trevor went out with other kids to look, but the part of me that has always wanted to shield my children from all evil has a pretty loud voice. I mean, I'm a therapist, for Christ's sake; I know experience is the only teacher and I know some of the worst parents in the world are the best intentioned; parents who try to protect their kids from living life as it is. But there's still a big growling mother bear inside me who wants to keep bad things away, who wants to turn my back on how hard I believe this world can be.

"So what do you guys want to do?" I ask once the car is moving.

"I've got summer basketball this afternoon," Emily says. She grimaces a little and I know she's worried about hurting my feelings. I planted *that* seed just after Sarah

19

and I split and I'm sorry it found a fertile bed. I was feeling sorry for me then, soothing myself with my children's care. I was being a jerk.

"Game or practice?" I ask, thinking if it's a game, we'll all go.

"Practice. And then there's the party tonight." She grimaces again.

I say, "Your face will stick like that. Look, I don't want you to miss things because it's your weekend with me. Ever. This back-and-forth stuff only works if it doesn't disrupt your life. Okay?"

She nods. We've had this conversation before. "Okay, Mr. Psychologist," she says. She believes me about as much as she believes Oral Roberts.

"How 'bout you, Mister Man?"

"Wanna shoot some hoops?" he asks.

"I'll kick your butt," I warn.

"You won't even see my butt," he says back, and I feel the rear of the car bounce as Trevor dribbles across the seat, spins, and stuffs his imaginary ball out the window to a running narrative: "Michael Jordan holds the ball in one hand, leaning forward, smiling at Manute's bewildered face."

"Bewildered?" I say. Where'd you get a word like that? Ten-year-old kids don't say "bewildered."

"I'm gifted," Trevor says. "You should go to my school conferences once in a while. Michael Jordan hip fakes one way and drives, leaving Manute standing flatfooted, lookin' the fool."

I check the rearview mirror in time to see him make an identical move across the seat and stuff out the other window. The boy needs a lesson.

"Don't call, me Manute," I say. "Call me The Doctor."

Emily looks over and smiles. "We'll call you *a* doctor," she says. "You're getting old, Dad. Basketball is a kids' game. Besides, you're a swimmer. You should stick with that, it's almost like a sport."

I fight launching into the story of the year I placed fourth at the small college nationals in the 1650 freestyle, but the kids are too quick. "We know," Emily says, and they chant, " 'I finished fourth in the sixteen-fifty at Nationals. Would have finished even higher if I'd hit all my turns.' "

I protest. "It's *true* . . ."

" 'Toughest field in five years,' " they chant on. Trevor leans his head over the seat. "You sure that wasn't synchronized swimming, Dad? You know, where they grease their hair and screw down into the water?"

"That's it," I say. "We're going to the store to buy asparagus and lima beans for your dinner. You children have no appreciation for true athletic competition. Man against himself. You play sissy sports where your team members can take up the slack."

"We play team sports because they're fun," Emily says. "Who wants to spend three hours a day staring at the black line at the bottom of a pool. And I've seen those pictures, Dad. You had *green* hair then from all the chlorine. No wonder you couldn't get any girls."

I'm beaten, as usual, and am not about to open up the subject of why I couldn't get any girls. I refrain from further attempts to elevate Aquaman to superstar stature. Besides, I absolutely love watching Emily grow athletically. My daughter is an amazing volleyball and basketball player, smooth as silk, with hands quick as a cat's paw, and a standing jump reach nearing thirty inches. She made varsity in both sports last year as a sophomore. My heart swells just watching her bring the ball upcourt. She's long and sinewy, with naturally curly auburn hair and a constant air of incredible assurance. If ever I could live out my real athletic fantasies, it would be through

Emily. But I'm a therapist, and I know better, right? Got into this business because saving the world seemed so much easier than saving myself. And my kids are part of that world, despite years of Sarah's loud cries to the contrary. "Anytime you think you can take me 'mano a mano,' " I say to her, "call for an appointment."

Emily laughs and says, "You got a car phone? I'll polish you off so fast you'll have time to get to the chiropractor before dinner."

God, I love my daughter.

It's well past midnight and I sit in my living room listening to the sweet strains of James Galway's flute floating through my massive speakers out across the darkness. Emily and I have agreed I won't embarrass her by waiting up, so I consider lying on the couch in my pajamas with my eyes closed as being in bed. She doesn't, but I'm the adult and she's the kid—an oft-used line from family therapy—and that's the best she will get. I have also agreed I will not go to the door when I hear her on the porch, and even though I fought that agreement vociferously, in truth it was a point easily given. I don't care if she wants to kiss on the front porch. In fact, the longer I can keep her doing that the better. When I *don't* hear her on the front porch, she can start to worry.

A hand on my elbow nearly rockets me to the ceiling. Trevor says, "I was looking for you in the bedroom. Where were you?"

"Right here, buddy, what's up?"

"I'm scared."

"How come?"

"I think I heard something outside."

I sit up and put an arm over his shoulder. "Think we should go look?"

He thinks a minute. "Maybe . . ."

"'Course if we're out there when your sister gets home, we may end up eating breakfast through a tube in the hospital."

Trevor laughs.

"Think something's really out there?" I ask.

He shrugs again. "Probably not. I just thought I heard something."

"What do you think it was?"

"I don't know," he says, and his eyes fill with tears. "Maybe it was somebody coming to get me."

I pull him close and lean back. His head slides into the crook of my arm and shoulder. "I don't think so," I say. "I'm a pretty dangerous dude when it comes to protecting the NBA's next slow white superstar. But I'll tell you what. Why don't you lay here awhile and listen to the music with me and then we'll go sleep in my room."

Trevor thinks that's a pretty good idea. I watch him there in the darkness, a near-spitting image of me at his age, bronze face and thick light red hair, sinewy muscles strung like a hundred-dollar tennis racquet, full of terror at what he does not understand. Or maybe he does. The universe gave us Corders all kinds of physical gifts, but it also gave us something of an unsettled edge.

"You been thinking about Sabrina Parker?" I ask.

I feel his head nod in my armpit.

"Scary, huh?"

I feel the nod again.

"That's not going to happen to you, kiddo. It's not. Not as long as there's breath of life in my body."

Trevor pulls himself in tighter against me and is quiet for a second. Then, "What about when you're not there?"

23

The only person who ever drowned, drowned on my day off.

"If I was a bad guy, I'd rather take me on than your mom," I say.

"But what if neither one of you are there? What if it's when I'm walking home from school or if I take the garbage out at night, or if I sleep over at Eddy's house, or Liz's?"

"Well," I say, "you'll just have to be real careful when you do those things. Take the garbage out during the day. Have you and Liz and Eddy made plans about how to ditch bad guys?"

He shakes his head. "Huh-uh."

"Think you guys might be able to come up with a good one?"

He looks up at me, thinking. "Yeah, I bet we could." He pauses a second, then, "I hate being a scaredy, Dad. But I keep thinking about how bad it would be if somebody stole me. And if they beat me up or if they killed me. She must have been really scared, Dad. I don't think she's alive anymore, do you?"

I hesitate. "Nope, son. I don't think she's alive anymore."

"Will they get the guy?"

"I don't know, Trevor. I really don't. I hope so, but I don't know. But I'll tell you one thing."

"What?"

"Even if they don't, he'll never get his hands on my boy."

He sticks his head further into my shoulder. "I sure bet she was scared," he says again.

I nod. I can't imagine the terror.

Three

I don't think I learned as much about therapy as I could have in college. There was a big push on behaviorism then and the idea of reducing psychology to a lab science or viewing the world as a giant Skinner box didn't excite me much. Truth was, I came to Lewis State University on a partial swimming scholarship, with no leanings whatever toward a major. I majored in psych because Sarah did, though I'm pretty sure it gave her better preparation for what she's doing today than it did for me. Learning to quantify behavior is a pretty good prerequisite for buying and selling, but the behaviorists' philosophy doesn't leave much room for consideration of that light—that power source—I believe exists in all of us and I didn't have a lot of use for a view of the world that didn't include it. In difficult times I had always turned to that light. Certainly there were professors with leanings toward Carl Rogers and Abraham Maslow and others of that ilk at LSU, but B. F. Skinner's *Science and Human Behavior* was the bible for the majority.

As undergraduates Sarah and I took the team approach. I covered the touchy-feely courses and she covered the rat courses, which left her with by far the lion's share of work. In grad school she went for a master's degree in business administration while I remained in psych, but she was acutely tuned to the fact that a little wellplaced psychology would go a long way in the business world, particularly with so few others using it, so she continued with her part of our undergrad agreement. Certainly *some* knowledge seeped through when I pored over Sarah's research to pass my orals, but the truth is I learned most of what I know now from my father, who taught me to pay close attention to what goes on around me and to reserve judgment. The rest I learned on the job. But I sure could swim fast.

The point is, my cheatin' ways may have been for the best. I learned from Dad—though he would never have used these words—and from my failed experience believing I could be the perfect husband and father, that my life is a lot like everyone else's, no better and no worse. I can sometimes help people with their lives by finding connections to my own, and I get as much as I give in doing that. And that is the nature of help. I think it is easy in this business to fall into the wisdom trap, and it is also hugely arrogant. Though we may have the words, our clients have the experiences—and experience really is the only teacher. Therapy is just another word for help. Beyond that, its existence has no purpose other than to help psychologists become rich people.

I have never dealt with a client, child, or adult who was not like me in some major way. Their fears of being truthful with their partners or their children or their parents, their struggles for control, their need for a safe place to hurt or for someone to trust, their need for answers when there are none, are my own. Much of my formal education taught me this is a detached, intellectual, hands-off business, when in fact it has proven itself to be an incredibly connected, intimate business.

26

* * *

A week to the day after his sister's disappearance, Jerry Parker runs into the kids' room like a shot. Outside in the hall he has belted three other children for reasons we could not detect because we couldn't understand the victims' words through their tears and snot. Now Jerry wears his four-year-old hardass face and stands with fists cocked in anticipation of giving at least one more parent good reason to bring legal action against the center. He is blond and thin, with the intense brown eyes of a gunslinger.

I whisk Little E from the path of a massive roundhouse, leaving Jerry nothing but air, then squat in front of him. My size means nothing to him, and he throws an identical left, which I catch in midair.

"Stand back," he growls, "I'm Kong. Rrrooooooww!"

"Can't let you hurt me, Kong. Wanna go to my room? Find some good things to beat up in there?"

He growls again and swells, hammering his chest until I worry he'll make a dent.

"Wanna?"

He growls, "Yes," and beats his chest again.

I point to the toy bins. "Wanna take some of this stuff?" Jerry stalks to the toy bins and chooses dinosaurs, gorillas, and several muscular superheroes—all bad guys. We fill a small cloth bag with them and stalk out, growling together down the hall. Three doors from my office John Sheldon pokes his head out to ask us if we can keep it down. John Sheldon was born in a herringbone tweed jacket with leather elbow patches and a pipe in his mouth. He is balding with wire rimmed glasses and a chin surely modeled from a javelin. He is a precise man, always in full control, and as a rule doesn't fare well with children. He is, however, laserlike with his diagnoses of adult personality disorders, and that makes him a valuable participant in the team approach to family therapy that we use.

Jerry snarls, raising his arms in a menacing stance. "Get back! I'm Kong!"

John glances at him, then back at me. "Can you keep it down please, Wilson?" he asks. "We're *trying* to have a session in here."

"Get back!" I warn, motioning my head toward Jerry. "He's Kong."

John pulls his door closed against his back in an effort to shield his client from these childish goings-on. He and I have struggled before—something about him *forces* me to give him a hard time. He's always right, but he never wins. "Corder," he says in a low voice, "I know you think you have to let your kids take this place over, but you're not the only person working here, all right? Now, I'd appreciate it if you'd take the rough stuff and the excessive noise inside the playrooms or to your own office."

Jerry's growls continue as he pulls me toward my office door, but I stop suddenly, placing both fists on my hipbones, elbows protruding to the sides, like the true He-Man. In a low, guttural rumble, I say, "Do you know who he is?"

John in unflappable. "We can take this up in Wednesday's team meeting," he says and quietly closes his door.

"Until then," I growl, as if he were still in the hall, "I'd suggest you get back in your office and cower like the milquetoast Jimmy Olson wimpburger you are. I don't remember if I told you who he is." I nod my head toward Jerry, who is still swollen in the chest but smiling. "He's *Kong.*"

"I know that guy," Jerry says. "I don't like him." He pulls me on toward my office.

Once inside, Kong takes on every monster he brought in. He begins each scenario growling, prowling, waxing invincible, and finishes conquering every toy in the place, stopping short of dismemberment only by my hand. Then he sends me for good guys, He-Man and She-Ra, which he dispatches with gorilla rocket flings across the room. He swells his skinny body until I believe it will burst and he conquers all, showing no mercy even though I, as voices for the fallen, beg for it. At the end of the hour, his thick light curls cling to his sweaty forehead, long lashes weighing his eyelids nearly closed. I'm nearly as exhausted as he is. The monster Kong will not be dissuaded; there will be no resolutions today. Jerry will not get out of empowerment play—that play which allows him to express it as he sees it.

At the sound of my phone, I drop my pen in mid-sentence, closing my eyes to visualize my last thought so I can return to my charting after the call. It's been a week since Jerry's first session, and nothing has changed. He plays his rage over and over, with no resolution.

"Wilson Corder."

"Hi, Wilson. This is Peggy Parker."

"Hi, Peggy, how are you doing?"

"Pretty well, I guess. All things considered."

"How can I help?" I ask. I've had no contact with Peggy this last week other than a few seconds each day when she drops Jerry off or picks him up. She has been missing her own group treatment in favor of other obligations that seem to favor the police and the media. I have had thoughts of her, however. Important pieces are missing from the puzzle of Sabrina's disappearance and I'm guessing Peggy possesses some of them, but she has become something of a darling to the media, who are unaware of her past woes with Child Protective Services and are painting her only as a grieving mom. If the cops share my suspicions, they're keeping it to themselves. In this kind of situation, the last thing they need is to appear intrusive. My final conclusions are on hold, though this business unfortunately requires that I be eternally suspicious. I would guess Peggy was drinking and drugging that night. If so, all bets are off. Under those conditions, her kids are on their own; she's proven that before. That's a cold thing to think of a mother whose child is missing, but another child is still with her and he's my first concern.

"I wondered if you worked with Jerry today," Peggy says.

"As a matter-of-fact I did."

"What did he say?"

"About what? I mean, he said a lot, Peggy. He was with me an hour."

"Well," she says, "you know, like about how he's doing."

"He's angry," I say. "There's certainly more beneath that, but he's not showing it yet."

"Well, did he say anything?"

About what? I think. "Listen, would you like to come in alone and talk? I don't feel comfortable talking about Jerry over the phone like this. For one thing, he's entitled to confidentiality just like you are, and I'm guessing you have some things to get off your chest. This must all be pretty overwhelming. Pretty awful."

The line is quiet, then, "Yes. I guess I would. That might be good."

I find an hour that doesn't exist in my schedule tomorrow. It will cost me my charting time, but I can make it up after work. I need to know as much as I can about what Jerry went through that night.

A beep in the earpiece interrupts our conversation on my end, signaling that someone is waiting on the line. They're stacking up. The phone rings simultaneously with hanging up. "Wilson Corder."

"Wilson, my man. You got any openings?" It's Don Cavett.

"For you I do. Might be a little wait, though."

"How long's the line?"

"I think I can still get someone in by the turn of the century."

"I need it a bit sooner than that."

Don knows he'll get it as soon as he needs it. Don Cavett is a Child Protective Services supervisor and he knows more about child protection that anyone in Three Forks, and that includes treatment needs as well as legalities. With a degree in social work as well as clinical psych, he's smart and he's precise and he's the man to have on your side when you can choose only one. He's been in the business for more than fifteen years and has contacts everywhere. He can get a type-in from the police department on past criminal activity of a suspected abuser in less than ten minutes. On many past occasions, when I've felt it made therapeutic sense to bring legal pressure on a suspected sexual offender, Don has persuaded the prosecutor's office to make threats when they would normally pass it up for lack of evidence. Don Cavett is a gem. He also knows I'm as busy as he is, and doesn't call in favors unless it's important.

I say, "How about tomorrow noon?"

"That's a little *too* soon. I've got a kid over at the burn center in Seattle. He won't be back until early next week. Got a real mess and I need someone to see the kid before we can make a decision about letting his dad around him."

"How did he get burned?"

31

"Dipped."

"How old?"

"Almost three," Don says, "but he's going on forty."

I grimace. "Dipped" is a term used when a young child is intentionally scalded in bathwater. The damage normally covers feet and ankles, butt and genitals. What I hate most is that it occurs often enough to have a name.

I'm never comfortable with my initial head movies. I generally develop empathy for the abuser after a period of time, when I uncover the incidents in his or her own history at least as vile as those they perpetrated. This nastiness doesn't spring from thin air. But in the beginning, when I don't have a face and a struggle and a tragic past, all I see is the act. Someone put an almost three-year-old kid in a scalding bath. In that furious instant somebody scarred a kid, inside and out, for life.

I hate the beginnings.

"How about lunch?" I say to Don. "You can fill me in."

"Can't today," he says. "How about tomorrow?"

"Great."

"I should warn you now," he says. "The dad is one of yours. He's got a private practice in town."

I grimace. "Stepdad or real?"

"Step."

"Great again. Anybody I know?"

"Wouldn't be surprised," Don says. "He's consulted for you guys, and he's presented a number of seminars. He knows I'm referring the kid to you, so you may get a call. I won't give you his name until the proper forms are filled out, so have fun guessing. Actually, it might help you to do this one blind."

The beep is back in my ear, and I want to reach down inside the earpiece and rip it out with tweezers, but I place my finger on the button once again, simultaneously with the ring.

I take a deep breath, close my eyes, and lift my finger. "Wilson Corder."

"Mr. Corder, this is Detective Palmer from the Three Forks Police Department."

"They couldn't be my prints," I say. "I had my fingers sanded in eighty-one. Cost a fortune."

"What?" A silence. "Oh. Pretty funny."

"I try to inject a little humor when I can."

Another short silence. Detective Palmer likely thinks I've been injecting something besides humor. He says, "I understand you've been working with the Parker boy."

I think quickly, considering my confidentiality obligation.

"I have a release from the mother," he says, as if reading my mind. "She's the one who gave us your name. I'll send you a copy in the mail, but I was hoping you'd talk with me a little now."

"Tell you what, Lieutenant . . ."

"Detective."

"What?"

"I'm a detective, not a lieutenant."

"Oh," I say. "Well, tell you what. I've got forty-five minutes before my next appointment and I get a little nervous talking shop over the phone. How about meeting me at Andy's Cow Patty Palace on Third in about ten minutes. It's two blocks south of the center, same side of the street. You can show me your badge and your release and hold your gun to my head and we'll do business. I got a couple of traffic tickets I need fixed anyway."

After correctly identifying that as another attempt at humor injection, Palmer agrees and I stack my charts neatly in the middle of my desk before checking out at the front desk and jogging the two blocks to Andy's.

Palmer slaps the release of information form Peggy Parker signed for him in front of me on the table. He was longer than expected getting here and I'm on my second cup of coffee with only twenty minutes before my next appointment. "You must be Wilson Corder," he says.

I glance around quickly. Apart from a woman I guess to be in her mid-eighties seated at the counter, I'm the only customer in the place. "That's good police work," I say, and put out my hand.

"They don't call us Three Forks' finest for nothing," he says.

"You have to pay them to call you that?"

He laughs, shaking his head. "Gotta tell you, Corder, if I ever need therapy, and there are those who say that time has come and gone, I'm coming to you. You're a funny guy."

"I know," I say. "My kids tell me I should go on TV."

"So they can turn you off?"

I nod. It's an old one. "So, Detective, what can I do for you?"

"Well, we really don't have much on this Sabrina Parker thing. A name. We're getting almost nothing out of Mom, and to tell the truth I don't care how credible she looks on TV, she seems a little elusive to me. I can't say that publicly because the media would eat us alive. Anyway there was a party earlier in the evening of the child's disappearance, kind of a neighborhood wingding in Whitman Park, probably fifty or sixty people in attendance at one time or another. It's a poor area of town, economically speaking, but somehow everybody brought some kind of dish, and from the sounds of things everybody brought some kind of drug. Things got a little wild. We have bits of information from some of the locals, but no one saw anything they considered particularly suspicious. Several witnesses remember a guy was hanging around Sabrina and making passes at her mother. No one thought it was strange at the time, given it's a public park. 'Course everyone was loaded to their eyeballs, so probably nothing seemed strange."

I repeat, "So what can I do?"

"Well, one of these witnesses says she saw Peggy and her kids leave the party with the stranger. Peggy says no. We're hoping maybe the boy knows something."

"Did you ask him?"

Palmer nods. "He looked straight at his mom and back to me and said, 'Wasn't no man go home with us.' "

I smile—that's Jerry exactly—and study Detective Palmer a moment. He is black, which I hadn't expected from his voice over the phone, and I make a note to get a better handle on my tendency to stereotype. A robust, powerfully built man—probably upwards of six feet two—with a beer keg torso and arms that strain the seams of his jacket, he is gentle but intense. He leaves no clues about himself from his dress, but he is a picture of competence.

I always find myself in a certain dilemma working with the law. Generally speaking, cops want information from kids while I want *expression,* and I often have to give up one to get the other. Plus, kids usually shut down when they think they're being pumped, particularly if they're already scared. On the other hand, nobody likes to see a kid killer on the loose. But when it comes down to doing for society or doing for my client, the client comes first, though that line is not always clearly drawn. If Jerry saw or heard what happened to his sister, saying so could put him in danger. Yet talking about it in a safe place could only be good for him psychologically. At this moment, no obvious conflict exists, but that could change in a second. I can count on things getting more complicated. At this instant, however, I hate what happened to Sabrina Parker as much as anyone does. "You said you had a name. For the guy who was talking to her?"

Palmer nods. "Marvin Edwards. There's no one by that name in our records, but we're typing him in around the country. My guess is we'll get a few Marvin Edwardses by the end of the week."

"I'll listen for his name," I say. "It looks like I'll be seeing Jerry every day for a while, along with Molly Comstock. If he knows anything he's either too scared to say, or too shocked to remember. Right now, he's just toughing it out."

"That's all I can ask for," Palmer says, and finishes his coffee in a gulp. "Got to get back to work. 'Preciate your help."

"One thing," I say as he stands. "This has to come at Jerry's pace. It may be slow, but it'll stand up better if he isn't pressured. Molly and I can only work from his point of view, and from his point of view, things look pretty confused."

Palmer nods. "You're the doctor," he says.

I wish I were, I think. *I'd work with rich people.* They can afford to hire someone to watch their kids when they go out to get blasted. But that's unfair. I don't know that Peggy was blitzed.

"Wanna go get a beer?" I'm finished with my evening men's group, or better, it's finished with me. Eleven men, most caught red-handed doing to their loved ones what their fathers did to them, struggling—in varying degrees of good faith—to change without losing their sense of

36

manhood. Planet Earth is a tough town. I'm sitting in Molly's office with my feet on her desk, waiting for her to get her things in order.

"A beer?" she says incredulously. "After today you want to get *a* beer?"

"Okay," I say. "A keg."

"That's more like it," she says, extracting some Weebles people and action toys from under the cushion of her small couch. Neither Molly nor I pay much attention to whether a kid picks up after him- or herself, and by the end of the day it takes an Easter egg hunt to get everything back where it belongs.

"But before we drink ourselves unconscious," she says, pointing out her window at my bike, "you promised me a ride on that. I want it and I want it now."

"You're so wishy-washy," I say. "Make your point."

"Go get your stuff," she says. "I'll be ready in two minutes."

As we slide onto the bike, I offer Molly the helmet, but she says if I'm planning to crash, *I* should wear it, and hooks it to the back of the sissy bar. "I want wind in my face," she says. "Go."

I take the back road to Northrup, a little wheat town about twenty miles west of Three Forks, where I know we can get greasy pressure-cooked chicken with fries and a cold pitcher at a good price. The Three Forks-Northrup highway is a winding two-lane with three long straight stretches and very little traffic, where I know I can show Molly what this hot little missile will do. She shares my passion for speed and wind and balance, though at times she scares even me when I pop the throttle and feel her long fingers float away from my waist and her knees slide apart, and I fear she'll fly off the back of the bike.

I asked her once if she ever worries about the speeds

we reach, or the fact that we're likely as not to ride home in a ninety-mile-an-hour blur after polishing off two pitchers. "Nope," she says. "That's not how I'm going to die." I figure if she's not going to die that way, what the hell, neither am I. *That* should sound great to the state patrolman who scrapes our brains off some eastern Washington back road.

"I may have to turn Jerry over to you for a couple of days," I say when the chicken is ordered and we're settled into the oak booth in the Iron Horse Tavern with a pitcher of dark. Molly gets inside kids faster than anyone I've ever seen. She doesn't publicly admit to using witchcraft, but this woman takes a cosmic bypass on her way to kids' hearts and souls. I'm not a believer in much of anything I can't see, hear, or touch, and I avoid the idea of a psychic reality as if it were herpes complex 4000, but what I see Molly do with kids on a regular basis is un-goddam-canny. I'm considered pretty good in this business, but I'll stand out of her way anytime.

"How come?"

"He just did monsters today. Big, tough, growling monsters. After he kicked the hell out of everyone in the kids' group, he kicked the hell out of my office." I laugh. "I almost turned him loose on Sheldon, but John was overmatched."

Molly smiles. She joins me in my war with those in the business who consider child therapy to be junior therapy, which, though he denies it, John does. And he is certainly not alone. "Jerry could rip John Sheldon a new one on a *happy* day," she says.

The beer begins to take the edge off the day, a fact I'm certain the people over in Drug and Alcohol Treatment would find interesting, and I move in a little closer to Molly. We don't hide the fact that we're lovers, but we don't advertise it, either. I can honestly say I've never made a professional decision in which our relationship was a factor—we've had plenty of disagreements—and neither has she. Hopefully I'll never have to choose, because it is a relationship that quiets me. Molly is the one woman I've been with since my divorce who understands in much the same way I do, the dilemma of men and women getting together. Each of us believes the more that happens *outside* the relationship, the better we are *in* it. We have each tried it the traditional way, and in both our cases the results were dismal. There are parts of Molly's life she would never invite me into, not because she keeps secrets, but because I don't fit there. She spends a night a week volunteering time to an orphanage run by a local psychiatrist who is also a Buddhist monk, and another night with a group of psychics. I don't need that kind of confusion in the rafters of my mind; my feet are planted firmly on *western* ground. And generally speaking, we keep our families separate, not for a good reason necessarily, but because it's simpler that way. This relationship restores sanity to the one part of my life I thought I'd never get under control and the last thing in the world I need to know is why.

"So why do you want me to work with Jerry?"

"I think he can get to what's really going on inside faster with you. He gets stuck with me being a man—wants me to help kick the shit out of everybody, but that leaves the rest of him shut down. And he really trusts you. I'm great for monsters, but you could help him to resolution."

She nods. We pass kids off to each other all the time, depending on what they seem to need.

"Besides," I say, "I'm feeling a little like a cop on this one. I don't want that to make me push him too fast and lose him. That'll never happen with you."

"I'll give it a look tomorrow," she says. "We can decide then."

I drop Molly back at the center to pick up her car. We won't stay together tonight because, even though her kids are teenagers, she doesn't like to leave them alone too often, and more important, likes to feel our separateness.

I pull back out onto the street, nearly running a red light wondering where this is all headed with Jerry Parker. The blast from the horn of an oncoming car jars me into the present, and I pull over to the curb, reach back for my impact-tested helmet.

I back the bike tight against the curb on the street in front of my house a little past ten. The neighborhood is quiet save for the songs of the crickets, and the street is empty of traffic both ways. The air has begun to cool slightly, and though my miniature red two-story Victorian stands peacefully behind the dark green shrubbery and the sweet smell of freshly watered grass tickles my nostrils, *something* doesn't feel right; I don't know what. My front porch is dark and something in the shadows there sparks an uneasiness in me. I approach warily, knowing I'm often prone to paranoia and probably it's nothing. That notion changes dramatically when I pull open the screen door to find Ballou, my cat, gutted like a fish and nailed to my front door with a long spike.

Four

Certain risks go with this job. Involvement with folks who solve their problems violently often means dealing with people who don't want, or believe they need, your services. It didn't occur to me for a second that Ballou's fate may have been the result of an angry neighbor's revenge for her late night garden raids, or even a vicious childhood prank. In the years I've worked at the center trying to help hurt, angry people rehabilitate themselves—often against their wishes—my tires have been slashed twice, the front of my house egged, six windows broken (four car, two house), and the aerial to my car radio snapped off an average of twice a year. Child Protective Services, as well as the courts, rely heavily upon our recommendations to make decisions that have a tremendous effect on our adult clients' lives and egos, more specifically, whether or not their children should be returned home. *We have thumbs up or thumbs down on whether a person gets his or her child back.* When things don't go the clients' way, they can get pretty upset, and some are quite used to expressing their upset violently.

Though I took that in stride ten years ago when I sat in Personnel listening to my official job description—providing therapeutic services to dysfunctional families, many of whom may be reluctant—it's worn thin over the years. Ballou was seven years old and she's been with me since she was two weeks. I cannot describe the grief and rage I felt, pulling the spike from the door, catching her limp body before she could drop to the cement.

Therapeutic considerations for the perpetrator aside, which, believe me they are, I want somebody's head.

The police have come and gone, but whoever did this left no tracks; no terrorist groups have called claiming responsibility, and the cops left me with the impression that I'd have been better off calling the ASPCA. They have more pressing problems than kittycide, and unless something happens to add to what I've given them, I'll likely not hear from them further.

Now, a single streetlamp shines through the window of my darkened living room. I have buried Ballou in my back garden and all her things, two kitty-condos, three scratching posts, the covered litter box, have been either discarded or stored in the basement. I realize half the furniture in this place belonged to my damned cat.

I can't believe the colossal sadness below my rage. The nature of relationships is confusing and complicated. Women return on a regular basis to men who beat them senseless. Children will die to please their tormentors—return time after endless time to earn love that doesn't exist. I once had an eight-year-old client who looked forward to being hit by a car. I asked her why on earth she would want that.

"Because that's when you get stuff," she said.

"What kind of stuff?"

"Juice. Warm cereal. Your mom."

"Why do you have to be run over to get those things?"

She shrugged. "I don't know. That's how Jody and Robert did it."

Sure enough, a little research revealed that both her

42

siblings had been run down, one in the family driveway by an errant uncle and one by a reckless teenager on the street in front of the house.

We live strangely conditional lives. Half my work lies in discovering those conditions. But Ballou was unconditional with me, as I was with her. She came to me for what she wanted and what she needed. I did the same. Sometimes the other responded and sometimes not, but nothing in the relationship ever changed. I am absolutely crushed by the revelation of how much I need that warm simplicity. Music does not soothe me, the darkness will not envelop me. I think of calling Molly, or even Sarah, but can't imagine getting words out of my mouth.

I remove my appointment book from the saddlebags, paging through, hoping for some clue. I rule out all the young children, after considering each of their parents. The few adults I think might be angry enough don't seem capable. Nothing. I start through the book a second time, but suddenly fling it against the wall. To hell with them. This is what you get for trying to help. Fuck it. I'm out. I'll give the center thirty days in the morning. I can sell Amway, I really can.

Yet, even the thought of escape doesn't quiet me, and I'm suddenly in that menacing state of rage that is so familiar, and which has always fueled me. Before I know it I have laid waste to my living room, turning over tables and chairs, leaving a lamp shattered on the hardwood floor. By God, if some son-of-a-bitch wants to play *this* game, bring him on.

My phone rings as Molly sticks her head into my office. She arrived ahead of me this morning and I didn't tell her about Ballou when I said good morning passing her office. As long as I've been here and as many train-

43

ings and self-help courses as I've taken, when I'm feeling shitty, I keep it to myself. Unless it's used in conjunction with food or drink, "sharing" is not my word. I'll talk about this when I can do it safely, which means without breaking down. I'm a man, I show 'em cool imperturbability. The guys in my men's group would love this. That's okay, I'll lie and tell 'em I cried and asked for sympathy and nurturance.

I hold up five fingers to tell Molly how long I'll be and she nods and whispers, "I'll get the kids into the room." The want ads lie open on my desk, Amway is circled, along with sales positions at three different health spas. I shake my head and close the paper, stating my name into the phone.

"Mr. Corder, this is Dr. Jeff Banner."

"Hi, Dr. Banner, what can I do for you?"

"Do you know who I am?" he asks.

If you work anywhere in the field of clinical psychology in the state of Washington, you'd have to spend your days in a sensory deprivation tank to not know who Dr. Jeffery Banner is. He presents seminars all over the Northwest on domestic violence and anger management, and has published three moderately successful books on those subjects. Dr. Banner is Three Forks' answer to Joyce Brothers. "Yessir," I say. "Of course I know who you are. I've read your books and attended several seminars." Truth is, I've always been something of a fan of Dr. Banner.

"I trust they were helpful."

"Very helpful," I say. "They were great. What can I do for you, Dr. Banner?"

He is silent a moment, then, "Craig Clark is my stepson."

No bells ring. I wait.

44

"He's been referred to you by Child Protective Services. He was burned. Scalded."

Bells ring. "So, how can I help you, Dr. Banner?"

He is quiet again, then, "Needless to say, this is difficult. I've been in practice more than fifteen years. As you can imagine, this is my worst nightmare. I'm a highly visible man and all the world loves a sordid story."

"I *can* imagine," I say.

"I don't know what Craig will say to you," he says, "but I want you to know I didn't burn my stepson intentionally. Believe me, I know you hear that from the outset with nearly every case you work with, and I could certainly come up with a more believable story by merely looking through my files, but in my case it's true. I made a horrible mistake—"

I break in. "Excuse me, doctor. I will want to hear what you have to say, but I think I need to see Craig first and get whatever impressions I get. You're right, I do hear that all the time, but on occasion it's true. Accidents happen. I want you to know I'm aware of that. You and I will have the chance to sit down and sort things out."

"Just let me . . ."

"Really, Dr. Banner, I don't mean to put you off; this isn't about you. It's about *me* and my style. I'll need to talk to Craig first. I know it puts a lot of stress on you, and I'll get it done as soon as I can. When I do, I'll get right back to you."

He is quiet another moment. "You're doing what I'd do," he says finally. "I appreciate your integrity. We'll be in touch then. Thank you for your time."

"You're welcome."

I walk into the kids' room to find Molly strategically placed between Jerry and the rest of the children while she helps the nursing students from Lewis State University organize breakfast. Many of these children don't get enough to eat at home, so we always provide fruit and cereal and juice first thing. The room is large and well lighted, divided into several sections to accommodate more active and aggressive kids as well as quiet and introverted ones. A second room, off to the left through a short hallway, stands nearly empty except for punching bags and padded clubs and other safe replicas of instruments of violence. What happens in these rooms is usually not pretty. Hurt kids have to express their pain and fear and rage toward the savagery—or worse, the abandonment—that has been leveled at them or they will never be congruent in the world. Under any circumstances, four-year-old expression is not very often attractive, and it's incredibly helpful to have the assistance of students and volunteers to keep safety limits in place, though I'm sure they recoil at what they see us letting some of the kids "get away with."

"Clark Kent is here," I tell Molly, Jeff Banner's words still playing in my ears. "With kryptonite in all four pockets. I'm going down. Jesus, the world is getting *really* strange. You want to take Jerry off somewhere?"

"I'm taking *her* off somewhere," Jerry growls. "Stand back or I'll kill her here."

I start to say, "Go ahead," but there is a time and place even for gallows humor. "Where you taking her?"

"You never know," he growls. "Stand back. I will. I'll kill her."

My hands shoot into the air and the two of them disappear.

This is an experienced group; most of the kids have been in treatment three hours a day, three days a week, for at least six months, and more often than not they set the group direction themselves. Today Christopher is working on his fear of his father and he has chosen other

46

kids to play family members and policemen and CPS workers. The nurses and practicum students have built him a jail with paper bars in one of the toy shelves, where Christopher's father (played, in the performance of his career, by Chris himself) is held. The man consistently beat all the children in the family and sexually abused Chris over a long period, by ejaculating on him, then ordering him into the garbage. ("Get in the garbage!" Chris constantly imitates. "You're garbage! You're shit! Get in there!")

Today Chris is jailed by Conrad and Melinda, the cops. He remains confined a short while, cussing and growling, before he rips the bars to shreds, storming to freedom and scattering the other players. And they do scatter, because Chris will put a serious hurt on them if they hang around. The students rebuild the set and the saga replays itself.

Little E, Eric's two-and-a-half-year-old, watches while attached to my leg. Though he is big for his age, and certainly dressed for a part in this play, he is really too young for this group, and I keep him close when things get wild.

As an infant Chris was removed from his home for neglect three and a half years ago, and his parents came into treatment here at the center. At that time the sexual issues remained buried in traditional family secrecy, and Chris and his brothers were eventually returned to their parents. He was removed again at three for physical abuse, and once again returned home after six months. Again the sexual issues went undiscovered. He was last removed four months ago. He now knows adults will never protect him and fully expects to be sent back to his hell. The jail game never changes because he believes his father is far too strong and too powerful to be kept away from him. I think he's out for good now, but it will be a long time before *he* believes it, and I guarantee he'll blow out of several foster homes before he finds one that can tolerate what he has become. For now, his sole means of expression lies in playing out the desperation of his life over again and again. When he collapses, one of us will be there. Down the line, when Chris gains some sense of trust—assuming the system gives him reason—he may put a different outcome on the game and we'll know we're getting somewhere. Not a day passes that I do not deeply regret the role I played each of the times he was returned to his parents. Suffice it to say, I would not like to have Chris's life stretching out before me.

Suffice it to say also that I'm really glad Jerry's not in here now, because, in his current condition, he would escalate this game beyond *conventional* warfare in a second.

When snack time is over near the end of the session, I leave the nursing students to read stories with the kids and I head back to my office to grab a few seconds of quiet sanity before seeing my first individual adult client, and to write down what just happened in the playroom. Dr. Banner's call rattled around in my brain throughout the session, pictures of Ballou danced before my eyes, and I fear I was less than effective. Play therapy has great impact, not only on the child directing the story, but on all the players. It isn't fair for me to be semipresent. I promise myself to do a better job tomorrow; then I sit down to write what I remember.

Mary, the receptionist, rings to inform me my client has checked in, at the same moment Molly knocks on my door. I tell Mary to give my client *People* magazine and tell her to sit tight a few minutes, while Molly plops into the chair next to the desk.

"So tell me," I say, dropping into my therapist's tone, "did your mother love you?"

"My mother deserted me three weeks before my birth," she says. "I never knew her."

"You and Jerry have a good time?" I ask. Molly's dark curls are plastered to her forehead and she displays vast, damp circles under each arm. I'm guessing life with Jerry was a tumble.

"He finally let me be the monster," she says, "for maybe the last ten minutes. He tried on every superhero he knows, but they all ate dirt. He didn't just sleep through whatever happened that night. He knows a lot, keeps using the same phrases over and over: 'Stand back.' 'I'll kill her here.' I checked it. Every time I didn't say those things as Kong, he stopped the game and corrected me, once by biting my leg."

I remember his saying those same things to me. "God, I wonder if he saw."

Molly takes a deep breath. "He saw something. When do you see his mom?"

"This afternoon. I'll see what I can get."

She stands to leave.

"Somebody killed Ballou."

"What?"

"Crucified her feline ass," I say, attempting to keep it light, instantly deciding I have probably jumped the gun on my control and may be about to spill the emotional beans. My throat fills, but it's too late. "She was nailed to the door when I got home last night."

Molly says, "Oh, no," and moves to put a hand on me.

I let out a few tears to bleed off the pressure of the dam in my chest. "I don't have a clue who did it," I say, and take a deep breath. "I hate it. I just hate it."

Molly stays a moment, slides easily in under me, and holds me tight. I fall against her. Her fingers run through my hair as she pulls my head against her breast, kissing my forehead, and my tears run. At least now I can be

49

honest with the guys in the men's group. I could stay like this forever, but life would go on anyway. "Can't keep this up too long. Half the world's out there kicking the shit out of the other half."

She stands. "I'm sorry, Wilson. I really am."

"I know. Thanks."

I meet with Don Cavett at Winchell's Donuts for lunch. Don is a man who believes (with the zeal of an elderly, bedridden Social Security recipient mailing her last pennies to Jim and Tammy) in sugar as nature's perfect fuel for the human body. "What people should know," he has told me on several occasions, "is that sugar is only bad for you if you don't get enough of it."

I arrive to find Don perched over two apple fritters and a cinnamon roll like a desert vulture over a wagon train surrounded by Indians in an old western.

"Great spot," I say, squatting on the stool across from him. "Eat here often?"

"Just for the atmosphere, really," he says. "Go ahead and order. Then we'll talk."

I go with coffee. I like sugar as much as the next guy, but when I make a lunch of it, come about two o'clock I have to insert toothpicks to keep my eyes open. Two of those doughnuts and by midafternoon I need a pair of glasses with eyeballs painted on the lens to trick my client into thinking I'm conscious.

"So," I say, "give me the hot poop."

"Actually, I really don't know too much about the kid," Don says. "Name's Craig. Been over at the burn center in Seattle. Should be back in a couple of days. Fred Cronk believes the stepdad's intent was harmless and wants to put the kid back when he gets here."

"I take it you don't believe the stepdad's story."

"Under normal circumstances, what's to believe?" Don says. "It's the *who* that's got my head swimming. The stepdad's version of the saga goes something like this: Kid peed his pants. Stepdad was going to put him in the bath to wash him off. He turned on the hot water as the telephone rang, and he ran to answer it. Kid crawled into the tub while he was on the phone. Stepdad ran to pull him out when he heard the screams. Says the kid couldn't have been in the water more than four or five seconds. I've heard some version of that story so many times I almost recited it along with him."

"What do they say at the burn center?"

"They say the burns are consistent with four to six seconds in about a hundred-and-forty-degree water, though it may have been longer. The cops tested it. Hot water alone was a hundred and forty out of the tap."

"Any legal charges?"

"Nope. Prosecutor's office saw the kid and said they were going after the stepdad, then they talked with him and all of a sudden it was an accident. Same thing at the burn center. Doctors took one look and said it was a classic dip job. Next day it was consistent with an accident. Needless to say, I've got a few alarms going off in my head."

I stand to pour myself another cup of Winchell's fine coffee, spilling a drop on the back of my hand—maybe a sign from God. Hot water hurts. "So you want me to see the kid," I say, sitting back down, "before Stepdad has a chance to get to him."

"Right."

"Almost three, huh? How verbal?"

"The next Donahue. Talks nonstop. Tough kid, too. Says exactly what he wants. The kind of kid you'd put on an ice floe if he had the goods on you."

"So why doesn't Fred listen to him?"

51

Don leans back. He's an angular man, maybe five feet eleven, with a thick gray beard spreading beneath his chin like a silver bib. He thoughtfully picks pieces of frosting from it and eats them, not unlike a monkey snacking on parasites. "Probably should save some of this," he says when he sees me watching. Then with a squint, he says, "Off the record, Stepdad's got a true believer in Fred. He doesn't listen to the kid because he can't believe both. I told you he was one of yours."

"Yeah, he called me yesterday."

"So you know who I'm talking about. What did he say?"

"Not much. I didn't give him a chance. I told him I needed to see the kid first. But I gotta tell you, Don, Jeffery Banner is a nationally recognized figure in the area of anger management. And he really knows his stuff. I've seen some strange goings-on in my years here, but if Jeff Banner scalded a three-year-old kid, he gets the record."

Don picks absently at his beard. "Yeah, I know. Most folks in the department think I'm out of my mind, but this system isn't set up to deal with people who appear to be functional, and I've been with Craig three or four times. Wait till you see his burns. If Banner's story is good, it'll hold up. My job is to protect kids and if a three-year-old walks into my office and points the finger at Jesus Christ himself, then I'm going to do a thorough investigation of Jesus Christ."

Believe me, Don is not exaggerating his commitment. "So, tell me when Craig is coming back and I'll clear out some time for him that day."

"That's the other problem," Don says. "Fred is planning to return him directly home. Margaret Drollinger is his supervisor and she wants this done quietly. Figures

52

it could blow up in the department's face, plus she claims she has no reason to question Fred's judgment."

"So what do you want me to do?"

"I want you to go over to Seattle and talk to Craig there," he says. "I caught Fred off guard in an inter-departmental staff meeting where he couldn't say no to that because it made too much sense. The department will cover it."

"When?"

"How about tonight? There's a commuter flight out at six. You could see Craig at eight and be back here before midnight." He smiles. "I'll wait up."

"I've got Men's Group at six-thirty," I say, thinking out loud.

"Cancel it," Don says. "We've got one shot here, Wilson. I need someone with credentials to make a recommendation that will stick. If that kid goes back, the window closes and we won't hear another word until he *really* gets hurt." He stares directly into my eyes. "I don't have a lot of backing for this in the office," he says. "Part of it is personal, but what I'm asking from you is strictly professional."

Don's emotional investment surprises me. He's always been precise, and little gets past him, but a person can't survive in his business if he turns over every rock in every case. But he has long been vocal in his belief that the Department of Social and Health Services protects poor kids a lot better than middle- and upper-class kids, and there is little about his job he hates more than that.

"So I get what's behind door number two," I say, rising. "No days and one lovely night in beautiful Seattle, Washington, compliments of the simpleminded taxpayers of the great state of 'WA.' Hope I can still get on that plane."

Don digs quickly into his briefcase and hands me a ticket. "You can still get on that plane," he says with a smile. "Thanks."

Five

I shocked myself the first time I cheated on Sarah. I couldn't believe it as I got into my car, heading for a secret rendezvous, and I couldn't believe it when the deed was done. An absolute in my life since adolescence was if ever I got a shot at Sarah, I wouldn't blow it. In high school, back in my small lumber town in central Idaho, I thought there were two kinds of guys in the world: those hopelessly in love with Sarah Campbell, and queers.

So what was I—devoted husband and father of the world's two most precious kids—doing driving my ten-year-old VW Beetle to the apartment of a woman I barely knew, for the simple reason that she had asked if I wanted to be another notch on her belt?

Sarah and I had been together eight years.

I remember as if it were yesterday my thoughts and feelings the day back in 1972 when I moved my few belongings into her apartment, and a year later when we committed to marriage; remember the trembling in my heart when my daughter sucked in her first breath as Sarah lay laughing and crying, her hair clinging to the sides of her head like a year-old corsage in a prom book. There would be no others of significance in my life; this was all I could ever want.

I remember this with equal clarity, eight years and another beautiful baby later, the electrical surge in my groin, short-circuiting all meaningful activity above my neck, when Ali Nettleson whispered her gunslinger's challenge into my ear. To this day I remain amazed at the power of erotic longing, and how it can displace the subtler feelings of what we come to call love.

Love. What a trickster that word is. Conquers all. All you need is. Will keep us together. What is this thing called. It adorns either end of a sentence like pearl earrings on the finest lobe, like a pencil-thin gold band on the most delicate finger. I counted on it to keep me free of my baser human instincts, and when it failed, decided it was absent. It took me years to realize it wasn't absent at all, only camouflaged.

It ain't what it appears to be.

The damage I did in its name keeps me now and forever from judging violent or abusive or negligent people, regardless of their transgressions. Time and again our clients put their children and their futures at grave risk because they don't understand the nature of what brings people together, what a fine line there is between the good and evil of human connection. Though I have never hit a woman or a child, I couldn't have kicked Sarah in the stomach any harder than I did the day I told her I hadn't been faithful.

I'm back from the burn center and what I got for Don Cavett was two for one. From almost-three-year-old Craig, I got more information than even the dullest social worker would need to understand the motive behind his scalding. And Carrie, his exquisitely delicate, twenty-year-old child-mother, provided me an intricate internal map of her own emotional terrain, and a glimpse of the vast chasm between her attachment to her son and her desperate need (which she called "love") to keep Dr. Jeffery Banner, a wonderful man who was "better than I ever thought I'd get."

I met with Craig alone in a makeshift playroom, though I never travel without my own tools of the trade, drawing paper and colored markers, a collapsible house full of miniature plastic inhabitants, replicas of enough different animals to fill an ark, and dinosaurs galore.

Craig went directly to the heavy artillery. In moments he had mommy and daddy and baby dinosaurs spread far and wide. The daddies terrified the babies, who constantly ran to the safety of the mommies, only to be disappointed when the daddies marched right past—or *over*—the mommies to wreak havoc. Daddy dinosaurs bit babies' tails, threw them into the air, and pushed them into the "boiling river" when the babies pooped. When I sought the whereabouts of the mommies during this mini-holocaust, Craig simply moved them out of sight. Finally, when all data indicated mommy dinosaurs simply don't cut the mustard as protectors, Craig filled a small pillowcase with daddy dinosaurs and began beating it against the wall, screaming, "Die! Die! Go to jail!"

"Do you want all the daddy dinosaurs to die?" I asked.

He looked at me as if I had just dropped onto his plate from the back of a bird, rolled his eyes, and said, "Jeff."

I nodded toward the pillowcase clutched tightly in his hand, entertaining for a split second the wild thought that I may have stumbled across the truly accurate account of the extinction of these marvelous beasts. "Are all the dinosaurs in that bag Jeff dinosaurs?"

"Yes!" he yelled, bringing the bag high over his shoulder and down onto the floor with a thud. Then he leaned toward a rubber shark with a huge open mouth bearing

56

razor-sharp teeth, out of reach on the floor beside him. I put the shark into his hands. "Seecut," he said.

"Secret? What is it?"

"Shark tell."

He put the shark close to my ear. "Psst. Psst. Psss, psss, psss. Psst."

"That's a secret, all right," I said. "Can you tell me what it means?"

Craig threw the shark against the wall. "He get me," he said. No seecut today.

Craig blew through the remainder of my bag of tricks like a tropical storm. At his instruction, I drew Mommy (very small and alone), Daddy Jeff (behind bars), and Craig (far off to one side). He wanted tears falling from Craig's eyes because he "soiled" his pants, a term with which few three-year-olds are familiar. Daddy Jeff sported a "mad mouth" and "mad eyes" and repeated in a stern tone: "You bad. Pants soiled. *Consense.*" (I finally deciphered this as "consequence.") Next, we played a game with bears in which the daddy bear took the baby bear for a bath after he had "soiled" his pants and the baby bear screamed, "Too hot! Too hot!" As Daddy Bear, he said, "Okay, okay, I'll put some cold in," turning an imaginary faucet. "There. It's just right for you now, son." Baby Bear refused to get in by himself, waiting for Daddy Bear to take action, but immediately screamed, "Oh, no! A trick! A trick!"

I was proud of the session. I think of play therapy the same way I think of spelunking, though I've done the latter only once. A friend of my father's—a career air force man named Roger Stallings—took me to some caves near his home in New Mexico when my family was on a visit there. I was fourteen and the dark inside the cave was so thick you could almost feel it on your skin. My eyes never adjusted because there was nothing to adjust to.

"The ridge you're about to step onto," Colonel Stallings said, "is about a foot and a half up, and less than two inches wide. I want you to find a way to stand on it."

I stepped onto the paper-thin ledge, attempting to hug the damp rock above it, slipped, and barked my shins as my toes slid off. Colonel Stallings heard me cuss, and laughed. "Don't hug the wall," he said. "You have to push back, not too hard and not too easy. Too hard, you'll land on your butt."

Nearly two hours later when my shins were scraped to the bone and my butt felt like it had been hammered all afternoon with a board, I got it, and in the inky blackness of that New Mexico cave with Colonel Stallings gently urging me on, a calmness shivered the length of my body as my fingertips bore feathery pressure against the cold stone, and suddenly I knew I could stand on that ledge as long as I wanted. Anytime I wanted. It was a feeling I have since come to rely upon, in almost any situation, to tell me I'm on track.

My session with Craig was a classic example of that light touch. I merely did as I was told, following Craig's lead and throwing in a gentle kick start when things bogged down. I didn't lead him and never once thought he felt threatened by me. Craig's perceptions were crystal clear.

When we were finished, I asked him if he wanted to go home to his house and he said, "Yes. With my mommy."

"You want your mom to be there."

"Yes."

"Do you want your dad to be there? Daddy Jeff?"

He pursed his lips and said, "I no go."

58

"Where will you go? Where will you go if Daddy Jeff is at your house?"

"With you. I go with you." He gripped the pillowcase one last time and whacked all the Daddy Jeff dinosaurs against the wall.

Because his burned feet still would not support him, I carried Craig back to his room, where his mother waited in a state of high anxiety, nearly unable to sit still.

I lay Craig on the bed and asked if he wanted to tell his mother what we talked about. He appeared reluctant, glanced to her, then back to me, making no verbal response.

I turned to her. "Is it all right for him to tell you?"

"Of course. He's my baby. He can tell me anything."

I asked Craig if he believed her.

He said nothing, made no motion.

"Do you have a way to let him know it's safe to talk?" I asked her.

"He knows he can talk!" Carrie shouted, catching herself in mideruption. Then more calmly, "He's just mad at me and wants you to think I'm not a good mom."

"Carrie, he's only three."

"This is his way of getting rid of Jeffery. He's had me all to himself for three years and now he's jealous."

I repeated his age.

"You talked to him. You must know how smart he is."

I smiled. "Yeah. He's real smart all right. But he's still only three. And Carrie, you're really important to him. He can't afford to try to make you look like a bad mom, okay? Whatever kind of mom you are, you're *his*."

She seemed to relax a little, and tears welled in her eyes. "I'm scared," she said. "I don't know what to do." She nodded at the bandages on his feet. "Look at him."

"I'd be scared, too," I said. "Right now see if you can

59

find a way to let your boy know it's okay to talk to you. He needs to know you can take it."

Carrie remained caught up in all she had to lose. "You know, he's already said he wants to come back to me and Jeffery, that he wants Jeffery to be there."

"Do *you* want Jeffery to be there?"

"Of course," she said, as if I were from Mars.

"Craig *knows* that. You're his mother, Carrie. He can't afford to lose you. He's going to say what he thinks you want to hear. What you need to do now is let him know it's safe to talk to you, and tell you the truth. Unless it isn't."

Craig was not exactly following the script, having rolled over on his side, his back to us, as if to say, "Let me know when you guys get this worked out." Then, as Carrie groped for words, he turned over. "Daddy Jeff go to jail. He hurt."

Carrie reached over and touched him. "Daddy Jeff loves you," she said. "He . . ."

Craig turned his back.

Very quietly I said, "It's not safe to tell you if you don't believe him. Don't worry if you think what he's saying isn't true; it's true to him." I took a deep breath, lowering my voice. "There's a lot riding on this, Carrie. This is important to your relationship with your son."

She began to cry but quickly regained control, closing down all access, so I put a hand on her shoulder and said I had to leave. I got up and gathered my things, touching Craig on the shoulder. "I like the way you talked to me, guy. You're a brave boy."

In the hallway by the elevator, she caught me. "What are you going to say when you get back?"

"I'm going to tell CPS that if Craig is coming home, Dr. Banner shouldn't be there."

"I knew it!" she said between clenched teeth. "This

was a trick. This was a trick to get my son. And I know you're after Jeffery."

"Who told you that?"

"Nobody told me that," she spat. "Nobody had to tell me that. It's clear."

"It isn't a trick, Carrie," I said. "Your son has serious injuries. We have to be sure he doesn't get hurt again."

"He's *lying*," she said. "Jeff couldn't have hurt him! He's a psychologist, for God's sake. He's a *teacher.*"

I refrained from asking her something that had bothered me from the moment I saw how young she really was: What a psychologist and teacher was doing marrying a student nearly twenty years his junior, whom he had met in his Psych. 101 class, all information I had gleaned from Don's referral. While Carrie had been over legal age when they met, still, Banner had stretched the limits of professional ethics to hook up with her.

"Look," I said as the elevator door opened and closed, "you're talking to the wrong person. I don't know Dr. Banner well and I don't have any history. I'm just operating on what I got from Craig. Based on that, I have to make an initial recommendation. This isn't finished by any means, Carrie. If Jeffery is willing, and he certainly sounded like he is, maybe it can be worked out. But let me tell you something *really* important that has nothing to do with Jeffery. If you go back in there and tell your three-year-old son he's a liar, you'll damage your relationship with him for a long time. I know you're hurt and I know you're angry and I know you think Craig is the reason. But somewhere inside you have to know he's only three years old and that's not true. Now, I would suggest if you can't let him talk, just hold him. Just be his mom. But don't try to shut him up. You'll pay in ways you can't even dream of."

She turned to go.

"Can you do it?"

She turned back, her ambivalence covered by contempt. Before she could speak, I walked back toward her. "This isn't about me, either, Carrie. Look, frankly I'm as confused as you are. I'm certainly not predisposed to believe that a man of your husband's reputation and stature goes around scalding little kids. I do know that from my own point of view, kids belong with their parents. But they also deserve to be protected, and when they get hurt this badly, we *have* to look into it. Every adult has to protect every kid." I caught myself heading for the soapbox, so I cut it short.

"I know how much this hurts, at least I think I do. I don't want you to lose your boy, but you're going to have to show you can choose Craig's needs over your own even when you're hurting this much. Now, I'm not going to go back and say Dr. Banner burned the boy intentionally. I don't know that. What I'm going to say is that Craig *believes* he did, and we have to honor that if he's to feel protected." I waited. "Now, can you do it?"

Carrie touched the doorjamb for support. "Yes. Tell me one more time what to do when I go in there."

Relief washed over me so fast I got goose bumps. I believed I was leaving Craig in kinder hands than I had thought moments earlier, and it felt good.

Staring out the window of the nearly empty 727 into the moonless, star-spangled sky, I let my mind run. Banner was a puzzle. He was a topnotch seminar leader with an absolutely spotless reputation in the field. But his getting hooked up with Carrie put a small crack in all that. I also knew my work with Craig was on the money. I had liked Banner on the phone earlier; he was willing to let me do my job. But Craig's perceptions were absolutely clear. He had specific and intense fear of the man. But, but, but, but. . . . There had to be more. I did figure out that if he was guilty of this abuse, he made a big mistake choosing Craig.

It was two-thirty in the morning when Don Cavett's phone receiver crashed to the floor after the fifth ring, giving me a certain satisfaction that we were *both* awake. I said, "You said you'd wait up."

"I lied."

"Come over to my office at two this afternoon," I said. "I'll fill you in."

The kids' group is over and I'm back in my office with the blinds pulled, lying flat on the floor, hands folded on my chest, eyes closed, trying to meditate three hours' sleep into a two-minute break before I collect Peggy Parker from the waiting room. Last night's plane ride robbed me of valuable sleep. Jerry just spent two solid hours unsuccessfully battling Kong, who has hidden his sister. In one variation he has eaten her. I try hard to clear my mind, as Molly taught me, straining to hear the cosmic hum she swears by. What I get is the hiss of steam from water heating and dripping through my automatic coffee maker. Deep breaths will work. Please, O Master of the Universe, give me just two minutes in a deep coma.

The Master of the Universe is not in. Dragging myself to my feet, I make a mental note to let Molly know what I think of witchcraft, take a deep breath, and head for the waiting room.

I glimpse Peggy before she sees me. She sits, bouncing her foot to a hummingbird's cadence and twisting her ring on her finger like a miniature Hula Hoop. Her face is pinched, her eyes sunken. When I speak, her head snaps up. "Hi, Peggy. Come on in."

Peggy has consistently avoided serious therapy. She

has long maintained it was her brother-in-law's fault that Jerry was left at home for those two days when she was initially referred to CPS—that he had agreed to pick Jerry up—and she has refused to take responsibility. She is guarded, almost visibly fearful, in the adult group, lacking the ego strength to say she made a mistake. She has always been polite, yet distant and defensive, and I'm constantly aware of the unresolved question of drug and alcohol use that was the original focal point of therapy when she left Jerry alone for those two days.

This session is no more productive. Peggy seems preoccupied and unable to focus. Several times I ask her to concentrate on her feelings of loss, or fear, but she comes up blank. She has been deluged by the press in the past week and seems, quite apart from her despair, fascinated with the idea of celebrity, constantly directing the conversation back to the anchor man on Channel 6 or the female newspaper reporter who has spent the better part of three days with her. Peggy is tall and blond, and would probably be physically quite beautiful, were it not for the worn blanket of alcohol abuse and hard times covering her face. Her eyes dart like a hawk's throughout the session, and thirty minutes into it I find myself absorbing her agitation.

"You're going to have to help me out here, Peggy," I say finally.

She eyes me suspiciously, then glances away. "Did Jerry say anything?"

"He's doing pretty much the same things," I say. "How does it help to know what he's saying?"

"I don't know," she says quickly. "I'm not afraid or anything."

"Afraid of what?"

"Nothing. I'm not."

I nod. "Listen, Peggy, this must all be horrible for you.

You haven't said anything about what's going on inside you. I can't imagine not knowing where my child is."

She agrees, without emotion.

"So, can you tell me how you're feeling?"

She shakes her head. "Numb, I guess."

"Is that all?"

She hesitates, as if scouting internal territory, then nods. "That's all."

I say, "I'm stuck. I don't know how to help."

She shakes her head again, rising. "I guess you can't."

"Would you like me to take a stab? Make a few guesses?"

"Sure," she says, as in, *what the hell.* "Go ahead."

"You might be feeling pretty guilty. You said you saw this guy talking with Sabrina at the party. No one there seems to have known him. You might have questions about your judgment."

"It wasn't my fault," she says quietly, sternly, and her nervousness vanishes. "We don't even know that was the man who took her."

"I didn't say it's your fault. I'm just saying you may be feeling some guilt."

Peggy bursts into tears, shouting, "All I care about is finding her! That's all I care about! It's not my fault." She pulls the door open.

I say, "Wait," and she stops. "You're obviously not ready for this. If you get ready, call and I'll set up a time. I'm not sure what you're afraid of, but if it's *me,* I can set you up with someone else."

She shrugs and is gone.

"You ever think we're in this business just for ourselves?" Molly and I are lying stark naked and sweaty

65

in her bed, exhausted from the kind of lovemaking intended to purge reality.

She says, "The business of fucking?" Molly is the only woman I've ever met who likes to make love more than I do, and is thoroughly comfortable saying so.

"No, mental health."

"Same thing."

I'd reach up and grab her throat, but my head is next to her toes and I haven't nearly the energy.

"Child abuse. Domestic violence. You know, fun and games in the trenches."

"Yup."

"There *are* times when you think we're in it for ourselves?"

"I always think that."

I decline to pursue it, deciding my energies are too low for philosophy.

She taps my stomach with her fingers. "Come up here."

I start, but fall back. "You come down here," I say. "I'm old."

Molly brings her mouth close to my ear. "That's why I just work with kids," she says. "I *learn* by letting them go and following them and working where they want to work. It's as much for *me* as for them. When I'm on, we all get something. It's easy if you can stand a little chaos." She traces her finger down my sweaty belly. "If I did kids *and* adults, I'd be confused all the time just like you are. Adults always want to complicate things with words and explanations." She bites my chin. "Adults are a pain in the butt."

"Ah," I say, waxing wise, "but where would kids be without them?"

"If they could find transport other than the Sperm and Egg Express into this world, they'd be just fine," Molly

66

says, and I sense cosmic considerations on the horizon. I know only one thing that will head those considerations off, so I scoot down, tracing the perimeter of that magical expanse between her belly button and her hip bone lightly with my tongue and we are, without delay, back from outer space.

Six

I glance around the circle of nine men in my Tuesday night men's group, wondering if any of them offed my cat. It seems unlikely. True, it can be a surly group, but though rage sometimes ricochets off the walls like a racquetball, hardly ever do we call it a night without at least partial resolution for the issues of the evening. Some of these guys are pretty tough—the Duke himself would throw back a straight shot of testosterone before swaggering into this room—and most are perceived as dangerous in one way or another to their children and their wives/girlfriends, but none seems particularly sneaky or treacherous, and I'm guessing the desperado who brought the curtain down on Ballou is not from this wild bunch.

A quick check for pressing issues proves fruitless, and I sit back. "Well, I suppose we could sit here for two hours, but I've been up a long time. I might get sleepy."

Carl says, "Why don't we just say fuck it and go home?"

"We could do that too," I say back. "Might not sound too good at your court review hearing, though. Comes under the heading of 'resistance.'"

Carl's eight-year-old daughter—now safe in foster

care—has recently accused him of molesting her on several occasions over a long period of time, though he was originally referred for physical abuse. He is angry, and blame sprays from his mouth like BBs from the muzzle of a 12-gauge shotgun, aimed at the Department of Social and Health Services, foster parents, Three Forks Mental Heath Center, the guardian ad litem for the child, and the governor, whose office Carl called in the heat of his rage. "This happens every time," he steadily maintains. "They get your kid and make up stories, then they fry your ass with them."

It is not lost on me that Carl has "every time" with which to compare.

"Anybody else want to say fuck it and go home?" I ask.

"Everybody *wants* to," Eric says. "C'mon guys, let's get this show on the road. I could start, but it's the same old shit you heard from me last week." I love Eric because he does my job for me. He's court-ordered into the program like the others, but Little E is back home with him now. The state can't drop dependency for another six months, and they're requiring him to remain in treatment that long, but Eric is definitely in the home stretch.

When Little E was six months old, Eric flew into a rage because he wouldn't stop crying and shook him senseless, and though the boy bled from the ears and later began having seizures, most of the damage has proven reversible. Eric's guilt has not. His words and ideas are by far the most powerful in the group because, though he took some time admitting what he did—and his frame of mind when he did it—since that admission he's asked for no pity and given no excuses. As much as some of the others fight going through that process themselves, they respect his honesty. I do not know anyone, client or friend, who loves his or her child more fiercely than Eric loves Little E. He made a mistake. He shook Little E to avoid hitting him, not realizing how delicate and fragile the floating brain of an infant can be. And now, not a week goes by that he doesn't stand to face the music. "I don't ever want to forget," he says. "I'm tellin' what I did loud an' clear till the day I die. That'll make damn sure I'll never do it again." I think ol' Eric is a lifeguard, too. Also, he's easily six-two, two-fifty. Tattoos cover his arms like horses on cowboy wallpaper, and his shaggy brown hair and beard, along with the diamond-studded earring in his right ear, say he's not particularly interested in what other people think.

"What about you, Jockey Boy?" he says to Miles. "Give us a kick start here."

Maybe a hundred and three pounds soaking wet, Miles idolizes Eric, a man roughly the size of the stepfather who brutalized Miles with astonishing malevolence over a period of ten years, leaving him full of so much fear and insecurity he has held only the most menial jobs, and never for more than six months at a time. When Miles joined the group, Eric intimidated him so badly it took Miles three months to say so. But that changed in the space of one group session.

"What about you, Jockey Boy, you ever gonna say somethin' in this group, or you gonna sit there till your caseworker decides you're a fuckin' artichoke an' hands your kid to someone who ain't?" Eric was feeling pushy, tired of other group members scrambling to make themselves look good.

Miles squirmed, and part of me wanted to save him. "What do you mean?" he asked, glancing at Eric, then directly at the floor.

"You been here three months. You ain't said shit. You got another six, maybe eight, before they give up an' farm your kid out for good. From the looks of you, you got at least that much work to do, so I'd get with it."

Miles glanced from side to side, avoiding looking at the other group members, who were more than willing to let Eric go after him instead of one of them. His eyes finally settled on mine for a brief moment, then went back down. "What should I say?"

"Why don't you ask Eric what he has in mind?" I said gently. "He's been over this ground himself."

Miles looked to Eric. "What should I talk about?"

"Talk about what got you here," he said, his intensity reeled in a notch. "Talk about what you ain't proud of. How'd you lose your boy?"

Miles hesitated, then, "I beat him up."

"Why?"

" 'Cause he wouldn't do what I told him to," Miles said, dropping his head again.

"Bet you'd do that different if you could take it back," Eric said.

Miles glanced to the side again, then back. "Would if I knew why I done it in the first place."

"You done it 'cause it was done to you," Eric said.

"How you know that?"

"It's the law," Eric said gently. "It's the law. That's what you need to talk about first, what was done to you."

Miles appeared lost a moment, his eyes exploring the room, as if an answer might lie in a corner of the ceiling, then he patted his thighs gently with both hands and shrugged. "Dad left when I was four," he said and went on to tell us of his mother's bringing in a twenty-year-old, two hundred seventy-pound stepdad—a baby himself at the time—with a fury too huge to be contained even by his mammoth carcass. "It was like Mom gave me to

71

him," Miles said. "Once when I was five, just after I started kindergarten, she came to school to get me 'cause I pissed my pants. She had to come from work an' she was real mad 'cause it was a new job, an' she wouldn't even talk to me in the car. She just stopped in front of the house to let me out."

"Was anyone else home?" I asked. "You said you were five, right?"

"Right. Nope, no one else was there. They left me all the time. Anyway, I went in and put my clothes in the washer like I always had to do an' then I went upstairs and waited in the closet 'cause I knew I'd probably end up there anyway."

Out of the corner of my eye, I saw Eric becoming agitated as Miles talked. He said, "They put you there a lot?"

Miles rolled his eyes and nodded. "I stayed in there 'cause I wanted to look like I was real sorry when Burt come 'cause if he thought I was real sorry, he might not hurt me as bad." He paused.

"So what'd he do?" Carl said.

"Well, when he finally did come home he didn't do nothin'. I mean he called me down to dinner an' didn't say a word about it then or all night. I watched TV, just waitin' for him to land all over me. I remember wishin' it wasn't Friday so I could get back to school the next day instead of havin' to be around him. Then, next day I get up real early 'cause I wanna be ready when he comes for me. I know this ain't over, I mean, I know he ain't just forgot, an' I come downstairs an' Burt's having breakfast an' he pours me a big ol' glass of juice an' tells me to sit down and talk.

"Now I been with him a year an' a half already an' I got the marks to prove it, so I know some shit is up, but I don't know what it is yet, so I sit. He tells me go ahead

72

an' drink up and I do, just so I have somethin' to do while I'm feelin' all nervous.

"Finally he says, 'Heard you had a little accident at school yesterday,' an' I say yeah."

Eric's eyes closed in anticipation.

"So he says, 'Your mom wants me to help you stop peein' your pants. Says she can't seem to do it.' I wait some more. He stares at me a minute and says 'Tell you what, Miles, you ain't going to the bathroom till tomorrow night at six o'clock.'

"Well," Miles goes on, "I just stare at him 'cause I don't know what that means, but I put down that orange juice. I ain't dumb. So Burt says, 'Do you understand?' an' I say I do, but I don't really. I mean, I don't know how hard it's gonna be."

"Your stepdad told you you couldn't take a leak for two days?" I asked incredulously. "Jesus, Miles, what did you do?"

"Well, the second he tells me I can't go, I gotta go bad, an' it ain't long before my insides are burnin', so I go lay on the couch an' try to go to sleep and forget. I hear him in the kitchen tellin' Mom she better watch me every minute if she wants this to work an' that if she fucks it up he'll kick her ass, then he gets ready to go pheasant huntin' with a couple of his friends.

"Right before he leaves he sticks his head back in the living room and says, 'Miles, what's the worst thing ever happened to you?' an' I say I don't know an' he says, 'Think about it,' so I say maybe when they locked me in the closet that time an' wouldn't let me out to eat or go to the bathroom or nothin' for two days. 'That the worst?' he says, an' I say yeah. Then he walks over to the couch an' sticks his finger in my face an' says, *Well, that ain't nothin' compared to what's gonna happen if*

73

you pee before tomorrow. You understand me?' Man, he's so big."

Eric stood up and walked behind Miles's chair and, in a trembling voice, said, "What did you do, Jockey Boy?"

"Well," Miles said, "I rolled up into a ball an' just tried to forget, but it's like there's a hose runnin' in me, like I'm just fillin' up, you know? I think I might be able to let a little out at a time an' maybe it'll dry an' Mom won't be able to tell, but I try that twice an' I can smell it all over the damn place. I remember thinkin' maybe I could cry some of it out, you know, like tears are water, but nothin' worked. By the middle of the afternoon, I'm dyin' an' I know I can't make it to tomorrow, or even tonight."

Miles stops, tears filling his eyes, but no one speaks. He swallows hard, and continues. "I don't know how," he went on, "but somehow I made it till Burt got back. I hear the car drive up an' Mom disappears out the back door of the kitchen an' in a minute I hear her call in to me. She says, 'Come out here, Miles. Show Burt what a good boy you been.' Well, I can barely fuckin' walk, but I get up an' make my way to the porch. Burt is openin' his trunk to show Mom all the birds he killed an' he just looks up at me an' nods.

"An' right there it runs. Runs like maybe I think the porch is on fire. I start bawlin', but I can't stop an' it burns an' it feels *so* good an' I'm *so* scared."

"Fuck," Carl said. "What'd he do?"

"He says, 'Had to wait till I got home, huh? Boy, you got some guts.' I remember thinkin' at least it's over now. He'll kill me an' it'll be over. I see him comin' for me an' I just close my eyes an' wait for that loud bang in my ears."

Eric's fists opened and closed on the back of the chair, though he remained silent.

"Only I don't hear it. All of a sudden I'm up in the air an' on my back in his arms, an' it almost feels good 'cause I know he's going to throw me away, but he doesn't. Not exactly. I feel myself fallin' backward, an' then there's somethin' soft an' warm on my back an' my eyes pop open, an' I see the trunk comin' down. That fucker threw me in the trunk with them dead birds. Man, I scream an' scream an' scream, but the trunk slams shut an' ever'thing's black. An' you know the worst thing? The worst thing is I think I hear my mother laughin'."

Tears streamed down Miles's cheeks like drops on a rainy window. Eric placed his huge hand in the middle of Miles's back. "How long were you in there, Jockey Boy?"

Miles shook his head. "I don't know. It was light when my mom opened the trunk, so I know it was at least all night. Burt was nowhere around, an' Mom tried to say somethin' to me, like maybe she was sorry or somethin', but I just walked into the bathroom an' took off all my clothes an' got in the shower till the water run cold an' then I probably stayed a half hour after that." He looked up. "I didn't piss my pants at school again, though."

"Your stepdaddy still around?" Eric asked.

Miles nodded, drying his eyes. "Lives about five blocks from me. Comes over once in a while when he's drunk, but usually I hear him comin' an' turn out the lights and lock the doors."

Silence blanketed the room and I watched the members run Miles's story through their heads. I would not diffuse its power with words. We each needed to find our own way.

"You ever tell anybody this before?" Eric asked finally.

Miles shook his head.

Eric nodded, thinking. "Soon as this group is over," he said, "let's you an' me go over to your place an' load your stuff in my pickup an' you can move in with me an' Little E. Then if your stepdad wants to come around an' raise a little hell, I'll give him some to raise." He looked around the room at the other men. "Jockey Boy," he said, fixing his eyes on Carl, "you're a gutsy little fucker. Really gutsy, maybe even a hero. We could use a little more of that around here."

After group I offered Eric my paycheck, but he just laughed and said he wouldn't have my job for all the world.

"Well," Miles says now, "maybe I do have somethin' to start." He sits ramrod straight, hawkish eyes relentlessly scanning. He is handsome really, but could never hear that, and famous in every battered women's shelter from here to the Montana border. His every relationship has ended in violence within a year of its beginning, and he is recently coming to terms with the possibility that he may never share decent time with a woman. He seems safe only with Eric. Miles continues to fight for the return of his son, but unless a lot more of Eric rubs off on him, that will never happen.

"You know that Parker girl?" he says, "the one in the paper? Sabrina is her name, I think."

I nod. "Um-hmm."

"I was at that party the night she disappeared. It wasn't a party really, kind of a neighborhood barbecue in Whitman Park."

It's an amazing thing. There are two hundred fifty thousand people in this town, and both common sense and experience tell me child abusers don't run in a pack, but I get information on one client from another *far* more often than coincidence should allow. I suppose there are other common denominators.

76

Several members challenge Miles because he has repeatedly committed aloud to stay away from drugs and alcohol. Sabrina Parker's last neighborhood barbecue was obviously not a shindig for the clean and sober.

Miles's hands shoot up in defense. "I didn't drink. Didn't take nothin'," he says. "I just went because a friend of mine invited me. I didn't take nothin'. Really."

I say I believe him.

"Anyway," he says, "I talked to that guy they say was hangin' around her. He was sort of hustlin' the mom, but he kept goin' back to the kid."

If anyone in the world can scope out danger to a child it has to be Miles. Even apart from his car trunk story, his life has been a textbook chronology of a kid in the eye of a merciless tornado. Few acts of cruelty have passed him by, most perpetuated by his stepfather, but lots of rugged relatives, and even strangers, have had shots at him, too. It is a testament of unimaginable courage that Miles stands among us at all. Eric was right. He is a hero. He is also a potential front pager, and if Eric hadn't hauled him in under his giant wing, Miles might just have disappeared into his fear and rage.

"So what did you say to this guy?" I ask.

"I told him to leave her alone, that she's just a little kid."

"And . . ."

"He kinda surprised me. He threw up his hands and said, 'Hey, man, I didn't mean nothin'. Just bein' friendly.' Said he was just tryin' to get her mom's attention."

"What did you do?"

"I told him he shouldn't use a kid. He was big," Miles says, rolling his eyes. "Could'a kicked my ass across the room, but he just said, 'Okay, man,' an' walked away."

"So what's on your chest?" Eric asks.

77

"Well," Miles says, "I been watchin' all this stuff on television, where her mom says she just woke up in the mornin' and found her kid gone an' ever'thing."

"Yeah?"

"Well, she *left* with that guy."

Though I believe my face registers nothing, the tumblers of Peggy Parker's secretive behavior click into place. I ask if he gave that information to the cops.

Miles stares at me.

"You're not going to invoke the code of the streets on this are you, Miles? I mean, you're not thinking you shouldn't tell? Code of the streets doesn't apply to kid killers, does it?"

"We don't know for sure she's dead," says Matt, who paid his admission into this group by hitting his eight-year-old daughter fifty times with a belt because "that's how many she had earned" on the day he did it. She was black and blue from her shoulder blades to the backs of her knees, and Matt has yet to acknowledge one lick of wrongdoing. He claims he got the idea from a private family counselor, whom he refuses to name.

"From kidnappers, then," I answer. "Hey, do we protect kids or not?"

"Yeah," Miles says, "but the cops. I don't like to talk to cops."

Eric breaks in. "The rules have changed, Jockey Boy. Counselor's right, we protect kids. All of 'em." He smiles. "It's one of the rules for bein' in this group, an' it's one of the rules if you wanna stay with me and Little E."

It's agreed by most of the group that each would rather stand on his head to receive hot tar up his nostrils than say word one to the heat, but Eric really is a powerful enough man to write new rules.

Then I explain, for maybe the hundredth time, where

I stand. Either I report suspected abuse and neglect or I'm subject to a ten-thousand-dollar fine and up to a year in jail. "In other words, Miles, either you report it or I will."

Matt says, "Hell, let the counselor do it. That's what he gets paid for. No fuckin' wonder everyone's afraid to talk in here."

"If you're afraid to talk in here," Eric says, "it's 'cause you're chickenshit," and that pretty much ends it.

Out of curiosity, and remembering the neighbor's account of the man he saw on Peggy's doorstep in the early hours of the following morning, I ask Miles if the guy he saw leave with Peggy was wearing an overcoat.

He thinks a minute. "I don't remember for sure. I don't think so. I mean, it was pretty warm."

I let it go at that, thinking at least I have some information that will help me better understand what's going on with Jerry.

I wish what just went on with Matt in the men's group were unusual. I wish I didn't have to suspend my disbelief fifteen times a day to accept the different ways of thinking I'm exposed to. I wish I could be truly startled when I hear of one more person standing by while a child is hurt, or when the details of a new case surpass what I believed to be the previous record for inhumanity. But I know better. I have a client whose boyfriend squeezed her eighteen-month-old son so hard his insides broke, *after* he'd fractured the boy's skull, all because he wouldn't stop crapping his pants. My client lied for her boyfriend right up until the day he went off to jail (he got a year, for Christ's sake) and then *left a thirteen-month-old girl, whom she was supposedly babysitting, ALONE WITH HIM* two months after he got out on parole. And when this same guy brain-damaged and blinded another woman's child four months later, he want back to jail for *parole violation,* and is, on this day, free as a bird. The law stands by, too. I have a male client who raped his eighteen-month-old daughter because he was mad at his wife for the way she treated him—or didn't treat him, as he puts it—then kicked her across the floor and stuffed her into a garbage bag. Two of my female clients, independent of one another, have used daughters under the age of five to sweeten their prostitution businesses. And so on, as Kurt Vonnegut would say. And so on, and on, and on.

Eric stops me by the front entrance. He lays a huge hand on my shoulder and says, "Don't worry about it, Counselor, some days are worse than others."

I smile and say thanks.

"When shit gets bad," he says, "look at the good. If it wasn't for you, me an' my boy'd be goners."

I start to tell him *he's* responsible for getting Little E back, as I always do, but he raises his finger to his lips and shakes his bushy head. "It was you, Counselor."

At home, alone, I shove a microwave dinner in the oven and plop into the recliner in front of a situation comedy about a normal family with normal problems of boyfriends and girlfriends and SAT scores and menopause and male-pattern balding. (Is there *female*-pattern balding?) The farthest reaches of my consciousness record the microwave's three computer beeps when my dinner is ready, but I'm dead away and it's a full hour before I pop awake to a dinner almost as cold as it was when I put it in, and Randy Shaw is on Channel 6 with a teaser: "North side child missing. Stay tuned for details in one half hour at eleven." I reset the microwave and clear a spot on the coffee table in front of my couch so I can eat a late dinner with Randy Shaw.

Sure enough, Randy's got the hot poop on another downed kid. The details I waited a half hour for are sketchy, but another door was battered in and a five-year-old named Cindy Miller, last seen in Daisy Duck underwear, is no place to be found. The incident took place last night, but the mother didn't report it until late this afternoon. *That* will make it into the child protection system—if she has any more kids to protect.

I dial the number Detective Palmer gave me to contact him after hours—which I assume is his home.

"Palmer residence."

"Detective Palmer?"

"Here."

"This is Wilson Corder."

"Corder. I was going to call you in the morning. You got a minute?"

I say of course.

"I take it you heard about the Miller girl."

"You think it's the same guy?"

"Hard to say. He went in the same way, but we've got less on this one than on Parker. No witnesses at all. Mom says she didn't hear a thing. Claims she woke up late this morning and thought her daughter had already been picked up by her brother to go to a preschool summer recreation program, and then to her grandmother's. Couldn't figure why the doorjamb was broken, but thought the door was open because the daughter left in a hurry. Said she was going to chew her out for that when she got home. Mom said it was late this afternoon when she realized the rec program doesn't operate on Tuesdays. Took her another two hours running around in a panic before she called and reported. Trail's cold as my ex-wife's heart."

"Jesus. That's bad."

"Not so bad. She was a bitch."

"I meant . . ."

"I know what you meant," Parker says with a short laugh. "That was *my* attempt at humor. Listen. I don't have to tell you what kind of sorry shit this puts us in. If this is the same guy, it'll take two or three more killings for the department to put a profile together. He hit on the north side, which means we can't limit ourselves to an area. I'm telling you, Corder, when one of these random guys gets loose, we operate behind him all the way. Another kid has to die for us to learn anything new. Now I know I'm jumping the gun putting these two together. This Miller kid could show up in southern California with her dad in two days and we'll find out it was all some bullshit custody dispute. But I doubt it. I've got a feeling."

"What can I do?"

"Well, if you've got any way to hurry your boy along—any ways to help him remember *anything,* now's the time to go for it. I mean, he is the sum total of what we've got." Palmer waits for my answer.

The truth is I don't have one. The danger of paying the kind of attention to Jerry that Palmer wants me to pay is that I'll start putting ideas into Jerry's head, which won't help his therapy and it won't help in court. A good defense attorney will catch him between his experience of what really happened and his desire to please me, and his testimony will look unreliable as a wire mesh condom. With a four-year-old, there's a danger of that anyway. "I'll go as fast as I can," I say to Palmer. "And I'll give you what I get as fast as I get it."

"Good enough," he says. "Listen, get some sleep."

Sleep is hard to get. The news of another girl's disappearance brings back vivid pictures of the terror I imag-

ine Sabrina experienced. Sometimes I can block it out—
in fact, most times. But now I see her being dragged
away, helpless and screaming. I see a man's hand over
her mouth, robbing her of her one defense. I hear her
gasp for breath. I see her alone with him in some isolated
spot, see him tear her clothes from her body, Sabrina no
longer screaming, frozen with fright. I see him hurt her.
God, I see him hurt her. Then I see his hands on her
throat . . .

I believe the poisonous nature of my involvement in
this work lies in my ability to immerse myself into nearly
anyone's life and accept it; giving my clients' struggles
with the universe equal weight with my own. In other
words, my greatest strength is my greatest weakness.
Certainly that style was a large cost factor in the loss of
my marriage:

Trevor's fifth birthday. He was to have had a party in
the afternoon that included about twenty-five of his most
intimate friends (Trevor was a *popular* kid at his kindergarten, and so tuned in to others' feelings he couldn't
bear to exclude *anyone*), and then a family get-together
as soon as I could possibly get off work, which looked
to be about seven-thirty. Things were coming to a head
with Sarah and me—though she wasn't yet aware I had
been taking my physical passion elsewhere—and all
communication seemed to have closed down. Nothing
was left but tests, the focal point of which came to be a
competition between home and my work. What did I care
more about? How many times—and, believe me, she kept
an accurate count—did I choose work over my family?
It was a *perfect* setup to end it all, because when faced
with the choice of a crisis over a noncrisis, Wilson Corder takes the crisis every time. And when he has twenty

or thirty clients from which to choose, he can *always* find a crisis, and when he knows he's being tested, he may very well find one intentionally. So much for Wilson Corder in the third person.

Five minutes before the couples' group was to begin that night, my phone rang. "Wilson Corder," I said. "If I'm lyin', I'm dyin'. I'm dyin' anyway."

"Hi, Wilson. This is your dear, dear wife. You remember me. Dark circles under the eyes, varicose veins. Used to be kind of pretty."

"*Still* pretty." I corrected her. "What can I do for you?"

"Just checking to make sure you'll be home right after work. Trevor's climbing the walls already."

"I'll be walking out of here as the last word is spoken," I said. "In fact, I'll tell them when we start that I need to wrap it up ten minutes early."

"Okay," she said tiredly. "Thanks."

I could hear in Sarah's voice that Trevor's party had turned into a convention of five-year-old lunatics, and I intended to rush directly home after group and take over. "Listen," I said, "put yourself on survival mode. Let him open one gift about six-thirty. That ought to hold him. If it doesn't, there's Darvon in my headboard. Give him the bottle."

Sarah laughed. "Just get here."

I should have known the Devil had tapped my phone. As I jogged out of the group room toward my office, having stopped group ten minutes early as promised, I was met by twelve-year-old Wendy Strong and Jackie, the therapist who ran the eight- to twelve-year-olds' group. Jackie said, "We need to talk to you for a second."

"Good, that's just how long I have. Hi, Wendy. Where was your dad tonight?" Wendy's dad had been absent and left no message.

"He's home," she said. Wendy was a waifish little

mousy-haired girl whose eyes danced continually with trepidation. "He threw me out. He said if you were so da . . . so smart, I could just go live with you. He said if I come home and my attitude isn't different, he's going to knock me across the room and to he . . . to heck with my caseworker."

I didn't want to get into Wendy's attitude because I knew I'd face Sarah's later if I did. "Are you afraid?" I asked. "Does he sound serious?"

Wendy nodded.

"Call CPS," I said to Jackie. "Tell the night crew to come get her from here and take her to her old foster home. They said they'd take her back at a minute's notice. I'll call Wendy's dad and let him know what we've done."

"Our phone's disconnected," Wendy said.

Visions of Sarah and Trevor hammered into my consciousness like Jack Nicholson bashing into the bathroom in *The Shining*. I took a deep breath and squinted at Jackie. "Okay," I said. "You take care of getting her into placement, and I'll take care of her dad."

Jackie nodded and they left. I ran to my office, attempting to call Sarah, but the line was busy, so I hustled out to the front desk, got the address from the night clerk, and sprinted for my car, thinking I could call from a phone booth on the way. I thought briefly about going home first before driving to Strong's, but decided I'd feel pushed to leave before it was time and mess up Trevor's party.

I swear to God if you could have found the point on a map of Three Forks farthest from my home, it would have turned out to be exactly at the center of Roger Strong's roof. I ran yellow lights, tried shortcuts that proved to be long cuts, jumping out every five or six blocks to call from a telephone booth, but the line remained busy, and I felt myself sinking further and further into deep shit.

I know I could have said forget it and let Roger Strong worry all night, but combined with his fierce temper was Roger's fierce honesty. I had agreed at the outset of therapy to inform him prior to any change in course. He knew where Wendy's foster parents lived, which wasn't far from his house. No way I would sleep that night without the bases covered.

Roger reacted as expected, cursing me and threatening to fuck it all and move away and leave Wendy to find a family for herself and blah, blah, blah. When he finally calmed down, he agreed to meet with her and me in my office the following day, and I streaked across his lawn, jumped into my car, and raced for home. I almost stopped each time I passed a phone booth, but by now figured the best I could do was get there as fast as I possibly could and tell the biggest lie I could drum up. I actually thought of hitting a tree in hopes I would be found wandering dazed in the night, calling my wife's name. I didn't want to ruin Trevor's birthday with a fight between Sarah and me, and I didn't want the two of us to spend the rest of the night verbally assaulting each other. And I *knew* I didn't have a chance because I had once again failed a very simple test, one on which I could have easily earned an A. And on my son's birthday, for Christ's sake.

I walked through the door forty-five minutes late, a miracle in itself, if you had asked me. No one did.

Trevor slept in my chair, his presents unopened.

"It just never fails, does it?" Sarah said.

"Doesn't seem to," I answered. "There was nothing I could do about it, Sarah. You *must* know how much I wanted to be here on time. Let's don't do this. Let's just wake him up and have his party. Where's his sister?"

86

"She's in the TV room," Sarah said.

I said I'd get her.

The party came off as smoothly as possible, but I knew all of hell awaited me behind our bedroom door.

"What do you suppose it would take?" Sarah asked, pulling her nightgown over her head, and I thought, *Here it comes.*

"What do I suppose *what* would take?"

"What do you suppose it would take for something at your home to be as important as the *piddliest* little thing at the almighty mental health center?"

"Sarah, let's not—"

"Not even your son's birthday."

"Look," I said, trying to hold back my temper, "he had his birthday. It was just a little late."

"Do you know what my day's been like?" she asked.

"Your day was hell," I said.

"Wilson, I took a day off work to give Trevor this party. That means I'm a day's work behind, which will take me *three* days to make up. I had twenty-five four- and five-year-olds here for three hours this afternoon and only two other parents. I'd say on the average they had the manners of spider monkeys. They threw things, they cried, they beat each other. One girl got two little boys in the bathroom with their pants down. But no one died and there are no lawsuits that I know of and Trevor said it was a great party. All I wanted from you—no, all I *needed* from you—was to get here in enough time to take over for maybe one hour. No twenty-five monsters, no bloody noses, no greedy little boogers wanting to know why Trevor got all the presents. Just your family." Tears started down her cheeks, dripping from her chin. "I'm sick of it, Wilson. Do you hear me? I'm sick to death. You just don't care. You take care of people you don't even know and you leave your children to fend for themselves."

I looked up to see Trevor standing in the doorway, silently crying, and my heart sank right into the mud. "My party was okay," he said. "It was okay that Dad was late. It was okay."

If my look could kill, Sarah would have been reduced to subatomic particles. I motioned Trevor over, and he came slowly to the bed. "I'm sorry," I said to him. "I just couldn't get here any quicker. I'm sorry you had to wait and fell asleep and had to be woke up to open your presents, but you know what?"—and I looked directly at his mother—"It's probably never going to change. I'm a late dad, I guess."

Trevor said it was okay one more time and lay there with me while I ran my fingernails over his back, lulling him to sleep before carrying him back to his room. When I returned, Sarah and I started a marathon Convince-O-Rama during which she tried to show me how I'd used my son to get myself off the hook and I tried to show her she was a cold bitch. We were very near the end. I think I finally told her I'd been in someone else's bed because I was too chicken to detonate the freedom bomb myself and I knew she'd do it herself when I said it.

The problem was, Sarah was right. For me, that was always the problem. I did use Trevor to protect myself and I did choose to take care of others before my own family. In my reality, my family was well cared for and pretty capable of fending for itself in a pinch. When I looked at where to go for balance, it was always to help families about to blast apart. What ended up happening was, mine did.

* * *

"Have a seat, Peggy." I motion between the chair and the couch. She looks at each nervously, as if the decision is too tough. I say, "The chair is more comfortable, and there's a lot less likely to be kiddie leftovers on your pants when you leave."

She smiles, grateful for my attempt to relieve pressure, and chooses the chair, which is something of a bucket and forces her to be cradled.

I tell her I'm glad she came back. "You seemed pretty upset when you left."

She nods. "It's awful. My ex-husband called in the middle of the night the other night and said this is all my fault and he's going to try to get custody of Jerry. He won't do it—he's drunk or high almost all the time."

"But that can't make you feel any better."

"Right. Worse yet, I think my family agrees with him. My sister is talking about Jerry coming to live with them, and my mother hasn't spoken to me since Sabrina disappeared. We've never been very close—I told you I was kind of the black sheep—but it seems worse now, with all this."

I say that must be incredibly difficult.

She nods and looks away, tears welling, and snatches a Kleenex, dabbing below her eye.

"Want to talk about it?"

"There's something else I have to talk about first," she says. "I wasn't completely honest the other day when I was here."

I wait.

"I might have encouraged that Edwards man. He was hitting on me at the party and I knew it. I'd had a little too much to drink and I didn't notice that . . . well, maybe he was paying too much attention to Sabrina."

I nod.

Peggy glances up and holds my eye for a second before looking away.

I say, "Is that all?"

She hesitates, grimaces. "Yeah. That's all. I'm just saying it might have been partly my fault."

I reported the information about Peggy leaving the party with Edwards last night, two hours after group, just as I said I would. Obviously CPS hasn't confronted Peggy. I ask her how I can help.

"I just thought it might help working with Jerry," she says. "He might blame me, too."

"We've got the bases pretty well covered with Jerry, Peggy. Certainly we appreciate all the information we can get about that night, but you might consider getting help for yourself."

She darts back into her old song. "I didn't do anything wrong . . ." but I raise my hand.

"I keep getting this feeling you're telling the truth, but you're not telling all of it. You seem scared, and you have a right to be. But I'm guessing the thing that's scaring you most is the thing you won't say."

She looks away.

"Peggy, listen. I have some information that I had to report to the state. Somebody who's a client of mine said you left that barbecue with the man they think took Sabrina. Now, I don't know if it's true or not but I do need to let you know I've reported it."

Peggy's eyes are frozen on me. I continue. "Look, Peggy, if you come in here with a little bit of the truth, you get a little bit of therapy. If you go to the authorities with a little bit of the truth, you get a little bit of action. You must know more than you're saying or this would all make more sense. I don't know who you'd feel safe in telling, but if I were in your shoes, I'd figure that out."

"Is it confidential?"

"It's like all therapy," I say. "Nothing you say leaves this room unless it's new information about current abuse or neglect. You know I have to report that."

She nods, closing her eyes. "I did leave with that man. But I didn't take him home. I was pretty messed up, but I straightened out enough before we got home to send him away." She breathes deep. "But then I went home and drank more. I passed out. That's why Jerry couldn't get me up. I'd had too much to drink and I just passed out." She looks at the floor. "I may have taken some drugs, too. I was feeling pretty crazy."

I nod and take a deep breath of my own.

Peggy bursts into tears. "I can't lose my last child. I can't. I just can't. Jerry's all I have left. *Please,* Wilson. Don't tell them to take Jerry."

"I don't tell them to take kids, Peggy. They decide that for themselves. I just report, and I do have to report this. It's a repeat of how you lost him before."

"Please don't report it. I couldn't take it, Wilson. I couldn't take it."

"What would you do?" I ask.

Peggy knows better than to threaten suicide unless she means it because then we have to talk about evaluating her, and consider hospitalization. Jesus, people are left with ghastly choices sometimes. She says simply, "I don't know."

I sit back. "Look, Peggy, let's go at this from a different angle. First, I think it would be a bad idea for Jerry to be out of your house. He's attached to you and he already feels partly responsible for what happened to his sister."

"Did he say . . . ?"

"Wait. Let me finish. I also think if your alcohol and drug use is so great that you're passing out when you need to be there for the kids, it's dangerous."

91

Peggy breathes in sharply.

I hold up my hand again. "Now, just wait. A better thing would be for you to report it yourself. You're already in treatment and I'll let CPS know you've talked to me already. My guess is they'll recommend substance abuse treatment because that's what I'm going to recommend. If you comply, I can't imagine they'll take Jerry away. If you do comply, I'll strongly recommend that they leave him in your home."

Peggy nods, digesting what I've said.

I say, "Things are out of hand, Peggy. It's time to get control."

She sinks back into the chair and nods.

What the hell, I think. I decide to go for it. "Peggy, what do you think happened to Sabrina?"

"What do you mean? I think she was taken. Kidnapped."

I take a deep breath. "Do you think she's alive?"

She flares. *"Of course . . ."* But it trails off. "I don't know. I have to keep thinking she is."

"Do you want to know?"

Peggy's eyes snap up at me.

"Do you?"

"Yes. I don't know. I'm not sure. I mean, as long as I don't know, there's a chance. You know what I mean?"

"Um-hmm," I say. "I do know what you mean. And I'll tell you what else I know, or at least what I think. I think unless you go all out to find out everything you can, and tell the police and me *all* you know, you're going to be completely eaten up with guilt when everything's out in the open. The issue of Jerry is different from the issue of Sabrina. You must know the longer she's gone the less chance she's alive."

"I know that."

"You heard about the second missing girl?"

Her gaze drops to the floor.

"Then let me say this. If it makes you mad it makes you mad. I've worked with you and your kids a long time now. Almost every time I get the feeling you're hiding something—holding back information with silence—it turns out you are. I'd say *every* time but there might be one that slipped by me. And I'm telling you now, Peggy, I've got that feeling and I've got it *big.*"

Peggy stares.

She doesn't storm out, so I continue. "Whatever it is, it has to do with what happened after you left the party. Now, I may be crossing some lines here, lines between therapist and detective, but I feel fine about it because all this secrecy isn't good for Jerry and I doubt it's good for you. If it *is* good for you, it's because you know something pretty awful."

Peggy still doesn't detonate, which surprises me a little, but she offered no more. She agrees to call CPS, and I tell her I'll have to check to be sure she does. My deadline is twenty-four hours from the time I receive the information, but I give her only until four-thirty. That way I can contact her regular caseworker before quitting time.

I feel better as she leaves, but still unsettled. The trouble with Peggy Parker is that she is tremendously skilled at disclosing exactly what she thinks other people might already know. Nothing comes out completely on its own, which means there's more. If I know what that more is, I can be there when Jerry falls, and maybe I can clear my head of all the wild possibilities of what I believe were Sabrina's last hours.

Seven

"Can you say for certain that Mr. Creason deliberately abused this child?" The public defender fixes a hard stare and I squirm in the leather swivel chair on the witness stand. The judge watches impassively. It is my first time in court.

"Yes," I say. "I can. Based on the work his son has done in therapy, and Mr. Creason's unwillingness to cooperate, I can say I believe that Mr. Creason physically abused him. My opinion is based on state guidelines for physical punishment."

"Are you aware that Richard Creason has a history of lying that is documented not only at home, but by his teachers and counselors at school?"

"I'm aware of that."

"So how do you account for arriving at your conclusion?"

"I've spent more than a hundred hours with Richard. Based on the therapeutic relationship we have established and information I've received from other agencies, I believe my conclusions are true."

Richard is twelve. He sits in the courtroom, next to his aunt. As I finish my sentence, he stands, speaking loud and clear. "I lied. The bruises on my eye were from

94

a fight at school. I was mad at my dad so I said it was him. I lied."

Outside the courtroom, Mr. Creason puts two thick hands on my shoulders. He's a large and powerful man, some would describe as simple. "I know you wanted to help," he says to me gently. "But you can hurt people when you don't know what you're doing. You might not be as smart as you think."

I pop awake. The actual events were more complicated, but the dream is the truth. Mr. Creason's blazing look filled me with humiliation. He was correct. I thought I was pretty smart. I thought I was *right*.

It is a recurring nightmare. Sometimes I scream my accusations of abuse over a wildly protesting public defender and a judge's gavel, before falling to my knees to beg Bart Creason for forgiveness. I can't imagine being wrongly accused of hurting a child.

The work Craig Clark did with me in Seattle indicates intentional abuse. However, I don't know enough about him to know if he's been abused before and is confusing Dr. Banner with the abuser, or if some odd set of circumstances I can't fathom occurred to cause him to say what he's saying. That would be unusual, but certainly not unheard of. He is remarkably articulate for a three-year-old and his sense of cause and effect is that of a child much older. If I were to write my impressions solely from that interaction, I would say it is a near certainty that Dr. Banner intentionally scalded him in some kind of power struggle over potty-training. But today the CPS caseworker held a meeting of interested parties, and I have to say I'm having trouble with my initial assessment.

Fred Cronk called for the staffing at the request of Carrie Banner, and we met in a small room over the Department of Social and Health Services building shortly before noon. I knew Fred was predisposed to believe the Banners. Don Cavett was not present because he was not directly involved with the case, and he had already informed me that Fred's immediate supervisor, Margaret Drollinger, had no reason not to back Fred. Luckily I'd had the chance to veto the presence of the Banners' lawyer. I've had more than my share of experiences meeting with public defenders and private attorneys only to have them later select certain sentences and parts of sentences to kick my ass in court, and at this point I wasn't even sure which side I'd be on if court time came.

"I've called this meeting," Fred said, "because of the unusual circumstances surrounding this matter and because Dr. Banner and his wife are interested in getting it settled as soon as possible. I should add that they've been cooperative in every phase of my investigation."

I glanced over at Banner, who sat comfortably in his chair. He is tall and dark, built a lot like me really, only shorter and a little less muscular. I remembered from his seminars that he always dresses casually but well, and he was looking good today in a tweed sports coat over an open-collar shirt. I nodded and smiled slightly, and he returned the smile. Carrie sat stiffly beside him, her hand in his lap.

"I've gone over this matter time and again," Fred continued. "I've talked with Dr. Banner and Carrie at length, and quite frankly I'm convinced that Craig's scalding was an unfortunate accident. Horrifying, but accidental nevertheless."

I believed I was expected to fill the silence. I didn't.

"So where do we go from here?" Fred asked the group.

All eyes turned to me, and I smiled. If battle lines were to be drawn, I wasn't going to be the one to draw them. At least not yet.

Fred's supervisor peered at me over her reading glasses. "Mr. Wilson, I understand you have some thoughts on this."

"Wilson's my first name," I said. "And I do have some thoughts, but I'm feeling a little distressed."

"And why is that?"

"Well," I said, "normally a staffing is held to put all the information out on the table and make an objective assessment." I nodded to the Banners. "No offense to you, Dr. Banner—and I really mean that—but I'm not hearing any information, other than what Fred has already decided."

Fred opened his mouth, but Banner broke in. "Wilson is exactly right," he said. "He knows everyone here aside from himself is of the same mind and he's right to want it done correctly." He sat forward. "And for my part, I don't want my position in this community or in this business to impede a complete investigation. If there's to be any integrity in our field, we have to police it."

Fred looked surprised. I thanked Banner for his words and raised my eyebrows, nodding toward Fred. When he didn't respond, Banner said, "I've told you some of this, Wilson, but let me fill you in on what I've told CPS and the police. I had been trying to teach Carrie to potty-train Craig because she was worried she'd never get it done, Craig being her first and all. We played some potty games and made some reinforcement deals, and he was actually doing quite well.

"He was naked from the waist down on the couch that night to air out his diaper rash. I was working on some research when I glanced over to see him hosing down our brand-new couch." Banner sat back and smiled, then pinched the bridge of his nose. "I have to admit, I was a little put out. Carrie was at an aerobics class and I knew I'd have to interrupt my work to clean him up, and the couch would certainly have to be cleaned professionally. I think I was madder at myself for leaving him there than I was at his mistake, though I was probably a little rougher on him verbally than I should have been, because I remember he looked at me and shrank back, which only served to increase my anger at myself." He looked directly at me. "I'm sure you know the feeling that goes with making mistakes in your area of expertise, Wilson."

I smiled. "It's a feeling I know well."

Banner went on. "I decided the easy solution was to just drop him in the tub and clean him there, so I hurried upstairs to run the water. Just then the phone rang and I ran into the bedroom to answer it and I'm afraid I got caught up in the conversation. Then I heard Craig's screams. I couldn't for the life of me think what was wrong, but I was there in seconds. Craig had managed to get himself into the tub and was sitting there screaming. That was the point I realized I'd never turned on the *cold*. I snatched him out immediately and rushed him to the hospital." Banner took a deep breath. "I just couldn't believe it. I mean, I don't bathe Craig often, but enough to know to be far more careful. There's no excuse for this." He looked directly at me. "And believe me, Wilson, I thought immediately how this would appear. Think of the number of times you've heard stories exactly like the one I just told, from men who savage their families."

I nodded. "You're right. I hear them a lot." Now I knew why everyone believed Dr. Banner. *I* believed him. At least based on what he'd just said and the sincerity with which he said it.

Fred reclaimed control. "We'd like to come to some resolution to this soon," he said. "There's a lot of pressure on the Banners, as you might guess, and as a matter of policy we like to keep a child out of the home for as short a time as we can."

I nodded.

Fred pushed. "Based on what you've heard, Wilson, do you see any reason not to send Craig back today?"

"I want to see him again first," I said. "For whatever reason, he's pretty frightened. Anytime a kid goes through that kind of trauma, whether it's intentional or not, he needs to feel some power over what happens to him next. When will he be out of the burn center?"

"That's why I called the meeting today," Fred said. "He's coming back on a plane with a student tonight. I'd like to return him to Dr. Banner and Carrie then."

Now I'm feeling really uneasy. Dr. Banner seems vulnerable, and I believe I can truly imagine what it must be like to have your professional life on the line like that. And to tell the truth, I'm a bit intimidated by him. Irreverent as I may be among my peers, I ain't quite so smart for my britches with fame in the room. Besides, I've attended Dr. Banner's seminars and I've read up on some of his work on anger management and domestic violence. He's well respected and he's smart as hell. His private presentation of himself seems congruent with his public image. *But* I'm a lifeguard first. I shake my head. "I can't go with that. I know you can do it, but you'll have to do it against my recommendation."

Carrie looked surprised and started to speak, but Banner put a hand gently on her knee.

"The one thing I know about kids' therapy," I said, "is that it's done from *their* point of view. I won't be specific about what Craig said and did when I saw him, but he needs to deal with this relationship in what he considers a safe place. He said he's afraid to go home with Dr. Banner in the house and I think we need to respect that."

"I'm mandated, if there isn't danger of imminent harm, to put him back as soon as possible," Fred said. "Are you willing to state there's imminent harm, Wilson?"

I started to say no, that technically Fred would be within proper boundaries to do so, but once again Banner stepped in. "Wilson's right again," he said. "The fact is, the *harm* has already been done."

I nodded. "And I'm not making accusations, Dr. Banner. I want you to believe that. But I think it would be in everyone's best interest if you voluntarily placed him. There must be relatives . . ."

"Certainly," he said. "He can stay with Carrie's mother." He turned to Carrie. "Or your sister. What do you think?"

Carrie appeared confused. As much as she wanted her boy back with her, she clearly deferred regularly to Banner. "I . . . I guess. Not my sister, though. My mother."

"I have one other request you might not like," I said.

Fred was visibly irritated. "What is it?"

"I'm going to recommend that visits with Dr. Banner be supervised."

"Why on earth . . . ?" Carrie cried. "What's the matter with you, Wilson? Do you actually think my husband is going to try to hurt my son on a visit? My God. What's the matter with you?"

Once again Banner stepped in. "He's right again," and I'm thinking, *Three for three.* "We don't want to say anything that will inadvertently make Craig think he has to lie to protect us, particularly you. This is as much protection for us as it is for Craig. No one will be able to say we've coached him. Or frightened him. I'll agree to that, Wilson." He smiled. "You do good work. I have to admit I was worried Craig would get some inexperienced mental health worker coming in like a gunslinger looking to make a name, but I'm not worried now. I can see you're doing your job by the book. I have nothing to hide, and I appreciate your holding the line."

Within five minutes, we drew up the specifics of the agreement and were out the door.

Banner caught me in the hall, ready to push through the outside doors. "Corder," he said, and I turned. "I meant what I said in there. I hope when this is all over we can get together and swap war stories."

"I'd like that," I said. "Count on it."

On the way back to the center, I stopped by my house to change my sweat-soaked shirt.

Eight

I get on my bike after work tonight, peering carefully in all directions. Nothing looks out of the ordinary, but I feel like taking no chances. I strap on my helmet and ease out of the parking lot like a ninety-year-old lady renewing her license in Phoenix. Molly sits on the back, calling me a pussy.

I pulled a "confidential" envelope out of my mailbox in the staff room today, and found a snapshot of Ballou inside, just as I discovered her, tacked to my front door. A note in cut-out newsprint read: STOP SEEING JERRY PARKER. Jerry's name was cut out in individual letters. The envelope carried no stamp, meaning it must have been hand-delivered.

I canceled my next client and called Detective Palmer, who came directly over and questioned the front desk staff, as well as a few clients who happened to be in the waiting room at the time. No one claimed to have seen anything or anyone out of the ordinary, though "out of the ordinary" around here would be a sight to behold. Coming up empty after nearly forty-five minutes nosing around, Palmer requested the photo, in the unlikely event it harbored fingerprints. He dropped by later to say it was smooth as a baby's butt, and I told him not to bother returning it, that I had dropped the idea of blowing it up to poster size. He correctly identified that as an attempt at more humor.

"So, what are you going to do about this?" he asked.

"Quit picking up my mail," I said.

"I mean about Jerry Parker."

"What I've been doing," I said. "What are you going to do about Wilson Corder?"

"What do you mean?"

"Well, between us, Molly Comstock and I have a pretty good chance of getting information you won't find anywhere else. I don't know about Molly, but I gotta tell you, Detective, somebody keeps offing my pets, I could get gun shy."

"You asking for protection?"

I consider a moment. Channel 2 had led the eleven o'clock news for the past two nights with stories of manpower cutbacks in the police department due to inadequate funding. It's a sore spot among the rank and file. "I sure would be if I thought I could get it," I said. "But I guess I'll have to settle for being kept informed. I mean, what do you know about this Edwards guy?"

"Not much. We obviously think he's in town now, due to that note and the disappearance of the Miller girl. We've got a make on one Marvin Edwards who hails from a Podunk town in Mississippi. He's got several molestation charges, but they were all reduced to Communication with a Minor. Word is, he's a drifter with friends here. We've got his picture and we're out to get him in a big way." Palmer laid a beefy hand on my shoulder. "Corder, I've been told I have a pretty laid-back style and it's probably true. But don't confuse it with indifference. I want this guy and I want him bad. One more kid disappears and this town's under siege." He dropped his hand and started to walk away, but turned and winked. "I'm *gonna* get him."

I told Palmer I believed him and that I had never considered him indifferent. "How 'bout if I drop by and take a look at that picture," I said. "Might as well have a face in my head."

"Might as well," Palmer said. "Stop by. Probably better bring your partner. My guess is, this guy wouldn't be above creating a little nightmare on her street, too."

So, with the evening's work behind us, Molly and I head over to the police station. Palmer won't be there, but he's left instructions to show us their shots of Marvin.

The desk sergeant cites Edwards's vital statistics as we gaze at his mug shot. I don't know exactly when they held this photo session, but they caught Marvin in a *bad* mood. With a ragged scar running full length down his left cheek, matted curly dark hair, and a week's growth of stubble, Marvin's is not a face I'll likely forget. "He's pretty good-sized," the sergeant says. "Probably a little under six feet and pushing one-ninety. He's been small time up to now, but if he did this one, he's a *bad* actor. I'd consider him dangerous."

I tell the sergeant I have no problem considering him dangerous.

Molly and I take a short spin out the north end of town, settling back, gliding through the evening glow, each, I think, considering the possibilities. We still have a few hours of daylight left and it would be nice to keep right on traveling north, but I promised Trevor I'd take him to a movie tonight, since his sister is out of town at a basketball camp and he claims we need more time alone together for "male bonding." Male bonding occurs when I spend money on that bandit. The more I spend, the tighter the bond.

I drop Molly off back at the center, and we talk a few

moments about what we've been avoiding: our fear for our kids. If it was Edwards that killed my cat, it's just a few steps . . . The cold reality is that most likely, the same man who murdered Sabrina Parker—and we're both convinced she's dead—is out to scare me away from Jerry, at the very least. If that's true, he'll soon be out for Molly, too. The few times I've been threatened personally by a client—and it really hasn't been often—the threat has been directed at my kids. Something about the way we hold children aloft, give them voice, directs potential aggressors to our point of weakness. And believe me, that *is* my point of weakness. There's nothing more terrifying in this business than the tormenting realization that someone can get to me through my kids.

"He'd have to be out of his mind," Molly says when I finally mention it, "to come to my house. Alex went in for his prefootball physical the other day. He's almost two hundred and thirty pounds."

"I would say kidnapping a six-year-old qualifies this guy as out of his mind," I say.

Molly shrugs, raising her eyebrows.

"Jesus," I say, forgetting for a moment the issue at hand, "two-thirty. How do you feed him?"

She shrugs. "Just strap those little bags over his ears and wait till he chews through the end, then give him another. Not much to it, really."

"Well," I say returning to the present, "my guess is this guy's not afraid of much, but I also think I'm the one he sees as a threat right now. Just be careful, okay? Like keep things locked up at night and all."

"Yes, Mom," Molly says with a smile, touching my shoulder. She pulls out of the center lot as I glance around automatically in search of long black cars with dark tinted windows. Heading home to exchange the bike for my car, in the event Trevor wants to go to the drive-in, I tell myself maybe I should watch less television.

Molly and I seldom mix time with our kids. Neither of us has a need to create a Brady Bunch and we're both completely comfortable allowing the different parts of our lives to remain in their natural compartments. We don't want to be married and we don't want to be with each other all the time, though we do want the time we spend together to be good. Since a lot of what I do with my kids involves Sarah, and since neither of us intends to introduce the other to our kids as a stepparent, this seems to work best. There is clearly no "right" way to do this, but neither of us wants the other to ignore his or her history. It is incredible to me how taking certain expectations out of the relationship has allowed this level of intimacy.

"I don't suppose you want to go see *The Last Temptation of Christ?*" I ask Trevor as we walk toward the car.

"Any chicks in it?"

I grimace. "Why don't you go back and ask your mother that? In those exact words."

He asks do I think he's crazy.

I say, "It has a few 'chicks.'"

His eyes narrow. "Where is it?"

"At the Magic Lantern."

Trevor wrinkles his nose. "That's the place where you have to read the movies. If I wanted to read, I'd go to summer school."

"This one's in English," I say.

"Yeah, but it's about Jesus, right? Like it's about the Bible."

"Sort of." I start to explain a little of Kazantzakis's ideas, then remind myself that even though this kid is

106

nagging me about "chicks," he's only nine years old. His sister and I have tricked him into going to the Magic Lantern—Three Forks' only so-called art theater—with us a few times, but never that I didn't wind up buying him ice cream and taking him to a video arcade afterward to make up for the rotten time he had. I don't really expect to take him to *The Last Temptation*.

We settle on the East Sprague Drive-In, which features an Arnold Schwarzenegger film festival. Trevor considers Arnold to be the finest actor of his time, and can't understand why when the Academy Awards roll around, old Arnold never gets picked. Trevor has decided the Academy must be full of screwballs and sissies, an opinion he insists Arnold also holds.

When the lights go up around one A.M. and Arnold has significantly reduced the world's population of bad guys, I wake Trevor up to tell him it's time to go.

"Those were good, huh, Dad?"

"I've never seen Arnold better. They would have been twice as good if you'd stayed awake."

"I was awake. I just rested there a little bit before the end."

"Which you knew anyway," I say, "having seen those flicks at least ten times."

"Only three," he says. "Is all the popcorn gone?"

I assure him it is.

"Hey, Dad, do we have to go right home?"

"Why?" I glance at my watch. "You hungry?" I can't believe he is, having consumed seven times his body weight in remarkably expensive junk food.

"Huh-uh," he says, shaking his head. "I just don't want to go home yet."

My son's specialty is ambiguity; he's getting to it, but it'll be a minute. "You want to stay at my place?" I ask. "I can call your mom."

"No, that's okay."

"What, then?" We're nearing the exit, ready to jump the freeway back to town.

"You think we could go to Whitman Park?"

"Whitman Park? What for? Trevor, it's almost one-thirty in the morning. What are we going to do at Whitman?"

"I don't know," he says. "Just look, I guess."

I start to ask *for what?* when the fog lifts. Whitman is the county park closest to Sabrina Parker's house, the site of the barbecue the night Sabrina was taken. It was also the takeoff point for most of the organized searches, including the one in which Trevor's scout troop participated, searching for a lost girl whose name is fast becoming a synonym for terror among the children of Three Forks. Trevor hasn't been back there since that day. "This is about Sabrina Parker, huh?" I say.

He nods. "I think she was there, Dad. I think we just didn't see her." He stops, then chokes out, "I keep dreaming about it. The park, I mean."

"And Sabrina?"

He nods. "Sometimes when you're scared of something, you can't get it out of your mind, and you need to see it in real."

I nod quietly, staring into pleading eyes that fear I'll give the adult answer he expects. And I *want* to give that answer. I'm *not* excited to hang around Whitman Park at this time of morning. For one thing, hoboes sleep there during the summer, and it's a spooky park at night anyway. "How about if we just go drive around it? Would that help?"

We pull into the parking lot, having wakened Sarah from a phone booth to tell her we're going to be late and she should go to bed. She politely informed me that had already happened and why didn't I take him to my house and avoid dismemberment. It was a good idea.

Streetlights illuminate the parking lot and we sit, staring past the playground equipment into the shadows. The developed portion of the park stretches like a golf fairway almost two hundred and fifty yards toward a recreational baseball diamond, then slopes upward, gently at first, then steeper into an undeveloped woody portion, a perfect place for kids to explore the thick forest and giant rocks.

Trevor says, "Could we get out?"

The moon has not cleared the trees and I gaze into the dark expanse of the clearing. "Are you out of your mind?"

"Maybe she's here, Dad. Maybe we just missed her. What if she's still alive but she's hurt and she can't move? What if you were all alone in the dark here and nobody came?"

My best judgment tells me this is where any good dad draws the line and says, "It's not safe to wander around county parks late at night because bad guys hang out there." But the picture of an unnamed child discovered dead and frozen in a refrigerator box in a vacant lot outside Pittsburgh, Pennsylvania, in the winter of my eleventh year, flashes by as if 1957 were yesterday. Daily I searched out my mother's new hiding place for that issue of *The Saturday Evening Post* just to stare at that boy's face, above the caption DO YOU KNOW THIS CHILD? As tormented as I was, I couldn't stop looking at it. I couldn't let it go. I know how Trevor feels.

I remove a flashlight from the glove compartment, and we step quietly out of the car, heading across the dark expanse for the woods.

For nearly a half hour we search the rocky underbrush, uncovering nothing more than empty beer cans and a few skittish nocturnal animals. Trevor works like a search-and-rescue pro, leaving no shadow or dark corner un-lighted. He stays close and I am captivated by his intensity. "It's easier at night," he says. "You just look where the light is. Your mind doesn't wander."

I agree—though my mind is indeed wandering—before setting a deadline, fifteen minutes more.

"You think we should call for her, Dad?"

"I think if we call for her, the people who live in those houses beyond the trees will call for the police," I say. "Besides, if she could call back, she would've already." The intellectual side of me knows we are searching for something we're not going to find, but another childlike, hopeful, fearful part is intrigued. Fifteen minutes pass. "We need to go, Trevor. I don't think she's here, do you?"

"No," he says. "Probably not. You think I'm crazy, Dad?"

"Nope, it was a good idea. She's just not here, that's all. We should go now, okay?"

"Okay," he says, but pauses. "Could we go on Big Rock for just a few seconds?"

What the hell. We haven't been ambushed so far, and I'm going to be bone tired in the morning anyway. The half-moon has risen above the tree line now, and as we scramble up the back of Big Rock, I shut off the flash-light and we finish our climb by moonlight, then sit, staring back across the grassy expanse to the parking lot, the freeway beyond, and into the lights of the city. It is strangely peaceful.

Trevor slides in under my arm, and we sit a moment in silence. "Do you ever get ascared, Dad?" he asks finally.

I say sure, that I get scared.

"What of?"

"Oh, I get afraid for you and your sister sometimes,"

I say. "I get afraid that I haven't done things just right. Or sometimes I get afraid that you won't have all the best of everything because of something I forgot to do. Things like that."

"But do you ever get ascared in your house? Are you afraid to be alone?"

He's asking it it's always going to be like this for him, or if there will come a time when he doesn't have to be paralyzed from all that moves in the dark. "I don't get afraid in my house," I say. "I don't get afraid alone anymore. I used to, though. Just like you."

"When does it get over?"

"Oh," I say, "it just gradually goes away. Little by little. One day you just kind of notice you're not so afraid anymore. It helps to get bigger. It helps to feel strong."

"I hope it happens soon," he says. "I'm really tired of this."

"I hope it happens soon, too," I say, and the picture of the frozen, lonely, unknown Pittsburgh boy breezes again through my head.

Trevor presses closer. "Do you ever talk to the people at your work about me?"

"You mean like the other therapists? Of course. I talk about you all the time. Half of them are sick to death of you and they've never seen your face."

"No," he says. "I mean the ones that are your patients."

"Clients," I say.

"Clients. Do you ever talk to *them* about me?"

"Sometimes."

"What do you tell them?"

"I say I can understand why people abuse their kids."

"I should go there and talk to them," he says, ignoring my feeble humor. "I bet it would help them to know you're a good dad. I bet if I told them that, they'd listen to you better." Trevor has always been fascinated by my

111

work because it's so hard for him to understand about kids getting hurt on purpose. He tells me time and again how he can't see why if his dad tells them to stop, they don't just stop. I tell him I don't see why, either.

"They might," I say. "They just might."

We're quiet a few more seconds, and I'm about to suggest once more that we call it a night while it still is, when he pushes into his last leg of tonight's internal journey. I am absolutely fascinated by the way a child's mind works, the way it juxtaposes things adults try to keep apart to avoid dealing with them.

"Do you ever wish you and Mom were still living together?"

"Sometimes. No, not really."

He says it's okay if we don't, and I say good and give him a squeeze.

"Do you still hate yourself that you played around on her?" he asks, and instantly I wish the kids hadn't been dragged in on the details, but the fighting was so vicious and ugly then that nothing was kept from them. I'm still humiliated by my lack of integrity then.

"Yup," I say. "Yup, I sure do."

"How come?" he asks. "It was a long time ago. You tell me to let things go all the time, but you never do it."

I ruffle his hair. "I feel bad because I didn't tell the truth," I say. "That's the hardest part for me. I didn't tell the truth. When you love somebody, you should always tell them what's real to you. Then they know they can trust you." I feel myself being guided back through my life's toughest journey with a soft, slow hand.

He says that's hard sometimes, always telling the truth, at least for him.

"It's hard for everybody. Maybe that's the reason we should try to do it. Because it's hard."

"Why *didn't* you tell the truth?" he asks. "Grown-ups are supposed to, right?"

"Everybody's supposed to," I say, desperately hoping he'll understand, and forgive. "I didn't tell the truth, son, because I was ascared."

Nine

John Sheldon's eyes burn into the side of my face as we sit around the long table, waiting for the team meeting to begin. My head is down and I'm trying to concentrate on my charts, but for the most part I'm feeling John's displeasure with me. John is still upset about the incident with Jerry in the hall, and this is the first time he's had a chance to deal with it. Though any good therapist knows communication is the key to a happy workplace, a socially arrested part of me—a part which at times can make up as much as sixty percent of my personality— likes to push it. Since that day in the hall, I've delighted in remaining noncommunicative, pretending when I see John that I don't remember the incident ever occurred and ignoring the fact that he'll barely speak to me. In fairness to John I really believe he's one of those people who went into psychology in hopes of ferreting out the source of his own insecurities, and remains at least partially baffled. He works very hard at the *mental* aspects of the business while remaining bewildered with regard to the spiritual aspects.

Whatever. I don't have much energy for his concerns.

Carla Montande, our team supervisor, sweeps through the door toward her customary seat at the head of the table, spreading papers before her. Carla is a large black woman, always impeccably dressed, with a strikingly attractive face, probably the most "on task" person I know. She glances around the table. "Sorry I'm late. Does anyone have anything for the agenda?"

John's hand shoots up. He *raises his hand,* for Christ's sake.

Directly to Carla, and with a straight face, I say, "I think we need to talk about common courtesy among therapists."

"My sentiments exactly," John says and launches into an account of the events in the hallway a few days ago. "I realize," he says when he has completed his summary of my insensitivity, "that we have to find a way to coexist here and I realize kids sometimes make noise. But Wilson did nothing to quiet this child. In fact, Wilson, in my opinion, you exacerbated the problem, and you did it purposefully. I don't mean to be inflammatory and I'm aware that may sound like an accusation, but that's the way I see it."

I sit quietly in the face of his charges, trying not to smile. It doesn't occur to John that I couldn't care less. I don't have much to worry about with Carla; she's been putting up with my childish pranks for nearly ten years. If ever she intended to rein me in, she'd have done it the time I jammed Sheldon's office door while he was inside with a claustrophobic client diagnosed with a paranoid personality disorder. But John's opinion of me and my prehistoric style may have a following in this room, and I certainly don't want what seems to me like a minor incident to get out of control. On the other hand, I can't resist one more shot. "I admit that part of what John's saying is true," I say, "and I should apologize to the entire team. I do exacerbate, usually purposefully, but almost never in the halls. I work very hard to keep it under control, which is why I get up so early every morning. I exacerbate at least three times before I come to work. So you see, there's no way I could exacerbate again before late evening. I'm plumb tuckered out."

John turns beet red, his carotid artery swelling like a fire hose, before he explodes. "That's exactly what I'm talking about! One cannot be sober with this man. This is serious business. People who come here are in a great deal of pain and all this . . this . . . this . . ."

"Asshole," I fill in.

"You said it! All this, this *lunatic* can do is *play.* I resent working with people who don't take this business seriously! I resent it! I spend incredible time and energy trying to make this center *professional* and what I get back is Wilson acting as if these premises were the back lot at Disney!" John gathers his papers and stands.

I am impressed that John even knows who Disney is. "Go to your room," I say under my breath as he reaches the door.

Only Carla hears my last comment. She shakes her head, gazing hopelessly at the agenda sheet she has prepared, then closes her eyes. "Wilson . . ."

"I know, I know. God, I just can't help myself."

The remainder of our group of approximately a dozen stirs and twitches uncomfortably. While most are weary of John's dead seriousness, there are a few who think I should mow lawns and shovel walks for a living. And they may be right. But when John gets on his high horse, all I can think to do is ambush him. This business has no room for those who don't know the degree to which life and play are the same.

Carla stares at me. "Now how am I supposed to fix that?"

I sigh. "You're not. I'll fix it. I was out of line. It's been a tough week."

116

"Every week's a tough week," she says. "It's been a tough week for John, too . . ."

"I know. I said I'll fix it."

She waits.

"You want me to fix it now."

She nods.

In John's office, I offer my Look-Sometimes-I'm-Just-a-Jerk speech and tell him I understand what a distraction it must have been the other day. I do not address his arrogance, nor my belief that had John's client been raging out of control and disturbing *my* session with Jerry Parker, I would have been expected to understand completely. John understands adult pain. He does not understand child pain. I simply say I will do my best to keep kids quiet outside his office from now on and apologize for being insensitive in the meeting.

John accepts my apology reluctantly. A voice in the back of my mind won't let me forget the rough time Molly's going to give me when she finds out I made amends. She would much rather I'd have come down to John's office and driven a wooden stake through his heart. Molly believes deeply that if you can't understand a child's heart you have very little chance of helping mend an adult heart, and probably you belong in Sales. What the hell, I'll lie. "It's been a tough week," I say to John by way of excuse. "On top of everything else someone killed my cat and I may be a little on edge. I may have brought that to work."

"I heard that," he says, shaking his head sadly. "That's unfortunate. Do you have any idea who did it?"

"Someone who doesn't want me working with Jerry Parker," I say, realizing I'm bothering to share this information with someone I care so little about only to create the illusion of professional respect—and get my-

117

self off the hook. "I would guess it was the guy who got his sister."

"That's a vicious thing, to kill an animal," he says.

"It's a vicious thing to steal a kid, too."

"Indeed," John says, rubbing his chin. "So, are you going to stop working with him?"

I shake my head. "Nope."

"You're a brave man, Wilson. Sometimes probably too brave for your own good. I mean if a man—a *killer*—is making threats . . ."

"I just don't see where we can stop working with someone because we get threatened."

John shrugs. "We can't save them all, Wilson. It would be nice, but we can't."

"I know that . . ."

"I think we have to draw the line when it comes to personal safety. If we had wanted to be policemen . . ."

I nod. "We'd have gone to the police academy. I know."

"It's just that from a professional standpoint I think we have to set some limits."

"I agree. You and I just disagree on where the limits should be set."

John shrugs again. "Certainly it's up to you. I don't have an investment one way or the other, really. Even though you and I don't always get along, I hate to see one of my colleagues threatened."

I stand to leave. "I appreciate that, John. I really do. The limits are hard to set sometimes. I've got some pretty crazy cases right now."

"Yes. I understand you have been seeing the Clark child," he says as I reach for the doorknob.

The name doesn't register immediately, then, "Oh, yeah. Actually, I'm not exactly *seeing* him. I've seen him once."

"What do you think?"

"I think he was burned pretty bad. How do you know Craig Clark?"

"I'm acquainted with his stepfather. Dr. Banner. Of course you've met him. He told me about the staffing the other day."

"You must know him pretty well."

John swells with the pride of a man on the periphery of celebrity. "Actually, yes. Well, not *well*. He called just recently to consult with me on a diagnosis. We belong to the same health club. I'm certainly not in his league professionally, but he relies on my diagnostic abilities occasionally."

I nod. That makes sense. John Sheldon is nothing if not an extremely competent diagnostician.

"He mentioned that you did an admirable job in that staffing. He thought it took a lot of courage to take the stand you did."

I nod. "Tell him I appreciate it."

"You don't actually believe he burned the boy purposely, do you?"

"I don't believe anything yet," I say, thinking I don't want to be discussing this with John. "It's pretty confusing."

"It's inconceivable, don't you think?"

"Stranger things have happened."

"Maybe," he says, "but this would be awfully hard to imagine."

I nod again. "Well, I gotta get back up to the meeting? You coming?" I know he isn't. John Sheldon *hates* to lose even the slightest control before his peers. He'll be particularly courteous in the hallways and the waiting room, engage us individually in conversations, pay compliments and feign interest in issues he generally considers drivel, then appear at next week's meeting as if nothing happened. I open the door to leave. "Say, Wilson," John says. "You don't think Dr. Banner will actually be blamed for that unfortunate incident with his stepson, do you?"

"I don't know. Why?"

"It would just be a shame to put him through such an ordeal."

I don't argue, though Craig's "ordeal" flashes through my mind. I say, "Like I said, I don't know" and continue my attempt to get out of John's office with my ears intact. "I gotta go, John. If Dr. Banner just made a mistake, I'm sure that will come out and he shouldn't have anything to worry about." *Finally,* John's door closes softly behind me.

It was likely my father's influence that led me into this business, though I doubt he knew what it is a therapist does. If he did, he'd have had razor blades slid under his fingernails before seeking one out for professional services. But it was Dad who taught me to simplify, to cut through the bullshit.

Sometime around my fifth-grade year, shortly after television came to Samson Falls, Dad sat my brother Albert and me down in front of *Highway Patrol* and turned off the sound. At short intervals he questioned us about our perceptions of the program's characters and the goings-on in general. Which were the criminals and which were the victims? Was Broderick Crawford happy or mad? How could we tell? (It wasn't easy, Broderick ran a pretty short emotional gamut.) Without looking at the clock, could we tell when it was about over? After that night he required us to watch a different program each week with the sound off. My observational skills increased geometrically as a result of my father's expertise at using television as a teaching tool.

* * *

I walk back upstairs to the meeting from John Sheldon's office with a familiar feeling in my stomach, the one I get when the cards aren't all on the table. John Sheldon hates my guts. He would never admit that straight out, at least not to me, but he has no respect for me or anything I stand for, and one thing I can be sure of is, what he really wants won't be what he asks for. I have no idea what his interest in Craig Clark is, or for that matter, why he would spend more than fifteen seconds talking to me about Jerry Parker. He also doesn't give a rat's ass what happened to my cat. When John Sheldon is cordial to me, engages me in any conversation other than to tell me what an immature oaf I am, it's time to turn down the sound and pay very close attention. If I don't, he'll get me for sure.

Thanks, Dad.

A harsh ring jars me from sleep. The red numerals on my digital radio alarm clock read 3:17. Thinking—hoping—it was part of a dream, I drop my head like a rock to the pillow. The doorbell rings again and I stumble in the dark for my bathrobe before feeling my way down the stairs. Flicking on the porchlight I see Eric—Little E wailing in his arms—staring back at me.

I open the door. "Eric."

"How ya doin', Counselor?"

"Okay, I guess. A little bleary-eyed, but hey"—I can see he's wrecked—"come on in."

"Thanks."

I stare at his bloodshot eyes as he sits on the couch, which creaks under his considerable bulk. "What are you on, man?"

Little E continues crying, and Eric sits him to one side. "Booze. A little grass. I can't do it, man." He looks at Little E's tear-streaked face. "I can't shut him up without hurtin' him."

"Did you . . . ?"

"Naw. I stuffed him in the sidecar an' brought him here."

"Gotta stay straight to take care of . . ."

"I *was* straight. I took the shit to calm myself down."

I can see Eric's anger cranking up. "Tell me what happened," I say quietly.

He leans forward and stares at the rug, then up at me. "This is the third night in a row, man. I been up an' down with him the last two nights. Got maybe three hours' sleep total. Then my boss gets on my ass at work today 'cause we need to get these three Harleys ready for a show by the weekend an' I can't stay late to catch up 'cause I gotta pick *him* up before six." Eric nods at Little E, who is quieter now and appears to be eating his fist. "We start to argue an' I threaten to make him eat one of the fuckin' bikes part by part, an' next thing I know he's screamin' at me I'm fired. I say, fuck it, it's too late 'cause I already quit. Then I go get Little E. Man, I know I'm on the edge already an' he's still bawlin' when I pick him up, just like when I left him this morning an' I know goddam well it's gonna be another all-nighter."

"Eric, that's when you have to get yourself some help."

"I did get myself some fuckin' help, damn it. I called this chick I used to see off and on, an' told her to come over an' me an' Little E'd cook her up some chili. She said okay an' she come on over. Evenin' was goin' great—little shit actually went to sleep while we was watchin' a movie—an' Ella decided to stay. Shit, man, I ain't been all night with a woman since I got him back.

So I get him in his bed, over in the corner in my room, an' one thing leads to another, an' pretty soon Ella an' me are makin' it. Man, this is the *first* time in more than three fuckin' months."

He looks over at Little E and shakes his head. "Well, you know what happens then. Ella gets hot an' she ain't one to keep the moanin' down an' next thing this little shit's wailin' and screamin' an' Ella stops right in the middle. Says she can't fuckin' make love with him bawlin'. I say I'll move him into the living room for a minute, long enough to finish, for Christ's sake, but she says no, she's out of the fuckin' mood an' she puts on her goddam clothes an' is gone before I can figure what the hell happened."

He leans back on the couch. "Well, I know I'm hot, but I get his bottle an' stick it in his face an' hold him awhile, but I'm really pissed so I stick him back in his bed. I sleep maybe a half hour an' off he goes again." He closes his eyes. "Man, an' then I feel it. It's just like when I fucked him up last time. There's this knot in my chest that's tight and hot an' it just don't give a shit. I don't *care* if I hurt him again. I got no fuckin' job. I ain't gonna be able to feed him. He's fuckin' up my sex life." Eric stops to laugh. *"What* sex life? An' I just want to throw him through the fuckin' wall. I fix him another bottle but he won't take it. I try to stick it in his face three or four times but he just spits it out an' keeps right on with the goddam screamin'. That's when I grab him by the shoulders." Eric's head drops. Pain constricts his throat tight, and he swallows. "Just like before. I'm gonna shake him till his head pops off."

I put my hand on Eric's shoulder, but he draws away.

"But I see his eyes," he says. "I see his eyes an' all that's there is *terror.* An' somehow that stops me an' I bring him here."

"Eric . . ."

"You should'a seen him, Counselor. My fuckin' kid's gonna be scared of me for the rest of his life."

I'm quiet a minute. Little E starts to fuss and I pick him up, which quiets him immediately.

"Little shit don't do that when I pick him up," Eric says.

"Little shit won't do it when I pick him up either, most of the time," I say back. "Eric, what do you want? What would help?"

"I want you to take him. Just take him. I can't do it. I'm a biker, man. That's what I'll always be. I just ain't cut out for this shit. Remember when you told Jockey Boy if he couldn't take care of his kid it was best to cut to it *now?*"

"Yeah."

"Well, maybe it's time to cut to it."

"Miles's kid is less than a year old," I said. "If he's going to give him up, he needs to give him a chance while there's still time for him to attach somewhere else. That time's gone for you."

Eric is quiet.

"Eric, you know I can't take him. If I *would* do it, I couldn't. The state would place him in a licensed foster home."

I place Little E back on the couch and he sits gazing up at his dad, his crying finished for the moment. They couldn't look more alike if Eric spit him out, hair to his shoulders, an earring, a sleeveless Levi's jacket identical to his dad's. I smile. "Eric, look at him. He's *yours.* Who would take him?"

"I can't do it, man. There's too much. I don't know the rules anymore. I'm confused all the fuckin' time. I get so fucked up I don't know whether I'd be better off usin' or drinkin', or who I should be runnin' with or any

124

goddam thing. There's just too many choices an' most of 'em are fucked."

I move to the couch beside Little E. "You straight enough to hear the truth?"

"Yeah. Fuck, I just had one joint an' a beer."

That is akin to me sniffing a wine cork. "Okay. Eric, you're wrong about all the choices. There are only two. You can step into the river of your life or you can stay on the shore and spew all that biker shit about free will and free spirits and free rides, because that's exactly what it is: shit. Simple as that. And you're past all that, Eric. You couldn't go back to it if you wanted to. Shit. You've been fired from that job fifteen times since I've known you. You'll go back there tomorrow and Stan will beg you to come back and you'll jack him up for another buck and a half an hour and that'll be that. And Ella's not the only hot chick in the world. Believe it or not, there are women in the world who would love to make love with you to the music of a crying child. You just need to find out who they are. This shit will look better by daylight, Eric. You know it will. Just forget the call of the wild. That's not even what it is."

Eric stares at me through bloodshot eyes, and I see him soften.

I try our common metaphor one more time. "Step into the water and ride toward grace, my man, or stand on the shore and rage about your fear."

He watches me, and I don't know what he's thinking. Whatever it is, he doesn't offer it.

So I say, "And you're a lucky man. You got a kid to keep you floating in the right direction. All you gotta do is follow. When you do for him, you do for you. No confusion involved."

His eyes go cold again. "You ain't hearin' me, Counselor. I said I almost threw him across the goddam room. I just can't let him be."

"If you hurt him, you hurt him," I say, hoping I won't be quoted. "But unless you kill him, you won't hurt him any worse than you will by leaving him. He's yours, Eric. He's attached to *you*, not me or anybody else. You rip him away from that and you might as *well* shake him senseless again. In fact, it would be a favor."

Little E is up now, exploring, and I get him some measuring cups from the kitchen. I swear to God, at two and a half he has his dad's swagger. "Look at him, Eric. Giving him away would be like handing some poor unsuspecting foster family an Eric Doll. That's *cruel.*"

Eric lets my humor ease him. He sits back on the couch and for the moment the crisis seems past.

I commit the therapists' cardinal sin of offering him a beer, which he accepts. "You know the difference between you and me, buddy?" I say, twisting off the cap.

He smiles and takes a swig, wiping the foam from his mustache with his forearm. "You mean beside the fact that I could crack your head in the crook of my elbow like a walnut?"

"Yeah, beside that."

"There's a lot of differences between you and me, Counselor."

"Not really," I say. "I think the big difference is that when I fell down my dad picked me up and dusted me off and pointed me back in the direction I was headed. Yours kicked you across the floor. And he didn't bother to teach you about the monster inside. I think that's the difference."

Tears well in Eric's eyes and he stares at Little E playing on the floor with the measuring cups. "I just don't want to kick him across the floor," he says.

"Then don't. Look. You've got the number for the Crisis Nursery. That's what they're for. We can call from here if you want."

"Naw," he says, "that place ain't good for him. Only time I ever took him there was when I was pissed. He thinks I'm givin' him away. You're right, Counselor. This little shit is *my* job. I was payin' attention to the wrong stuff, that's all."

Eric has come a long way. He puts himself back together much more quickly now. I pat the couch. "You guys want to stay? It's late."

Eric shakes his head. "That's okay. Thanks for the offer, though." He stands and I stand with him. He looks down at Little E. "They forgive you, don't they?" he says.

"Seem to."

He slaps his thigh and Little E bounds for him, falling against his leg. At the door, Eric puts a huge hand on my shoulder. "I don't know what I'd of done without you, Corder. I mean it."

"Don't worry about it. Just answer me one question."

He waits.

"Can you really crack a walnut in the crook of your elbow?"

Eric smiles. "Indeed I can, Counselor. Indeed I can."

Ten

It's Monday. Sabrina Parker has been gone four weeks. The search for Marvin Edwards has turned into an agonizing ghost hunt. There has been no trace of him since the note in my mailbox, no sign of Cindy Miller, the little girl who disappeared up on the north side. Someone tried to grab a little girl on her way to school about a half mile from the Parkers' house four days ago, but he wore a ski mask and escaped on foot when neighbors responded to her screams. The city is on edge and the law seems totally frustrated. Though the police haven't attributed all the incidents to one perpetrator, every would-be detective from here to the Canadian border has reported a Marvin Edwards sighting. He has been spotted in hobo camps, hitchhiking on the freeway, working as a dishwasher in the Greyhound bus terminal, and performing abortions in the Deaconess Medical Clinic. The entire eastern half of the state is enraged at his crime, though not one piece of sound evidence has surfaced to indicate Sabrina's final fate.

Jerry has been stuck in his monster play, unable to conquer the power of the colossal evil consuming him, Peggy has added nothing that might help him through, and generally all movement seems bogged down in thick, brown Jell-O.

And just when there's no light, you get blinded.

"Get the monsters!" Jerry demands, even before all the children are in the playroom.

"You talkin' to me?" I'm Robert De Niro in *Taxi Driver*. "You talkin' to *me?*"

"I'm talkin' to you," he says, pulling back his fist.

"You talkin' to *me?*" I say again, and his face starts to fall. I've gone too far. "You're talkin' to me," I say quickly and gather monsters with exaggerated speed.

When my arms are full I ask, "Where to?"

"Follow me." He shoves me out the door. I trick him into taking the back hall to my office, in the event he should contract another case of the growls as we pass John Sheldon's office. Jerry is easily tricked as long as we hurry.

"You want Molly?" I ask, thinking it's always been easier for Jerry when she's the rudder.

"Leave the bitch."

I nod. "Molly stays."

"The bitch stays," Jerry echoes.

"You got some mouth on you."

In my office, Jerry lines up monsters and dinosaurs and He-Man and She-Ra as usual—even G.I. Joe this time—all to fall with a swipe of Kong's huge paw. They lie helpless, bleeding and screaming.

Here the theme varies. Jerry digs into his front pocket, extracting a small figure in a skirt, sporting blond bangs and a removable sword in a plastic scabbard hanging to its side. It is a figure from an old Prince Valiant set, broken up months ago. He must have gotten it from the box of what most of the kids now call "Odd Ends." Compared to the other figures, the prince is tiny.

Jerry stands the figure on the back of my small couch,

saying, "This is upstairs . . . I mean, up the mountain." He entrusts Kong to me, with instructions to "kill them feed"—a term I have come to interpret as "eat them"—should any of his dead foes move. As Prince Valiant creeps stealthily down the back of the mountain, a couple of Kong's wounded enemies twitch, and Kong chomps their body parts. The prince seems grateful for the distraction, and sneaks more rapidly, silently drawing his sword, then leaping—with a scream that probably puts John Sheldon on top of his desk—onto Kong's back.

Jerry snatches Kong from my grasp, and I slowly retreat from the theater of war to observe the prince clinging to Kong from behind, stabbing the back of his neck and head as Kong roars with rage, unable to shake Prince Badass, growing more and more enraged, stomping and shaking and baring his teeth.

At the moment I believe Jerry will finally let someone conquer the dark monster haunting his dreams, Kong reaches back and gets a claw on his royal peskiness, working for a solid grip on his scrawny throat, then flings the prince to the floor, raising his huge foot to stomp out his life. But the junior monarch rolls away ninja style and comes up scrapping. For probably three minutes the two face off, circling, one desperately searching for an advantage over the other, until his highness leaps too close, and the huge gorilla gets him once and for all. In a quick and violent climax, the prince is clawed, bitten, and thrown across the room, to be crashed against the far wall with all the velocity a sweating, exhausted four-year-old boy can muster; one plastic arm flies high in the air, followed by a leg, followed by the head. As pieces tumble to the floor, Jerry whimpers, "Get up. Please, Mom, get up. Where are you? Get up! Get up!" louder and louder until he crumples into a sobbing heap.

I move to him quickly, sliding to the floor beside him against the couch amid the casualties of his wretched battleground. Jerry's cries are loud and long, extended to the limits of his breathing, his body soaked and limp.

I say, "Jerry, tell me what happened."

He only sobs his mother's name.

I wait for the desperation to recede. Then, "Jerry, it's okay. You can tell me. Tell me what happened that night."

"I . . . ca . . . can't."

"Why?"

He shakes his head. "I ca . . . can't."

"Jerry, you can tell me. You need to tell."

He regains partial control of his breathing. "I get in . . . trouble. They come take me. I . . . no get involved."

Involved. Not Jerry's word.

"Why not?"

He begins to speak, purses his lips, shakes his head, and we sit. "It's okay, Jerry," I say. "You can tell me. I think that's why you brought me in here today, I bet. Instead of Molly. You were going to tell me."

He stares into my face. He looks old. His eyes close.

"Tell whenever you want," I say. "Doesn't have to be today. Doesn't *have* to be ever," and still we sit.

"The door was banging and I was scared."

"At night?"

He nods.

"It keep banging but nothing happen. I yell downstairs to my mom but she don't answer."

"You sleep upstairs."

He nods.

"Got my own room, too."

"Anyone else up there?" I ask.

"Nope. I yell at Mom but she still don't answer and then it crash and I hear Sabrina yell."

"What do you do?"

131

"I yell for Mom some more, but she don't get up. I just hear Sabrina yelling, yelling, yelling."

"So what do you do?"

"I get out of bed and come down a little bit. About the top stair or a little bit more."

"Uh-huh. What then?"

"I see him. He gots Sabrina."

"Who?"

"That guy. He gots Sabrina and her yelling at me to get Mom."

"Jesus, Jerry, what do you do?"

"I run to get Mom."

"Yeah."

"But . . ." He searches my face. "But she don't wake up. I can't get her to wake up."

"So what do you do?"

"I run to the kitchen."

"What's in the kitchen?"

"Knife," he says. "A big knife in the drawer with the cat food. I get the knife and I come back out."

"What are you going to do with it?"

Jerry's shoulders swell as he raises an imaginary butcher knife with both hands. "Kill him," he says. "I'm gonna kill him. I growl, *rroooowwwww!* and tell him 'Get away from my sister, bastad.' "

Now the story takes Jerry over. "Stand back." The unrecognizably deep voice sends goose bumps dancing across my arms. "Stand back or I'll kill the bitch here." His eyes widen. "I take one step at 'em and Sabrina crying and telling me get Mom hurry and just get Mom and I 'fraid to tell her Mom's not there . . . I mean I can't get her up. He gots her on her neck, so I take one step closer."

"Stand back," and the mysterious voice returns. "Stand back or I'll kill her here."

"I take one more step," Jerry says, "and monster guy grab my arm and goes . . ." Jerry demonstrates his twisted arm shoved up behind his back. "Then he backs up to go out the door he busted and he goes out only he still gots Sabrina and her crying and screaming at me to get Mom, but I can't get her up."

"Oh, God, Jerry," I say. "What did you do?"

"Take my knife and go upstairs back to my room, 'cause I know that monster man guy coming back to get me." Jerry's look is cold and hard. "And I know I hafta kill him."

I have no words and I know my heart will pound through my breastbone and if that doesn't kill me I'm going to cry until my breath simply stops.

"You gots tears in your eyes," Jerry says.

I nod. "I sure do gots tears in my eyes."

"How come?"

"I'm thinking of how scared you must have been, and that makes me really sad," I say. "And I'm thinking about how brave you are."

"I not scared," he says defiantly.

"Maybe you're not," I say. *"I* sure would have been."

"Well, not me. If that monster man guy come back I gonna kill him. Gonna cut off his arms and his head." He raises his eyebrows and nods to let me know this is no bullshit, buddy. "I will."

"I believe you, Jerry. But it's time for big people to take care of this monster man guy. Little guys shouldn't have to mess around with 'em."

"Gonna kill him," he says.

"So when did your mom finally wake up?" I ask. "Did she get up in the morning?"

Jerry stares blankly. Nearly five seconds pass. "Go back to the room," he says.

"Don't want to talk about it, huh?"

"Let's just go back."

133

After Family Group, around eight, I call Molly to see if she wants to have some dinner. I can't get Jerry out of my head, sitting upstairs in his bed in the dead of night with a kitchen knife, ready for the return of the monster man who stole his sister. I feel like Jerry; I have to go over it and over it and over it until it either makes sense or I get tired enough thinking about it that I can allow it to be, and go on.

"I'm starved," Molly says. "We should ride to get there." Molly could eat a dozen meals a day and not gain weight. She runs and swims and lifts weights like a woman possessed, with the metabolism of a humming-bird. "Kids are gone," she laments into the phone. "I bear them, feed and nurture them through the hard times, the sadness and sickness of their Wonder Years, and what do I get? An absentee vote of confidence. Confidence dinner will be in the refrigerator. Confidence their clothes will be washed and folded. Confidence . . ."

"Feeling a little unappreciated?" I ask.

She switches. "Hell no, I'm glad to have them gone. Means I can go on lightning motorcycle rides with my boyfriend and drink beer and eat greasy chicken and pizza. I'm just telling it like it is."

In a booth at the Iron Horse, Molly combs hundred-plus-mile-per-hour rats out of her hair, grimacing as she listens to me tell Jerry's tale. "He told you because you're big. In his eyes, if anyone could protect him, it would be you," she says.

"Yeah. But I don't know whether I can fill the bill. Part of me thinks protecting him would be trying to get him out of there, if Peggy doesn't have any better judg-ment than to get messed up when there's no one to look after her kids. But if he were removed . . ."

"He'd think it was his fault and be *way* worse off than he is right now," she says. "Did you ask him if the guy at the party was the same guy who took his sister?"

I shake my head. "He finished before I had a chance, though I assumed it and probably wouldn't have asked anyway. You think there's a chance he wasn't?"

"Not much. It would be a big coincidence, but nothing surprises me anymore."

I'd feel a lot better about Jerry's safety if I thought Peggy were coming clean with everything she knows—and everything she thinks. "Now that CPS knows she was out of it when Sabrina was taken, maybe they'll make some threats and put pressure on her to stay clean and watch out for him. You know how Peggy is always sure they're going to take him. If her caseworker had put on a little more pressure in the first place, we might have been able to get some decent work out of her. Now I just don't know."

"It's a crapshoot, Wilson. It's always a crapshoot. But I'll tell you something. Whatever Peggy did that night isn't all that unusual. There are at least five other women in your adult group who could have been caught in the same position. No value. No money. No way out. You get a chance to party a little, numb the pain, you don't pass it up." She's right. Ugly as it is, Jerry's best where he is. The way he's behaving, if he *were* placed he wouldn't make it twenty-four hours in most foster homes. A more haunting thought, however, is that if Marvin Edwards is willing to threaten *me* to stop Jerry's information from getting out, what in the world is going to stop him from going after Jerry himself?

"I'll tell you something else," I say as the bartender serves the chicken. "There's more to come. There are a *lot* of missing pieces."

"No kidding," she says. "Peggy's covering her ass

135

somehow. She *has* to be. She's been on television two nights out of five for the past month, she's starting a chapter of the victims' support group in her neighborhood and there's even a community fund to raise enough money to help her move. If she's seen as an accomplice— even out of stupidity—all that goes down the drain and there's nothing left but shame." Molly shakes her head. "To tell the truth, I don't know many people who wouldn't do exactly what she's doing. *I* sure wouldn't want to be stuck with her choices." Then she looks up and rams an index finger in my chest. Women seem to do that to me a lot. "That's why I don't do adults, Wilson. I'd start feeling sorry for Peggy Parker and the next thing you know I'd be compromising Jerry to meet his mother's needs. You're crazy. Give up those adult groups and come do kid stuff full time with me."

There are times I agree. When you look at kids' needs and parents' needs, particularly when the state is involved, things get pretty convoluted. The very nature of our adversary legal system creates the illusion that what's good for the child is by definition not good for the parent, even though it should be obvious that parents' needs can't be met when their children are in danger simply by being around them. So, because of our administrative needs, kids get pitted against parents, and the members of the system line up on one side or the other. But what I also know is, you can take *any* of these parents, Peggy Parker included, and turn back the clock ten or fifteen or twenty years and you'll find the very child you're trying to save. That's a law. And there were damn few lifeguards on duty then, so though we're late, we still have to give them what we can. Still, though it's a decent thing to have empathy for abusers, we have to *always* act in the best interest of the child, or the shit just keeps rolling downhill. We save kids because they're the ones we can.

136

* * *

Sarah and I sit on either side of Trevor, watching Emily star for her summer league basketball team. Neither of us brings anyone else to these games. Athletics is one area all but untouched by the toxins of our breakup, and I think the kids get a sense of continuity for the part of family that does continue to exist. Molly never tests me. Going to my kids' games with my ex-wife doesn't mean anything about her. Molly appreciates history.

Emily is kicking ass. This kid can run and jump like a cheetah, and I love it, though my response doesn't approach Sarah's. Sarah: ever rational, always calculating pros and cons, studying cause and effect. Plant her in the grandstands of one of her kid's games and she instantly transforms into a fire-breathing beast. In ten years no referee has made a sane call against any of her babies; the opposing team is composed of devil children who deserve not only loss, but humiliation as well.

Today none of that matters. Emily can't be stopped. Her summer league team is led by a player/coach who played for Emily's high school three years ago and now starts for San Diego State. This team is without discipline, *highly* offensive-minded, and they're having a ball. They run and gun and laugh and cuss and everyone in their league hates them. They *always* win.

On the sideline after the game we invite Emily to go for pizza, which she of course politely refuses. She scored twenty-three points and hauled down thirteen rebounds and is not about to celebrate with two old people and a brat when she can hang out with the folks who appreciate her most.

"Dad," she says, pulling on her warmup pants over her shoes, "who's Jerry Parker? Isn't he that girl who disappeared's brother?"

"Yeah, why?"

"Well, I got this strange phone call at home this morning."

My heart vaults.

"Some guy wanted to know if you were my dad."

Sarah won't return my anxious glance but stares directly at Emily. "What did he want, baby?"

"Well, at first I thought he was a recruiter or something. He asked if I was the Emily Corder who plays basketball at Jackson High School and if I lived at 730 West Carlisle and I told him yes. Then he asked if you were my dad—no he just *told* me he knew you were my dad." She ties the string on her sweat pants. "Then he said to tell you to quit working with Jerry Parker."

Eleven

When you deal in other people's rage, you'd damn well better know something about your own. Sticking your nose into other people's business is not only presumptuous, it can be dangerous. In college, my Anger Control Therapy professor, Dr. Stevenson, presented a number of cognitive methods to step back from anger, let us role-play them in class, and helped us put together a practical therapy program.

What he neglected to teach us was correct information about the nature of anger itself. A completely controlled man as far as I could tell, Dr. Stevenson shared the common cultural belief that anger should be contained within any given individual through self-talk and willpower, then diverted. I devised a program that earned an A, and I did it without Sarah's help. My interest was selfish in that I, myself, possess a nuclear temper for which I have, throughout my early life, paid dearly in loss of friends, lovers, and damage to inanimate objects. If I could reclaim merely the *financial* losses I have suffered for punched-out car windshields, fist-sized holes in apartment wall Sheetrock, disfigured reluctant vending machines, and my high school biology teacher's brand-new

1965 Mustang, I could have bought my motorcycle with cash. I used to get *pissed*.

Like many students of clinical psychology, I attempted a good deal of self-therapy while earning my degree—did I say *earning?*—and never understood why none of Professor Stevenson's methods for anger control worked worth a shit for me. I learned to contain my explosions for more extended periods of time, but upon ignition they were no longer measured in tons of TNT, but rather megatons. I had only learned to expand the container.

I have since learned, from my own therapy, and from working with young children, that emotions demand expression at their *outset*. Since *that* light bulb flickered on, I have destroyed no valuable property and I believe I'm considered a lot more fun to be around.

And then my daughter tells me someone is threatening to get at me through her, and all bets are off.

I control my rage barely long enough to get away from Trevor and Emily, and only then because I don't want them to see the power of my reaction. I don't care what kind of badass Marvin Edwards is, if that son-of-a-bitch comes within two miles of anyone in my family I'll spread his body parts from city limit to city limit.

It was a bad time for Sarah to ask, as I left her house after dropping Trevor and her off following Emily's game. "What are you going to do, Wilson?"

"About what?"

"About Emily's phone call," she said.

"I don't know."

"You don't know," she said coolly, and vague feelings from the old days began churning in me, feelings of inadequacy, and of selfishness.

"What do you want me to do?" I said. "What is there *to* do?"

"Stop working with Jerry Parker."

"I can't do that," I said. "What am I gonna do, leave the little shit high and dry?"

"Wilson," Sarah said, and all slack in our connection drew tight. "That man is threatening our *children*. Now, you can save the world if you want to, anywhere you want to, anytime you want to," she said, motioning back toward the house, "as long as *we* don't get involved. I will not put myself or the kids at risk because you don't have the good sense to know when to quit." Sarah's voice was taut, her stare cold and rigid.

"Look, Sarah," I said. "I don't need you on my ass over this. It's tough enough as it is. I'll figure out something. Okay?"

"Not okay," she replied evenly. "Damn it, Wilson, there's nothing to figure out. Whoever it was said to stop working with Jerry Parker. So stop working with Jerry Parker."

God, I hate to be told what to do. I said, "Fuck it. I'll do what I do."

Sarah's face turned to stone. "If you want to see your kids on a regular basis, you stop seeing Jerry Parker. I'll be talking to my lawyer in the morning. I'll get a court order, Wilson. I'm willing to bet a judge will be on my side."

"Jesus Christ, Sarah, you think I'm doing this intentionally? You think I *want* the kids at risk? Who the hell do you think I am?"

"I don't give a good goddam whether you're doing it on purpose or not. You're doing it."

Behind her at the screen door, Trevor stood in his pajamas listening, and all the air went out of me. I don't know where that little booger gets his radar, but since he was two and a half, he's sniffed out every major outbreak Sarah and I have had. I leaned forward and, through gritted teeth, whispered, "Fuck it, Sarah. If you

want to take it to a judge, take it to a goddam judge."
Then I summoned the will to smile and waved at my
worried son in the doorway.

I'm dying for lack of sleep and guilt now in the kids'
group. Molly is keeping Jerry with the rest of the kids
today in large group activities, sending me the quiet,
withdrawn ones—one by one—so I don't go off the deep
end.

I've been with Kevin forty-five minutes now and I
have yet to understand word one. It's as if the kid took
his alphabet to the Customized Language Shop to have
the consonants removed. When I ask him, "What?" for
the hundredth time, he shrugs and moseys off atop his
leg-powered truck. Kevin joined group only three days
ago—a victim of severe physical abuse—and already
Molly and I, separately, have contacted our part-time
speech therapist. Little E took a shine to Kevin the first
day and follows his truck continually at a reverential distance.

Across the room, Jerry Parker organizes a party to
search for his sister, and all the kids except Kevin—and
Little E, by default—are gung-ho. Since Jerry told me
what he saw at his house that night, he has been more
manageable with the other children, and in fact has tried
several different methods to enlist their help. He may be
getting ready to move out of expressive play and take
some risks finding wishful answers. Today his sister has
been hidden in the woods by a large hairy monster. Jerry
knows that she's alive, but that they must find her fast,
because the monster didn't get breakfast and he's really
mean and he might just go ahead and have Sabrina for
lunch if he gets hungry enough, or if he just gets mad.
The potential exists for all the kids to gather power if

their search is successful, and all are willing to ride the crest of this monstrous wave. These kids provide tremendous emotional resources for each other. They're here three hours a day, three days per week, and any given one—after a very short period—knows the others' fears and hurts and hopes. It is probably more difficult for us adults to play out these violent fantasies than it is for them. But it has to be done. No expression, no healing.

Molly and the aides prepare to load everyone into the center van and head for the park, when she stops by the cardboard service station I have set up for Kevin. "You want to go, or just stay here with The Great Communicator?" she asks. "We've got it covered, do what's easy."

With indecision as my most functional tool, I watch Kevin *putt-putt* around the room on his truck—still trailed closely by Little E in his sleeveless Levi's jacket with "Heck's Angels" stitched across the back—lost in a world of eighteen-wheelers and CB radios, and I struggle to decide. Just as I tell myself it's time to "pull my head out," Kevin, staring intently into his imaginary rearview mirror, crashes his truck into my shin. He glances up at me, startled, and a flash of anger crosses his face as he says, in perfectly clear English, "What the hell, fuckhead?"

He holds my startled gaze. I look to Molly.

"He can talk," she says. "My, how he can talk."

Kevin drops back into his more familiar dialect and *putt-putts* away. Little E follows, with his father's swagger. Molly plants the idea into the group that Kevin's vehicle is actually of the search-and-rescue variety, and Jerry immediately directs both Kevin and his truck toward the van over Kevin's mild but unintelligible protest, and we're off to find Sabrina.

* * *

143

It irritates me that there's never enough time to draw a bead on one thing before something else pops up in the way. What I really mean is, I wish the goddam telephone wouldn't ring in the middle of *everything* I do.

"Got a minute?" I hear on the line. I have just this second hustled back to my office for my keys, and the phone rang before I could make my escape. The voice is Don Cavett's.

"Just about," I say. "Talk fast."

"Anything new on Craig Clark?"

"Poor little shit can't walk on his crispy pods yet," I say, "but he sure can talk. And he's *pissed* at his stepdaddy. Keeps talking about a secret that I can't get a handle on yet, though I think it's important. It's crazy, Don, because Banner sounds *good.* It's almost impossible not to believe him, but I can't believe him *and* the scenario I get working with Craig. Something's off here, and I hope I find it. A person wrongly accused of abuse sounds exactly the same as a smart abuser in denial. They both say they didn't do it."

"You think there's a chance Banner's telling the truth?"

"I do think there's a chance. He had one good chance to take me on—in a friendly crowd, too—and make me look like some kind of gunslinger, but he didn't do it. If he's lying, he's slicker than anyone I've ever worked with. I'm saying we need to be really careful. I think if I can continue to see Craig, it will get clearer."

Don is silent on the other end a second. "Well," he says finally, "see what you come up with. I got worried when I saw Fred getting ready to sweep it under the rug. Keep me posted. I don't want Banner going down because *I'm* wrong."

"I'll pay close attention, Don, don't worry. Like I said, either Dr. Banner is telling the truth or he's *really* slick. If it truly was an accident, he's showing the proper remorse. If not, he's a dangerous man. Did he take a poly-graph?"

"Sure did. Says he's telling the truth," Don says. "Doesn't really mean much if we go to court, but it might keep us *out* of court. Now Fred is hung up on *intent*. Banner already admitted to being put out with the kid, so that's not an issue."

"If we concentrated on *intent*," I say, "everyone would get off. Almost nobody 'intends' to hurt a kid. They just get out of control and do it."

"You know that and I know that," Don says. "But obviously my department hasn't trained Fred Cronk for shit."

"Damn, I hate this, Don. I can feel us setting some-one up here," I say. "If it's Craig, we get his trust, he dumps his information, next thing he's back home with a mom who thinks he's trying to destroy her marriage and a pissed-off stepdaddy who's gonna be way too smart to get caught again. If it's Banner, we ruin a career."

"A lot is up to you, my friend," Don says. "If we shoot for a state dependency and you go into court undecided, we're dead. In fact, I wouldn't even try for a dependency if that were the case."

I feel the subtle pressure Don's trying not to put on me. Don is a purist who has long thought his department treats the separate economic classes differently, that rich or well-established people can treat their kids any way they want to because they look better naturally and be-cause they can afford the best legal representation. He also believes his department doesn't require enough ex-pertise from its workers. I do trust, from years of expe-rience with him, that this is not personal. The guy is a pro.

Don pauses. "Listen, Wilson, if *you* had abused a kid,

beat him or scalded him or whatever, and we interrogated you about it, how would you handle it?"

I laugh. "Most of your workers wouldn't have a prayer. I know all the questions."

"Yeah, well, which questions do you know that Banner doesn't?"

I'm quiet.

"And listen to this," he says. "From now . . ." and a digital watch beeps in the earpiece followed by a long pause and another beep "till now, is six seconds. That's the *minimum* time Craig was immersed. If you heard a kid scream like Craig must have been screaming from the next room—and these rooms are *right* off each other—how long would it take you to pull him out?"

"Actually, that's a tight call. It might take a second or two to register . . ."

"Okay, I'll give you that, but there are no splash burns on Craig from thrashing around, and no burns on Banner's hands."

Don's a persuasive man. "Okay, Don. What I'll do is work with Craig. I'll come in strong with whatever I get. If we end up doing some family sessions, I'll get someone else on the team to do them so I can concentrate on Craig. Meanwhile, you slow Fred up so he doesn't dismiss this. He needs to consider the information from Craig. Judging from how he was in the staffing the other day, he's depending completely on Dr. Banner's words."

"I'll do what I can," Don says. "It may involve holding a burning cigarette to Fred's nuts."

I laugh. "That would give him an idea what Craig went through. I'd like to be there for that, but I don't smoke."

"Fred Cronk will," he says, pausing again. "I hate putting you on the spot like this, Wilson, I really do. But you and I go back."

146

* * *

The kids fall out of the van into the parking lot at Whitman Park like lemmings, fanning out to play on the swings or in the sand, or to run in the wide expanse between the lot and the rough where Trevor and I searched for Sabrina a few nights ago. Jerry is less successful organizing the search party now that he has a park full of playground equipment with which to compete. He cuts his losses, establishing instead an elite force of five, plus Kevin—with Little E in tow—in his search-and-rescue truck, to comb the area for his lost sister. Molly and the student assistants remain with the majority, while the seven of us set out to find Sabrina and do battle with the monster. The going is rough for Kevin, whose wheels stall in the high grass, then stop completely as we head up into the rough. Jerry is committed to the importance of the truck once his sister is found, however, and aids Kevin from behind whenever the indispensable vehicle grinds to a hopeless halt.

Once in the hills we search without incident, often distracted by chipmunks and birds and an old Safeway shopping cart.

"Ten more minutes," I say finally. "Then we gotta head back." I set the timer on my digital watch to ten, and hand it to Jerry. "Round 'em up when that goes off, okay, Captain?" That will get the deed done far better than I ever could alone.

As I hoist Kevin to the top of the slightly smaller rock adjacent to Big Rock, where an imaginary telephone booth has magically appeared, I catch movement out of the corner of my eye, though I can't look directly because I don't want to drop Kevin on Little E. Kevin, I have painfully deciphered, wants to call his uncle from the magical phone booth to come help. When he's perched

147

safely on the flat spot atop the rock, I look back, expecting to see some medium-sized animal, but there is nothing more than a branch moving slightly. I dismiss it and wait for Kevin to finish his call, my hand on Little E's shoulder. Sandwiched between Kevin's usual gibberish, the words can be heard—articulated clearly enough for the pickiest of diction coaches—"Uncle Mike? Yeah, this is Kevin. Get your fucking ass over here!" He slams down the imaginary phone and turns, opening his arms in the universal "catch me" signal, and leaps.

I catch another glimpse of movement in the bushes as I pull the three of us to our feet, but again see nothing when my eyes snap around toward the spot. *This* doesn't feel good.

A scream. Jerry shoots down the dirt path, paralleling the rock like a missile, followed by Melissa and Heidi, also screaming at the top of their lungs. Jerry clinches my leg. "I saw him! He's here! I saw him!"

"Who?" I ask. "Who did you see, Jerry?"

He starts to speak, but no words come out as he begins to hyperventilate.

I lock my arms loosely around him, scanning automatically for the other kids, who stand very close, waiting for Jerry to speak. Little E buries his head between my legs and I squat to get my arms around him. Melissa and Heidi, it turns out, saw nothing, but joined in sympathy shrieking.

"Who did you see, Jerry?" I ask again when his breathing calms.

"That guy! That guy what gots my sister. He was right there in the bushes! I saw him! It was that guy!"

"Are you sure?" Probably the dumbest question I could have asked.

"Yeeeeeeeees!" he screeches in a pitch that could summon wolves.

So I *did* see something in the bushes off the trail. "Okay," I say to everyone. "What's the best way to get back to the van safely?"

"All go together," Heidi says. "Stay close. Is that right, Wilson? Is that right?"

"That's right, you little wizard," I say. "We're going to walk back down very quietly in a line. I'll walk at the back with Little E and Kevin's truck. If anyone sees anything, what should we do?"

"Scream," Melissa says with a shudder.

"Sound like a good idea to everyone?"

There is unanimous agreement.

"Okay," I say. "Now reach back and take the hand of the person behind you, so we all know where everyone is, okay?"

There is jockeying for position. Melissa doesn't want to touch Raymond because Raymond is dirty and he poops his pants all the time. Indeed, there is no question Raymond has done exactly that. Raymond ends up between Kevin and me, mostly because Kevin's protests don't register, and in seconds we're moving down the hill like a prison chain gang. I have no idea what Jerry really saw, but I've been around kids long enough to know always to believe them. If you're wrong, you're safe, and they're safe.

Back at the center the story has gained momentum. Everyone in the search party actually sighted "that monster guy," and he is definitely hairy all over with big white fangs and blood-red eyes. He is also either eight or twenty feet tall and there is some question as to whether he was eating a dog. Back in the group room we turn the kids loose with paper and crayons and all the animal and human miniatures we have, to depict the event they have experienced. When they're settled into that, I sneak out to my office to call Palmer, though there is no possible way to tell whether or not the man they saw was Marvin Edwards.

Standing in the parking lot less than twenty minutes later talking to Detective Palmer, I hear, "Get your fucking ass over here," and look up to see Kevin's uncle motioning him toward the car. I make a mental note to cancel the call to the speech therapist. Kevin is only articulate with words that have meaning in his world. Watching his uncle shove him into the shotgun seat, I wonder what the father they removed him from must be like. I'll know in a week or so when he joins the men's group.

Little E sits atop my shoulders, scanning the entrance to the parking lot. When his dad's Harley roars round the corner, wheels to his sidecar six inches off the pavement, Little E nearly claws my eyes out to get down. I put Palmer on hold and follow him toward the bike, where I explain to Eric what just happened in the park. He dismounts quickly, squatting before Little E. "Have a little scare, hotshot?" he asks gently.

Little E's eyes widen as he nods. "Monser man," he says.

"No monster man gonna get us, Big Man," Eric declares as Little E moves in against his massive chest. "Okay?"

Little E nods into his dad's chest and Eric closes his eyes, holding him tight a second, before swooping him into the sidecar, where he plants E's helmet on his head and cinches the seatbelt tight. Eric hits the kick start and the two roar off like a modern-day James gang.

Twelve

Five-thirty A.M. Lap swim. I cut through the still, cold water of Witter pool, picking up speed and power with every stroke, and my mind runs. I haven't seen Sarah since last week when we parted mortal enemies. The kids now wait for me out on the porch. She hasn't gone to her lawyer yet, but that could happen soon. Especially with these goddam phone calls. Emily had one more and Trevor thinks he got one, too, only he slammed down the receiver the second he heard a voice he didn't recognize. If Marvin Edwards wants Jerry Parker off my client load, I wish he'd come straight out and threaten me, and quit fucking with my kids. I gotta believe he's getting off on the terror. *How* did he find out about my connection to Jerry in the first place? That's the piece I want.

Palmer says we'll know more about him when they find Sabrina and see what he actually did to her. That better be soon for his sake. Christ, there are newspaper editorials calling for more manpower, special task forces, and Palmer's head if he doesn't get results soon; neighborhood groups are threatening to arm themselves if the police don't give more protection, and wackos are coming out of the walls to report a Marvin Edwards sighting.

But I'll say this, if it's getting to Palmer, he doesn't show it. I thanked him the other day for not putting more pressure on me with Jerry, and he just said, "Don't worry about it, Counselor. Like you said, when we do get it, it'll be right." Palmer is the first cop I've ever known to believe that about kids, and I appreciate it.

I ran it all past the rest of the Child and Family treatment team the other day, but I got more sympathy than help. John Sheldon mentioned again that he thought it was crazy for me to take chances with this guy, so I asked if *he'd* like to take Jerry over for me, which would be like me taking over my own car repairs. Carla, our supervisor, did entertain the idea of taking Jerry away from me, but I put a *big* wet blanket on that.

"Wilson," she said, "we do have people without children of their own who wouldn't be as vulnerable as you are."

A part of me wanted to consider what she was saying; certainly it would ease the pressure on my strained relationship with my ex-wife, but Jerry has come to trust me and Molly, and he has chosen to tell me, alone, the events of his terrifying night. If I abandon him now, he may not connect anywhere else. His trust feels extremely fragile. "Tell you what," I said back to Carla. "I'm not feeling all that vulnerable, except that my ex-wife might give me a bloody nose. We don't know whether these phone calls really mean anything and we also don't know how far this guy's willing to go. If he's up to it, he can find something that threatens any person in this room as much as going after my kids threatens me. I'm not stupid, but as much as I'd like to just protect myself, I don't see it as necessary yet." Regardless of how fiercely I love my kids, I have trouble deciding their well-being is more important to the universe than Jerry Parker's. Repeating that aloud wouldn't be considered sane, and I don't. "If

I have to," I said, "I can send my kids out of town until this is over." Inside I shuddered, thinking what hell that would create between me and Sarah.

"Okay," Carla said. "For now. But I want you to promise you'll keep me up to date on any threats or gestures that come out of this. I'm not comfortable with this decision if you're going to keep me in the dark."

I agree to keep her up to date.

"I'd like you to make that agreement with the whole team," John said. "This affects all of us, if not directly then by implication." As an afterthought, he added, "And I'd hate to see anything happen to you, Wilson. Though we may disagree on a lot of issues I'd hate to see you come to any physical harm."

Right, John. But this isn't a good time to address John Sheldon's straightforwardness, so I agree for the sake of argument.

A thousand yards—forty laps—into my swim, my pace increases as I lose myself in considerations of what to do next. Was there really someone in the bushes at Whitman Park? Could Marvin Edwards really be gutsy enough to try to take Jerry Parker out in broad daylight? With adults around? There has been no psychological profile drawn up on him yet, mostly because so little about him is known, but he did a six-year-old girl in. Most guys who go after kids stay as far away from adults—particularly adult males—as possible. If whoever was in the bushes watched us come, he had to see me first, and I'm a pretty big guy. I *look* like I can take care of myself. If Edwards was there, he isn't just some squirrel who preys only on kids. Maybe terror *is* what makes him tick.

Of course, desperate times call for desperate measures, and these have to be desperate times for him. Sooner or later Sabrina will be found and he'll be tracked down.

Jerry gets older and more verbal every day, will look like a much better witness in court with every day he grows. Maybe old Marvin's just doing the best he can with what he has. Not all this has to make sense.

And if I don't come up with some answers pretty soon, my arms will fall off. The clock over the guard room says I've been swimming more than an hour, and the guard is blowing her whistle to get me out so they can start morning swimming lessons.

I stop at the front desk and retrieve a message to call Don Cavett ASAP and another to see John Sheldon, before Kids' Group starts, if possible. I dial Don's number, hoping whatever he has is lengthy. Pretending to be civil to John Sheldon is wearing a little thin.

"Fred wants to close the case on Craig Clark," Don says. "We need something in writing from you saying what a bad idea you think that is, and why."

"Roasting his nuts didn't work, huh?"

"I made a mistake," Don says. "He didn't have any nuts."

"Some days nothing goes right, huh?"

Don says, "It's a truth, Wilson. It's a truth. So what about it? Can you get me a letter?"

"How much time do I have?"

"Fifteen, maybe twenty minutes."

"Jesus." I'm instantly scrambling for blank paper. "Look, can't we schedule a joint staffing? Present both sides and let the higher-ups decide?"

"Call Fred and suggest it," Don says, "but do it fast. He's ready to move on this within the next couple of days. And between you and me, Fred's supervisor is barely a life form. You won't get any backing from her."

"How high up do I have to go?"

"I don't know," he says, "but if she won't agree to a joint staffing, copy the universe with your letter. That'll rattle *somebody's* chain. I'm serious, Wilson, if you guys ever wanted to take on the department, this is the time. This is embarrassing. Even if Banner does have a good explanation, we're doing as shoddy a job investigating as we're capable. And believe me, we're capable."

I begin the letter, concentrating only on what Craig has done in his play therapy, trying to block out the consequences it may have on Dr. Banner. Don is right in being embarrassed at Fred Cronk's actions. Whether Banner is innocent or guilty of abuse, Craig's work hasn't changed a bit since I saw him in Seattle, and it deserves to be given the same weight as Dr. Banner's words.

I'm barely into the first paragraph when my door opens slightly and I see John Sheldon's nose in the crack, a position I'm sure isn't unfamiliar to him. He says, "Got a minute, Corder?"

"Barely," I say. "I gotta get this letter out before group. Is it quick?"

"I think so. I just wanted to speak with you a moment about the Jeffery Banner situation."

"Come on in," I say. "That's what the letter is about."

"Can I ask what you're going to say?"

"Sure. I'm going to say the situation needs to be explored, and that the work Craig's been doing in his play needs to be taken as seriously as Dr. Banner's declarations."

"You think he's guilty, don't you?"

"He says he's guilty," I say. "At least of neglect. I really don't know what happened. Craig's stuff fits with every abused kid I've ever dealt with. Something's out of whack. I know Banner's a friend of yours, John, and I don't blame you for being concerned, but these were third-degree burns. I can't just let that ride." I'm hoping

155

that by my being civil with him, John will believe I'm hearing him and go away. I have very little time to put this letter together, and I'd like to do it well.

"The caseworker is willing to believe Jeffery," he continues.

"I'm not sure the caseworker is able to look at both sides from where his head is," I say. "I've sent him my impressions of every session so far, and haven't received one grunt in response."

John sits erect, thinking, then, "Do you know what this could mean to Dr. Banner's career?"

"If it happened like he said it did," I say, "it shouldn't mean anything; in fact, it'll probably never get out. If not, I'd say it could wash him up right quick."

"That's right," John says. "Sixteen years in the business wiped out by three-year-old utterances. Does that seem fair to you, Wilson?"

"It seems sad to me, John, but I wouldn't get too upset yet. The jury's still out. Nothing has been decided."

I feel John heating up, and I wish he'd go ahead and show me what a really big deal this is to him, because then I might know *why*. "John," I say finally, "what would you do? I mean, given what Craig is saying, what would you do?"

"I'm not sure," he says. "I just don't think a man's reputation should be wiped out with one incident."

"Scalding a child is hardly 'one incident.' " God, I wish he'd quit forcing me to this side of the argument. I don't *know*. The *unknowns* . . .

John's entire body stiffens, but he catches himself. "Well," he says, rising from the chair, "I've got work to do. Thanks for bringing me up to date. I truly hope this works out. Jeff Banner is a special man in this business." He stops at the open door. "Wilson, do you remember the Cabarton family?"

I nod and close my eyes. "Yes."

Actually, the Cabarton case has been rattling around among my dead brain cells for more than a week, warning me to be careful. It ranks up there with Creason as one I'd like to forget. Jessica Cabarton came to us through the state three years ago claiming her husband had sexually abused their four-year-old daughter, Merrilee. Merrilee was verbal and backed her mother all the way, saying Daddy did nasty things to her and sometimes they hurt. Jack, the dad, a decidedly passive man, said he must have done *something* to make his daughter say what she was saying, but he didn't know what it was. He tracked it down to letting her come into the bathroom when he was taking a leak. For more than six months, we all assumed that he had been sexually inappropriate and either didn't know what appropriate was, or was too embarrassed to say exactly what he did. Merrilee was vague and Jessica was aggressively righteous. The family lived in Shoals, a small wheat town about fifteen miles south of Three Forks, and within a very short time after they entered treatment, word leaked out to the members of the township and Jack immediately lost his job at the grain elevators, a job he'd held for more than fifteen years. When the dust finally cleared, he lost his house, most access to his kids, and what little self-esteem he ever had. I was a main proponent of the belief that the abuse had occurred. Then one night, maybe eight months after they entered treatment, one of the boys from Merrilee's group pinched her on the butt in the hallway as she prepared to leave. She whirled around and laid him out with a hard open hand to the ear, screaming, "That's nasty! That's nasty! Don't you *ever* touch me there!" Her reaction was so severe that I stopped her a moment to help her calm down, and as I looked into her eyes it hit me like a ton of bricks. I said, "What did he do that was nasty?"

She convulsed a bit, and instead of telling me she reached around and pinched my butt.

"You don't like that," I said, understating the truth in spades.

Merrilee shook her head so hard I thought I heard something come loose. "It's nasty."

I almost held my breath. "Is that what your dad did? Is that the nasty thing your dad did?"

Still convulsing, she nodded.

"Did he do anything else?"

Merrilee's head shook violently.

Turned out, Mom had gotten caught up in the current sexual abuse panic and asked Merrilee if her father had ever touched her "down there." Mom was so inexpert and afraid and embarrassed, she only pointed toward the general below-the-waist area. Merrilee said yes. Mom told her that was nasty and asked if it hurt. Merrilee said yes. Mom put two and two together and got five. By the time we got involved, the Cabarton case had come through the child protection system with no one pinning down the actual abuse. Assumptions were made. Another *two months* of exploration and meetings with CPS told us no sexual abuse had ever occurred, that Jack was just too passive and naive to know what it was. The system kept the man away from his children almost a year, cost him his job and his home. No matter how loud we shouted out the truth once we knew it, Jack Cabarton would never again hold his head up on the streets of Shoals, and he and his children had lost that time forever.

Those cases don't come along very often, and Jack was so passive he didn't even come out and blame anyone—or sue our asses off—but I don't care to be part of another case like that. I believe in what Don Cavett is doing, but I don't want to have anything to do with bringing down Dr. Jeff Banner without being sure. Some little unknown piece of evidence might bring everything into focus.

Sheldon brings me back. "That was an unfortunate set of circumstances. I would guess that family will never be the same."

I agree.

"I'm just saying, Wilson, let's be careful. Let's be sure history doesn't repeat itself."

I assure John I don't want to be part of history repeating itself in that way, and he thanks me and leaves. I am also aware as I continue writing my letter for Don that I may be letting John Sheldon color my thoughts *against* Banner. The more he argues in favor of accepting Banner's words, the further I move opposite him. I have to be very careful not to let Dr. Banner pay because I think John Sheldon is a bozo.

At the end of the day, I find a letter in my mailbox from my lawyer, Carol Salinger. I have yet to receive a piece of *good* news from Carol, so my spirits remain grounded as I drop my saddlebags, lean tiredly against the counter, and open the letter.

God *damn* it. Sarah's lawyer is getting a court order to keep me away from the kids until some compromise is reached regarding our current difficulty. Carol says, due to today's events, she feels Sarah has an excellent chance of success and that I should sit tight until we can all meet. She will call me.

Today's events. What the hell are today's events? I hustle back to my office and dial Sarah's home number. Busy. I wait, dial again. Busy. My daughter could be on a marathon call, but more likely Sarah has indulged her infuriating habit of taking the phone off the hook when she's pissed. God, that's the kind of thing that can put a guy's car windshield in danger. I remind myself I'm on the bike. I wait a few seconds on the off chance I'm wrong, and dial once more. Busy.

Carol's home number is on my Rolodex, and though I don't want to bother her there, I can't get through the night without more information. "Hi, Carol. Wilson Corder. I got your note. Thanks. What are 'today's events'?"

"Hi, Wilson. No one called you?"

I assure her no one did.

"Oh, my." She pauses. "Someone tried to grab your daughter. I was sure you knew. She was at some special summer math and science symposium at school. They called Sarah from there and I guess she must have said she'd contact you. I got most of this secondhand from her lawyer."

"Tell me about Emily."

Carol hesitates while I barely contain my stomach. "Carol?"

"Her arm was broken, Wilson. Some man grabbed her when she went for a run during the lunch hour. God, I can't believe I'm the first to tell you; I'd have called much earlier. I had one of our apprentices deliver the letter. He didn't know how urgent it was. I'm sorry."

I hold on. "Do you know where they took her?"

"Holy Family, I think. Wilson, I know this is awful, but if you think you're going to do anything crazy with Sarah, I have to advise you not to go."

I try to hear her, but I can only think of Emily, lying in a hospital bed with a broken arm, and who knows what else. I struggle to hold my temper. "There's no restraining order against me right now, is there?"

"No, Wilson, but . . ."

"I just want to see her. Carol, I've never hurt any*body*. I've only hurt things."

"Well, she may have gone home by now. I'd call ahead. If she's gone home and you decide to go there, take somebody with you, a witness." Carol thinks like a lawyer, but I know I don't have to worry about Sarah making up stories about me. I simply say okay.

Sarah stands outside a door about a hundred feet in front of me as I step off the elevator on the second floor of Holy Family Hospital. Her back is to me and from this angle her shoulders appear to be supporting a Buick. I take a deep breath and approach, laying a hand on her shoulder. "Hi. How is she?"

Sarah looks up and the tears run.

"How is she?" I ask again. "Can I go in and see her?"

Sarah breathes deep and exhales slowly. I can see she'd like to unload both barrels on me right where I stand, but she composes herself. "Trevor's alone with her right now. They wanted to talk a minute by themselves. I don't know what about."

"Tell me how she is."

"Well, she has a simple fracture of the upper arm and they're keeping her overnight to see if there's a concussion. She looks a little rough, has one black eye and some scrapes . . ." Sarah trails off into tears. I try to hold her, but she freezes ramrod straight.

"Could I have a few minutes alone with her?" I ask. "I mean as soon as Trevor comes out?"

Sarah looks exasperated, but says, "I suppose so," and glances away. Then, "Wilson, I'm so mad at you I could have you put to death. I told you. I *begged*."

"I know. Just let me see her alone a few minutes, okay?"

Sarah shrugs and shakes her head as the door opens and Trevor appears, "Okay, Mom, you can . . . Dad! Hi. I'm glad you got here. How come it took you so long? Did you hear what happened to Em? Where have you been?"

I lift Trevor and we hug. "I'll answer all your questions in a minute. I want to go in and see your sister, okay? You wait out here for me a minute?"

He nods and hugs me again. "Sure. How come it took you so long?"

I look carefully at Sarah, and say, "I just found out. Your mother had her hands full of you and Em and I'm hard to get ahold of sometimes. I came as soon as I heard."

That satisfies him and he moves close to his mother as I enter Emily's room. Emily brightens and smiles as I approach. "Hey, Dad, how you doin'?"

"I'm doin' fine. How about you?"

"Got into a bad tangle, I guess," she says.

"Feel like talking about it?"

My daughter looks really roughed up. Her left arm is cast past the shoulder, and the side of her face is bruised and scraped. She has the beginnings of a shiner that in all likelihood will turn into two shiners as it spreads across the bridge of her nose. "Sure," she says. "I was at that math and science symposium and I decided to take a run at lunch. Marsha was going to go with me, but her boyfriend came by and she went to lunch with him instead. I started alongside the student parking lot and then down those stairs that go to the lower lot and out into the arboretum. I thought I noticed this car behind me going really slow but I didn't think anything about it, and I still don't know if that's where the guy came from, but all of a sudden he was on me." She stops and shudders, choking back tears. "He grabbed my arm and started pulling me toward those thick bushes right at the entrance to the arboretum. I screamed bloody murder, just like you guys taught me but he slugged me. So I started kicking him where it hurts, but I don't think I ever got him. I kept screaming and then I felt this really awful pain in my arm. I think I heard it snap, Dad. God. Yuk. Anyway, the next thing I remember I was here."

I lay my hand lightly on Emily's forehead, brushing her hair back, unable to think, washed over with relief that she's alive, and dying of guilt.

"He didn't rape me, Dad. Don't worry."

"Are you sure?"

"Yup. They checked." She laughs. "Maybe I was too ugly. You know, with a broken arm and a bloody nose." She grabs for my hand. "Oh, Dad, I was *so* scared. I just couldn't get away. I tried. I really tried." She cries a second, then cuts it off. "Do you think it was that guy who got Sabrina Parker?"

"I don't know, Em. If it is, I'm really sorry I got you into . . ."

"No. It's okay, Dad," she says. "That's not why I asked. The police brought over some pictures. It was a guy named Detective Palmer. He said he knows you. He showed me some pictures, but I couldn't *remember.* It could have been that same guy, that Marvin Edwards, but I couldn't be sure at all. Partly it looked like him and partly it didn't or I just couldn't remember. I don't know . . ."

"Don't worry about it right now. Just get better. We'll have you out of here pretty soon. Probably tomorrow."

Emily smiles and squeezes my hand. Her courage pierces my heart like an arrow. "Want me to get your mom?" I ask.

"Just a sec," she says, and pauses. "Are you and Mom going to have a big fight over this? I mean, I heard her say to one of the doctors that it was all your fault—you know, about working with Jerry Parker and everything."

I look into her eyes. "I don't know, Em. I'd like not to fight about it, but I don't know. Your mom is pretty mad at me, and she has a right to be. Marvin Edwards wouldn't even know who you are if it weren't for my job."

"She said she might stop you from seeing us . . ."

"Let us worry about that."

"I *can't* let you worry about it. I don't want to not see you."

"We'll work it out, Em. I promise," I say, wondering how in hell we're going to do that. The damage is done.

"Well, let me tell you one more thing before Mom comes back in, okay?"

"Okay."

"If this is about you working with Jerry Parker, I want you not to stop, okay?"

I am incredulous. "What?"

"Remember that time I asked you why you work at the mental health center, you know, like why you work with abused kids and mean parents and stuff?"

"Yeah."

"Well, remember how you said the reason tribal societies were more healthy than us was because in tribes every adult was a parent to every kid? That families weren't so crazy because if you had a nutso dad, or no dad at all, some other man helped out with you?"

"You have a great memory, little lady."

"Don't stop working with Jerry Parker, please, Dad. This guy was really scary. I mean *really* scary. If you stop working with him, who will he have?"

I know that Emily's toughness and courage will crack someday. She's played the "good kid" in the troubled family for too long, constantly suppressing her true feelings in favor of others, but for now, I just drop to my knees beside my daughter, carefully sliding my arm behind her neck, and pull her easily toward me, and I hold her.

Thirteen

I stayed the night at the hospital, as did Sarah, and it has to go down as one of the top ten miserable twelve-hour periods in my lifetime. I drove Trevor to his best friend's house for the night and by the time I returned, the doctors had given my daughter enough pain-killers to let her drift off, and avoid the toxic waste hanging in the air between her mother and me. Sarah sat across the room, shooting icy swords at the perfect target of my conscience. In our twelve years of marriage she never looked nastier. I offered to let her go home, to stay alone with Emily. "I'm not sure you care enough about her that I could trust you to do that, Wilson." Those were our last words of the evening.

I wanted to kill her.

I wanted to kill me.

We passed the night that way, Sarah sealed in stain-less-steel armor and me devouring my insides with guilt.

This morning Emily went home, holding her cheerful countenance. I followed them to Sarah's house, gently held my daughter for a precious few seconds on the lawn before her mother guided her into the house and closed the door firmly behind them. As I released Emily from my grasp; she whispered into my ear, "Remember what I said about Jerry Parker, okay?"

I said, "Okay," but nothing in the world could have made me stay with him.

"That's it, Wilson," Carla says, breezing into my office shortly after noon. "Someone else will work with Jerry."

I tell her, without conviction, that my daughter wants me to stay with it.

"It's not academic anymore."

I don't argue. "Who you gonna get?"

She shrugs. "Maybe we can just let Molly continue with it."

"Why is Molly any safer than me? She's got kids, and she can get a lot more a lot faster out of Jerry. Seems like it's just a matter of time before Edwards starts in on her."

"Maybe he won't know."

"Maybe he will."

"Her kids are a little better able to take care of them-selves," she says. "At least Molly thinks so."

"You talked to her about it?" I ask, and for some rea-son that pisses me off.

"She talked to me," Carla says.

"I'll tell you something, Carla. I don't think this guy cares how big Molly's kids are. He'll do whatever he wants to do."

Carla sighs and sits in the chair next to my desk. "So what do we do, Wilson? Do we let it ride?"

I say, "We can't let it ride. Edwards already knows what Jerry saw. If he has to come after me, then he's got to go after him. It's a mystery why he hasn't already, but whatever the reason, we can't withdraw him from treatment, if for no other reason than to keep an eye on him. Molly and I set him up for this."

Carla leans back in the chair and lifts her feet onto my couch. I'm always amazed at how comfortable Carla appears, and still runs such a tight ship. "Sometimes we need to cut bait, Wilson. We're not the law, this part isn't our job."

"Yeah, well," I say, "Jerry Parker didn't ask us to gain his trust. He didn't ask to come to the mental health center to spill his guts so we could jump ship on him." It's a common argument, one any child abuse therapist could take either side of at any given time.

"I can give him to John Sheldon," she says, smiling. "He offered."

"Jerry'd have a better chance with the witch from the gingerbread house."

I like being able to kick things around with Carla this way. A huge part of me is sure I can't put my family in more danger just because Jerry Parker's mother got him involved with a madman. But another part screams out against the idea of throwing a kid to the wolves just because he's not my own. As much as I hate the idea, I'm relieved Jerry will still be with Molly.

When things get this crazy, I listen for Dad's voice. Dad would have cut through the shit here. He would have told me I could fight about right and wrong with Sarah until both our voice boxes turned bloody, and then turn around and do the same thing with John Sheldon, or Molly or Carla or Jerry Parker, for that matter. And I'd come up with a different answer each time because I'd be looking outside instead of inside. *Now's the time to look at what you can live with,* he'd have said. The truth is I can't live with my children getting hurt. So, once

168

again, the limit I set has to be on me. If I can stop myself before my work threatens my family, I've done well. If not, I haven't. I have no reason to be mad at Sarah. Her limit is set. Always was, always will be. Tribal fathers and threatened children be damned, I have to stop somewhere.

"I'm going to have you do some intakes for the next few months," Carla says. "I don't want you in the morning kids' group."

I protest. "I can work with kids other than Jerry," I say. "There's no reason to take me completely out."

Carla shakes her head adamantly. "We don't know how Edwards even knows you work with Jerry," she says. "It's possible he sees you go in there, or someone else does and tells him. There's no way we can control who goes in and out of the waiting room."

It's hard to argue, and I don't have a lot invested anyway. I feel like a traitor to Jerry and if I were to walk into that room and he wanted me to go with him, it would just be worse. I'm better off to put myself in Carla's hands.

"So would I be wrong to assume you have several thousand new clients waiting for intakes?"

"Never a shortage of new folks waiting to enter our pearly gates," she says. "I've got intakes scheduled up the wazoo. You need not worry about boredom."

It's two o'clock when I glance at my watch and realize Craig Clark is waiting. Craig gets uptight waiting and seems to have an uncanny sense of hours and minutes for a three-year-old. He has been bursting with good work and information for the past week, and I'm anxious to get on with it.

"I hate Uncle Sam," he says once in my office.

"Why do you hate Uncle Sam?" I ask, digging in my memory for some relative named Sam he may have mentioned, thinking—almost hoping—maybe Uncle Sam is the real culprit, letting Dr. Banner off the hook.

"He lie."

"Uncle Sam? Uncle Sam lies?" I ask. I must have been with this kid longer than I thought; he's beginning to adopt my political philosophy.

Craig's nod is so emphatic his chin nearly dents his chest.

I drag out a plastic basket filled with miniature figures. "Is your Uncle Sam in there?" I ask.

Craig promptly dumps the basket, digging through the figures in search of an appropriate Uncle Sam. He settles on a bridegroom in tails and a top hat, and it occurs to me that Craig's Uncle Sam and my Uncle Sam—indeed all of our Uncle Sams—may be one and the same. I dig quickly through another basket filled with plastic soldiers and army equipment and extract a small replica of an American flag, colors intact. "Does Uncle Sam have one of these?" Craig snatches the flag out of my hand. "Yeah!" he says, triumphantly.

"You are a precocious kid if you already know Uncle Sam lies," I say, but Craig looks through me as if I were a window. I've obviously exhausted the possibilities of further self-entertainment with that one. "What did he say that was a lie?"

"I hate Uncle Sam," he says again.

"You said that."

He brings a wooden block down hard on the bridegroom's head. "There." Then he brings it down again, and again. "There. There. There."

I say, "That'll teach Uncle Sam to lie."

He whomps him one more time. "There."

"Why are you mad at Uncle Sam?" I ask again.

"He 'sposed bring presents four July."

"Uncle Sam brings presents? You mean like Santa Claus?"

"Yeah."

"So how did he lie? What did he say that was a lie?"

"I say bring two good Jeffs."

"Did he bring them?"

"No!" he shrieks.

"Well, you sound really mad at him. Did he bring you anything?"

"Parker."

"What?"

"Parker!" he screams, and begins waving his hands in tight circles. "Oh," I say. "Sparklers. But you wanted two good Jeffs?"

Craig nods.

"Did he bring you any? Did he bring you one good Jeff?"

"No!" Craig shrieks again and does a final hatchet job on Uncle Sam's head before digging into the pile of miniatures in search of Bad Dad Jeffs, which he proceeds to load into the pillowcase for a good bashing. Then we draw pictures of a tiny Mom, a huge Bad Dad Jeff, and a scared Craig in the corner. We put Bad Dad Jeff behind bars, but he keeps breaking through them to hunt Craig down. At last we scribble out Jeff's face, only to have him reappear on the other side of the page where Craig is hiding. There is simply no hiding from Bad Dad Jeff.

We search Craig's stories for an acceptable outcome, first on paper, then back with the miniatures, then through dramatic violence with the pillowcase filled with villain psychologists. But they just ain't no keepin' them Bad Dads down.

In the end, with no time remaining in our hour, Craig decides he'll go home with me. We will tell Mom that I'm going to be Craig's dad from now on.

"I think that won't work," I say.

He frowns.

I shrug.

He asks, "Why?"

" 'Cause I'm not really your dad. I can be your dad here, but not at home."

Craig gives me a whack on the leg.

"You don't like it that I can't be your dad," I say.

He whacks me again.

Craig is walking a bit on his burns, so I let him guide me to the waiting room, where his mother sits. Carrie still hasn't decided whether or not to like me—she appears to be leaning toward not—but with the CPS investigation still pending, she has no choice but to bring her son to me.

"How'd it go, Trooper?" she asks, rubbing Craig's head, avoiding my eyes.

"I go with him," Craig announces.

Involuntarily, Carrie fires an accusatory look at me. I shake my head slowly. "His idea," I say.

"So what am I supposed to do when he says something like that?"

"Are you going to send him home with me?"

"Of course not."

"Then tell him he's not going with me."

Carrie looks embarrassed at the simplicity of it, and I remind myself to be a little more cautious with her sensibilities. She reads things into all that's said—she's awfully young—and has to be incredibly torn between her son and Dr. Banner. If there's truth in any of what

172

Craig is saying, Banner *has* to be pushing his explanation with her. No matter who's telling the truth here, Carrie Banner is in a tough spot.

In the staff room an unfamiliar envelope sends my stomach bouncing hard against my lungs. It is blank and unstamped. I breathe deep and let it out slowly, my panic intensifying. I turn it over in my hands a moment, then tear it open.

The note is cut out of newsprint, just like the last one. Whoever constructed it was impatient and couldn't find all the words needed, so he butchered some of the words letter by letter. "The olny way you can proof your not seeing Jery Parker is by leave. Save your children."

Shit. I lean my butt against the shelf filled with blank green charting sheets and breathe deep for control. A cracking sound fills the room as the shelf gives way and I'm on the floor like a shot put, covered to my chest in blank green charting sheets and feeling like a jerk. Suddenly John Sheldon's hand appears, offering me a lift up. My humiliation is complete.

"That's not very well constructed," he says, nodding toward the fallen shelf under me.

I agree.

"I understand you're going to let someone else work with Jerry Parker," he says.

"Looks like it," I say back, reaching up to take his hand, yanking harder then necessary in hopes I'll pull him down with me. The attempt fails and I feel a little foolish.

"That's good," he says. "I think we need to protect ourselves. We're not paid the kind of money it takes to put ourselves in that kind of danger. I think you're making a smart move, Wilson."

I kneel to retrieve the green sheets, stacking them atop an identical shelf a few feet higher. "I'm not trying to make any kind of move, John," I say. "I'm just afraid for my family. In fact, all this says to me is that we can be intimidated from doing our job."

"I don't see it that way," he says. "I think you shouldn't be quite so hard on yourself. Who's going to take him on?"

I find myself getting hugely irritated, and claustrophobic. I desperately want to get out of this tiny room with this monumental asshole. "I don't know yet, John. Look, it's not often we see things the same. Let's just drop it, okay? I'm not proud of leaving Jerry Parker high and dry."

His mouth opens, but I'm out the door before I hear a word, wondering what the hell I'm going to do now.

What I do is call Palmer to tell him about the note.

Fourteen

The latest message in my box, this afternoon: "You have 2 days." At least this time he spelled everything right. It showed up a couple of hours after the team meeting, in which I decided I would give myself a week to ten days to transfer my clients and tie up loose ends before taking an indefinite leave until things quiet down. It was as if the note were in response to the meeting, though I know that couldn't be true because only team members attend, and though I may not be the most popular therapist in the center, certainly no one is displeased enough with me to pass on information to Marvin Edwards, even if anyone *did* know where he was.

I put the note in my back pocket, deciding to keep it to myself for a while. *Something* is goddam fishy here.

Back in my office I had Molly paged to her phone. "Hi, baby," she said. "What's up?"

"Nothing much. My pen pal just dropped another note. Says I have two days to get out of the center. I need to talk with you about it after work, okay?"

"Sure." She was quiet a moment. "What's going on, Wilson?"

"I don't know, but I feel snakebit. I don't know what's a coincidence and what isn't, but there's a lot that isn't right. Keep it under your hat, okay? At least until you and I can talk about it."

"Okay."

"Sooner or later, whoever is delivering the notes is going to make a mistake and I'm going to come down on them like a wrecking ball. Till then, there's nothing to do but play it close to the vest."

I spent the rest of the day catching up on paperwork. I have only the two days. Tomorrow, whether anyone likes it or not, I'm going into the kids' group one last time to say goodbye to Jerry and the others. It would be inconceivable to leave him hanging. I've also scheduled myself to see Craig Clark once more so I can say good-bye and turn him over to Molly, who hasn't even met him, for Christ's sake.

Molly finished early tonight and we headed out west of town, stopping at a 7-Eleven for a six-pack before shooting down into the regional park for a little liquid picnic.

High temperatures have hit in the high eighties and low nineties for the past month, and the slight breeze blowing off the river was a welcome friend. We parked the bike next to a huge ponderosa on the edge of a rocky beach and sat, me against the tree and Molly against my leg. She ran her fingers high on the inside of my thigh and smiled demurely. "Is it conventional wisdom," she asked, "that high stress puts the clampers on one's love life?"

"I don't know," I said back. "We may be about to find out."

"If it is," and she slid her hand higher, "what say we go against conventional wisdom."

"I could abide that."

We sat quietly, sipping the ice-cold beer and staring at the early evening sun sparklers dancing across the river. I wanted to relax, to release it all and just *be* there, because that's what Molly and I do best, but persistent questions kept tapping at the door of my frontal lobe.

"It's happening already," Molly said, moving her hand higher.

"What's that."

"Conventional wisdom is taking over. I can feel it."

"Not completely," I said, running my hand over her shoulder, inside her blouse, and cupping her soft bare breast in my palm. "I think there may still be an off chance. Broad daylight in a public park, however, might not be the best testing ground. How about we go back to my place?"

So we have set conventional wisdom on its heels and now lie entangled in the twisted, sweaty sheets, trying to make sense of things.

"My kids are going to stay with their dad for a while," she says in response to my question. "This is the first time I've ever liked the idea that he's a card-carrying member of the NRA."

"Does he know what's going on?"

"Yes indeedy he does," she says. "And if your name is Marvin Edwards, you'd best stay a long ways from his backyard. My ex-husband is a shoot-now, ask-questions-later kind of guy." She laughs. "At least that describes our sex life."

I get a flash of Emily lying bruised and broken in her hospital bed. "Just make sure everyone's careful. This guy's a *rough* customer."

When Molly is gone, I call Sarah for permission to come talk. The kids are at friends' houses and she elects

177

instead to meet me at an all-night restaurant down the hill from her house.

"I stopped working with Jerry Parker," I say as she drapes her purse over the back of her chair.

She stares suspiciously.

"It's true. Stopped today. In fact, I'm taking an extended leave from the center."

"Why are you doing that?" she asks, her look softening. "All you were asked to do is stay away from the Parker boy."

"That was amended. I got another note saying I could prove myself only by quitting. Asshole gave me two days." For the first time I'm feeling the full impact, and tears gather. I can barely talk. "I was given *two days* to jump ship on every client I have. All that trust and connection down the toilet."

Sarah softens even more and puts her hand lightly on mine, but I pull away. I'm not mad at her, but my rage is all I have to keep me going. "When this is over, I'm going to get this fucker," I say between clenched teeth. "Nobody terrorizes me or my family. I'm going to put a hurt on this son-of-a-bitch even if I have to wait half his worthless fucking life for him to get out of prison. He'll beg the parole board to keep him in." My fist comes down hard on the table, rendering my water glass airborne. Sarah scoots her chair expertly aside as water floods to where her lap would have been.

"How can I help, Wilson?"

I shake my head. "You can't. I just wanted to tell you face-to-face that I stopped working with Jerry and . . ." I pause. "And that you were right. I was an asshole the other night."

The waitress comes to clean up the water, and I apologize before ordering coffee for us both.

"You know, Emily is really mad at me," Sarah says.

178

"Why?"

"Because she knows we're fighting about this. She's adamant that you should go right on doing what you're doing—that we should figure out ways to protect ourselves. She thinks we're all playing a 'really shitty trick' on Jerry Parker."

"That's my fault," I say. "If you and I are squared away again, I mean if it's okay for me to see the kids, I'll take them tomorrow after work and explain. That okay with you?"

"That would be wonderful with me," she says. "I get pretty tired of being the bad guy."

I put my hand on her head and say, "You're the best bad guy I know, lady," and for the first time I see the effect of this on Sarah. Though she doesn't sob—that's beyond my ex-wife—her cheeks are suddenly a windowpane on a stormy night, and I realize again how I've driven the stakes up.

"You're not the bad guy, Sarah. If there's a bad guy here it's me—like always. I have a good act. That just means I can get away with looking good while I do stupid things. You're just protecting your kids and that's all I could ever ask for. I'll talk to them tomorrow, okay?"

She nods. "You know what kills me, though?"

"What?"

"I'm the person keeping you from Jerry Parker. Just because I don't know him. Because my kids have good parents Jerry Parker can't be protected and cared for."

"That's the reason I stayed with him in the first place, Sarah. But truth is, Jerry Parker is just one of thousands of kids standing before the firing squad. The only difference between him and them is we know who he is."

So here I sit, using a version of John Sheldon's argument on my ex-wife. "Besides," I say, "Molly can walk Jerry through this as well as I can."

179

"Wilson, just tell me I'm not a selfish bitch."

"You're not a selfish bitch, Sarah. You're a kind and giving bitch."

She laughs, and the thick, oppressive cloud dissipates ever so slightly.

The kids and I sit at Bonanza, a fish and steak place with an all-you-can-eat salad and dessert bar. Our presence here tonight is a monument to Trevor's insensitivity. Even with her broken arm and raccoon eyes, Emily wasn't able to raise enough sympathy from him to let her choose without a fight. It was a short argument. "Trevor," she said. "Let's eat somewhere we can get *quality*. Dad's paying, for criminy sake. We can take him to the cleaners."

"Every time we go someplace to get *quality*," Trevor said back, and the word slides through his nose in a mimicky whine, "I get hungry again before we even get home."

"You need to realize, Em, before you continue with this," I said, "that to your brother there is no difference between quality and quantity. His taste buds are made of tin."

Em simply wasn't up for it and Trevor scored an easy victory. So as his sister and I sit, finished, Trevor is about to polish off his third extra-large Pepsi and his second make-it-yourself hot fudge sundae. I fear we're going to get Las Vegas card-counter treatment: Before we leave the waiter charged with refills will take Trevor's picture and banish us forever.

"Look," I say, deciding I can't wait for Trevor to finish, "the reason I brought you guys out tonight is to tell you what's going on with me at the center with this Jerry Parker thing, and also with your mom."

180

Both are quiet, waiting, though that doesn't stop the automatic shoveling action toward Trevor's mouth.

"I'm leaving the center for a while."

Emily opens her mouth to protest, but I raise my hand. "It's just gotten too crazy. I don't know for sure where it's coming from, but your mother blames herself and then she blames me. I blame myself and then blame her. You guys need to know it doesn't have anything to do with the two of you, except that we both want you safe." My eyes cloud. "I don't know what I'd do if something happened . . ."

"Where you gonna work, Dad?" Trevor asks. "How will you make money? Don't you have to pay for your house and stuff?"

Where does this kid *come* from? "I've got a little saved up. This won't last too long. Edwards won't be out there much longer before somebody gets him. And I can do private practice."

"What's that?" Trevor asks.

"It's where regular people come to me for help—people who just want to change their lives a little—and have money to pay for it."

"How come you call it private *practice?* Is it because you aren't very good at it yet?"

I prefer not to answer that. Emily sits tight-lipped, staring at her plate.

I say, "Talk to me, Em."

Her fiery eyes burn into mine and her mouth draws tight. With the bruising across the bridge of her nose and her arm encased in the plaster cast, she could pass for a cornered animal—not frightened, but ready to fight. "Your face will freeze that way," I say, and she throws down her napkin, hissing through gritted teeth. "That stinks, Dad. And you know it. That stinks."

"Em . . ."

181

"Don't even talk to me. Take me home."

"Wait . ."

"I said *take me home!*"

Trevor says, "Come on, Em . . ." but her look forces him back into his cushioned seat. Emily rises with some difficulty, banging the cast on the side of the table. She kicks the table to get even and picks up her napkin to throw it down again.

Trevor and I sit and watch.

"Take me home or I'm walking," she says and I rise, hoping to avoid a public scene. Trevor hustles to the dessert section for a Styrofoam cup to carry the remains of his sundae, and in seconds we're in the parking lot.

The ride home is mostly quiet. Trevor tries to thank me for worrying about them, but I glimpse Emily's eyes in the rearview mirror and quiet him. I don't want her to break that cast across the back of his head. As we pull onto their street, I quietly ask Emily if she'll stay in the car and talk to me a second after her brother gets out. She doesn't answer, which I take as begrudging assent.

"I don't know what to do, Emily," I say when Trevor is heading up the walk toward his mother standing in the doorway. "I can't win this one."

Emily is quiet. She's still mad and her anger has stuffed all rational thought and words deep into the pit of her stomach.

"Take a deep breath," I say. "We can get through this. It's really important to me, Em."

Emily takes three deep breaths and closes her eyes. I get out and move into the backseat beside her, taking her hand. "This is hard for me, baby. I hate it. I hate all of it."

"You know what's worse than being beat up?" she asks. "Do you know what's worse than being threatened like this?"

I shake my head. "What?"

"Letting him get away with it." She takes her hand away and her fists clench. "I screamed at that son-of-a-bitch that I'd get even. I screamed at him that my dad would get him. I screamed it over and over." She bursts into sobs. "And now my dad's not going to do it! I can't stand it, Daddy! I can't stand it if he wins! Please!" She falls into me and I hold her clumsily, avoiding her bruises.

She cries a while longer. Then, very quietly, "Please, Daddy. I'm afraid just like everyone else. But I'm *mad*. He shouldn't get away with this." She looks up at me. "What about tribal fathers, Dad? What about that? Is that just for when everything's okay? When everything's okay isn't when people need tribal fathers. They need them when everything's not okay and they don't have a *real* father. I hate adults. You have all the answers until the questions get too hard."

I know now why my daughter is such a stud athlete. She's goddam tougher than anyone I know. "Okay, Em. What about your brother?"

"What *about* him? He eats too much."

"That he does. But he's just as much a target as you are. How do you think he would have survived what happened to you? Tell me what to do about your brother."

"Send him away," she says. "Send him to Gramma's, or let him go to Minneapolis and stay with Booger or Scooter or whatever that kid's name is. Who would find him in Minneapolis?"

I open my mouth, but she stops me. "Listen, Dad. I know I wasn't supposed to hear this, but you remember when you were telling Mom about Jerry Parker not being able to get his mom up? About him waiting in his room with a knife for the monster man to come get him?"

"Emily, you weren't supposed to hear that. That's confidential. I broke the law when I told your mother that."

"Too late," she says, "I already heard it. What if that had been Trevor? What if something happened to you and Trevor got into a spot like that? What would happen then, Dad? Answer me that."

"Okay," I say, raising my hands in surrender. "Now what about your mom?"

Emily sits forward, accepting the challenge. "Make me a deal, Dad. If I can work it out with Mom, will you stay at work?"

"Work it out how?"

"Somehow. How about it?"

I take my own deep breath and blow out hard. "Emily, look. You're too young to know this, but you're too young to know a lot of things you seem to know anyway. My relationship with your mother is hanging by a thread. Now, we didn't do so well as marriage partners, but up until recently we've managed to carve out a pretty good friendship since then. One of the biggest worries either of us has is you kids getting into the middle of our squabbles. Now . . ."

"Mom and I have already been through this," Em says. "The last time was tonight, just before you came. She knows this is me and not you. And I bet she knows what we're talking about right now. You *have* to know if she didn't want us talking about it she'd be out here jerking me into the house by my good arm, right? So she has to be thinking . . ."

"Okay, listen," I say, sitting in wonder that my daughter has fought my ex-wife to a temporary draw when the best I ever did was put a quick end to my misery with a first-round knockout, "if we go along with this, you're out of the decision-making business. We'll decide if we do it and *how* we do it. And if you have anything to say, you'll just forget it and bite your cast. Now I'm drawing the line and that's it. I'll do what I can, but in the long run I'd rather have you hate me and be safe than love me and get hurt again."

Emily smiles and hugs me tight with her good arm. "I'll go in now, Dad. Thanks."

"Tell your mother I'll call her tomorrow," I say as Emily marches up the sidewalk.

It was my own tribal dad argument coming from Emily's mouth that got me. In 1962, Ron Canton stole fifteen cases of Lucky Lager beer out of the back room at my dad's service station. The beer was destined for the Idaho back country the next morning on the mail and freight run. Ron came in through the back window about three in the morning. It was a great heist, except that he left a perfect bootprint in the mud right below the window, and fingerprints all over every damn thing. Plus, Norman Dolan, who worked graveyard shift at the sawmill and was home for "lunch," saw Ron do it.

My dad gave Ron a job.

"I don't get it," I said. "I thought when someone pulled a late night robbery on you, you were supposed to call the cops and send them off to jail."

"That's one way," Dad said. "But I don't know how he's going to pay me for the broken window if he can't work for the money. And he can't work for the money in jail."

Nineteen sixty-two was the year Ron Canton lived with us. He was my brother Al's age—should have been ready to graduate, but he wasn't spending a whole lot of time at school, probably because he was bushed from staying up all night burgling people. Ron's dad was in the Idaho state pen for three to five. His mother was

185

dead. His grandmother and granddad, both easily seventy-five years old, were just holding on. There was no dad for Ron. So mine invited him to move in, after talking with his grandfolks, of course, and Ron was so blown away to be getting a job instead of reform school, that he gave it a go.

He barely tolerated four and a half months of our family rules—he'd had zero rules for seventeen years—and eventually moved back to his grandparents'. But his time with us kept him in school long enough to get him hooked on being the first in his family to graduate, and in the years since, I've heard him say nothing meant so much in his life as the chance Dad gave him.

Emily is telling me Jerry Parker is my Ron Canton. I wonder what kind of luck she'll have with her mother.

Fifteen

This odyssey, which seems to have begun with Sabrina Parker's disappearance, has taken me some strange places, both internally and externally, but even Molly couldn't have gazed into her crystal ball and seen me in jail. It was worth it, though. I did the right thing.

But I sure hope I get out of here.

The first time I ever punched someone—I mean *really* tried to put somebody away—was in seventh grade. Mike Sinclair wanted to meet me after school. He was a seventh-grader, too. The Sinclairs were poor people who kept to themselves, and Mike was one of those guys who can put a serious hurt on you, not so much because of his size or strength or speed—in fact, I had advantages in all those areas—but because he was a guy who didn't care. John Sheldon once called me a pit bull. Compared to Mike Sinclair, I'm a Labrador retriever.

The macho arena of junior high school pugilism is filled with legends. Some guys reach legendary stature because they can put you on the ground with one punch (they're often the guys who liked the first and second grades so much they took 'em twice and are now shaving and buying beer for their buddies), some guys because they're so quick they never get hit, and a few are both.

Mike Sinclair's strong point was getting back up. Word had it Mike had been in more than fifteen fights that year and it wasn't even Thanksgiving. He's been beat a few times, but not without doing serious damage first. If you weren't willing to go the distance, you'd damn well better not start in.

Our trouble started in a flag football game in P.E. class when Mike hammered Randy Roberts—my best friend at the time—instead of pulling his flags. Mike claimed Randy's belt was too tight and he couldn't get the flag out. On the next play, as an act of early adolescent fraternity, I knocked Mike on his ass, then jumped up and stood over him. He came up swinging, but Mr. Stone, the P.E. teacher, stepped in, called it all even, and told us if we didn't want to spend the next three years in detention, we'd play *flag* football for the rest of the day.

"After school, fucker," Mike said as I headed for the huddle, and I was feeling like hot shit for taking him out, so I said, "After school," right back.

Word spread through the halls before the last one was out of my mouth, and by three-fifteen the fifty-dollar seats under the apple tree in Mrs. Madden's front yard were filling rapidly. Mrs. Madden worked at the courthouse and lived out of sight of the school, yet close enough to provide a good after-school meeting place. Her apple tree dispensed the sweetest green apples anywhere in town and she liked kids enough to have left an open invitation for us to use her yard anytime.

I think she meant for peaceful purposes.

By school's end, I'd pondered what I might be getting into and conveniently lost interest, but the challenge had been issued before witnesses and I had to show. Mike Sinclair, on the other hand, had not lost an iota of his passion or intensity. He came to fight.

I started slowly, mostly pushing and staying out of his

way, hoping we could maybe call each other a few names and go home, each claiming victory. The crowd, which was now filling the balcony level, had other ideas. After a few moments of no blood, they began calling us pussies and demanding their money back. I was embarrassed; Mike seemed unaffected. He was there for revenge.

As those in the cheap seats began to leave, Mike's watchband caught a button on my shirt, and the pin broke. His brand-new Timex fell face down onto a tree root, cracking the crystal. I really do remember feeling, for a fleeting moment, very sorry for him. Sinclair kids had *nothing*. The soles of their shoes were invariably worn through to the socks, if indeed they had socks, and they seldom showed up to school in clothes some kid didn't recognize from his own abandoned wardrobe. That watch was the only new thing I had ever seen on Mike Sinclair. I started to pick it up for him, but Charles Boots, the captain of our junior high wrestling team and self-appointed head cheerleader for this event, snatched the watch and shoved it in Mike's face. "Look at that, Sinclair. The son-of-a-bitch broke your new watch. It'll never work again."

Mike's eyes widened and a growl rolled out, and he waded into me, leading with a roundhouse that looked more like a planetary orbit than a punch. My head exploded as his fist cracked into my jaw. No one had ever hit me in the head before, not purposely. I stood stunned, confused about what to do next, so I shoved him again. But by now de-escalation was out of the question for Mike; rabid spittle ran down the side of his mouth. The roundhouse came again, landing on the exact same spot, as if the first blow had indented a parking spot for it. The first blow had surprised me. The second one hurt. And out of the corner of my eye, I saw Sarah Campbell.

Check-out time.

I stormed him, bashing through his fists, and he backed away surprised, crouching, covering his face. I must have uppercut him at least ten times before beating through his forearms to his nose. A mini-vascular explosion splattered blood into the third row. Mike reeled, but stayed on his feet, falling back into his crouch. I uppercut again with all my power, again and again. He wouldn't fall, though his nose was pulp. I couldn't say how many times I hit him before first hearing the crowd yelling at me to stop, but it didn't matter. Finally someone wrapped me up from behind and, though I struggled mightily, pinned my arms to my sides. Mike looked up, his nose spouting blood like a tomato juice geyser, and came at me. He caught ahold of my hair before I could be released, and brought my face against his knee. I dropped like a bowling ball, darkness closing in. The fans screamed to warn me, and I rolled blindly, until light rushed in again, in time to see his foot coming at my head. I rolled once more, scrambling to my feet, knowing this was truly do or die. Time slowed before me. I saw Mike coming, saw in his eyes the direction of his next move. I waited. When he lunged, I drove my shoulder past his blow into his stomach and churned my legs, driving him backward through the crowd into the trunk of the apple tree. The thud of his torso was followed in a microsecond by the back of his head cracking into the trunk. I released and drove again, and again, and again. Mike Sinclair's air left his body and I stopped long enough to grab his head by the ears, ready to plunge it into the crotch of the tree, when I heard Sarah's voice. "Stop it! Stop! Wilson, stop! You're going to kill him! Stop it!"

I did stop, Mike's head firmly in my hands, eyes rolled back. I shook him, and his head fell to the side on a limp neck, and I let him drop to the ground.

Twenty-five to thirty junior high school students stared in silence, and I backed away through the crowd toward the street. Voices buzzed; someone jumped in to help him. Randy Roberts pounded my back in congratulations, and I brushed his hand away, watching Sarah, who stared back at what I was sure she saw as a monster. With my eyes locked on her, I knelt to reach for my jacket, and someone put it in my hand. I gazed a moment more, then turned and ran for home as fast as I could.

In the dead of night I awoke with a start, Mike Sinclair's new watch dangling before my eyes. A kaleidoscope of the day's events rolled slowly first, then accelerated to a dizzying speed. I buried my head in the pillow, thinking of other things, of TV shows and movies and I had read recently; anything to force out the picture of Mike staring at his new-broken watch. It *was* the only new thing I ever saw on him. My chest filled with such immense sadness I feared I would choke.

And immediately behind those thoughts stood a picture of my rage, of the mixture of excitement and terror that had accomplished it, of the way it took me over; and suddenly I was really afraid. I slipped out of bed and moved quietly through the house toward my parents' room.

Dad heard the door creak and, as though he were expecting me, said, "Come on in, Wilson. What's wrong?"

I said, "I don't know."

"Is it about the fight?"

"Yeah."

"Want to talk?" he asked.

"Yeah. But I don't know what to talk about."

We moved out into the living room. He said, "Feeling bad? Does your face hurt?"

"A little," I said. "But that's not why I'm feeling bad. I keep Seeing Mike Sinclair's watch, the one that broke."

191

Dad nodded.

"It was brand-new, Dad. Sinclair kids never have anything new."

Dad hadn't completely caught up yet. "You think maybe it was stolen?"

"I don't know," I said. "But that's not what I mean. It was new. It had to be special. It's no wonder he got so mad."

Dad nodded. "You're feeling bad because you broke a poor kid's watch. I see."

"Yeah," I said, and began to cry. "Then I beat him up *so* bad. And it felt good. It felt good when I was done. It was like it wasn't even me inside, but it was. I mean I recognized me that way. It felt good, but it felt awful."

Dad put his arm around my shoulder.

"And now," I said, "it just feels awful."

At my request, Dad got dressed and went over to Mrs. Madden's yard with me on the off chance that somehow the watch had been left; that I could retrieve it and have it fixed, maybe put an expensive band on it or something. But it wasn't there, and I knew there wasn't much chance it would be returned to him. No one liked Mike Sinclair very much. I didn't really know whether or not it had truly been broken beyond repair. All I knew was I thought I was.

My dad and I spent the rest of the night talking about rage that bounces around inside you, and bursts out screaming when you're not careful. He told me some ways to see it coming so I could recognize it and catch it before it got loose. He told me about safe places to scream and safe things to hit. One thing, he said, was I should never lose my picture of Mike Sinclair and his broken watch.

And then he said what I thought was a strange thing.

192

He apologized to me for not teaching me about it before it did a bad thing to me.

"You got it in you, too?" I asked.

" 'Fraid so," he said.

"How come I never see it?"

"Because I don't like to see it."

Mike Sinclair was not in school the next day, but I made it a point to look at his wrist when he did return, about a week later, and the watch was missing. And Mike had some bruises that weren't put there by me, I think. I saved money from working at Dad's service station after school for about two months, and when I had just over a hundred dollars, I went to the drugstore and bought the nicest wristwatch I could get for that amount. I put it in a box with a note that said *I shouldn't of fought you that day. I was just being an asshole. I got you another watch.* I just signed it *Wilson.* Mike never said a word, and I never saw the watch on his arm, which was hard for me to understand, until I got up real early one morning to ride into the back country with my dad to deliver a load of diesel to one of the mining towns. Mr. Sinclair was in The Chief having breakfast when my dad and I stopped there, and the watch was on his wrist.

I never hit another human being after Mike Sinclair in anything but self-defense until I incorporated it into Jerry Parker's treatment plan, and in comparison, Mike Sinclair could have been my prom date, and while I don't think kicking someone's ass will ever be accepted in the psychological community as a viable therapeutic tool, it got done what I wanted done. It also got me thrown in the slammer.

When I decided upon that particular course of action, I feared it would be hard to dredge up my old rage again—I've had Mike Sinclair's watch in my head a long time—but it spilled right out when the time came.

I don't know exactly what she said, but Emily got me an extension with Sarah on my job at the mental health center. Sarah called late the same night I took the kids out to square them up with my decision to quit work for a while. "Wilson, you're not going to believe what I'm about to say."

I'd been asleep and though I recognized the voice, I couldn't for the life of me remember whose it was. I said, "We need to get the crickets off that piece of land down by the creek some way. They're going to destroy us."

"What?"

"The crickets," I said again, at the same moment realizing my dream world was leaking all over a phone conversation.

"You were asleep."

"No, I wasn't," I lied. "Who is this?"

"Wake up, Wilson. This is Sarah."

I asked her to wait, stumbled into the bathroom to splash cold water on my face, and returned. "Okay," I said. "Sarah, right. Ex-wife. Good-looking chick."

She said, "Listen to me. I'm taking the kids on a vacation. I won't tell you where, but we all had a long talk tonight and we decided you should continue what you're doing with Jerry Parker."

"What?"

"You don't really want me to repeat it, do you?"

"No," I said. "Really?"

"You can thank Emily. The way she's acting I'd have to send her away anyway. I have almost a month's vacation time stacked up, so I'm going to take the kids and go."

"I don't know if this will be wrapped up in a month, Sarah," I said.

"Then I'll take some personal leave. We'll deal with that when the time comes."

"When will you be leaving?"

"Day after tomorrow. We'll be gone by the time you're supposed to quit."

"Sarah . . ."

"Wilson, I really don't want to talk about this. We've made up our minds and I want to leave it at that. Here, Emily wants to talk to you."

Before I could protest, I heard, "Daddy?"

"Hi, baby."

"You said you'd stay if . . ."

"I said we'd talk about it."

"So talk."

I laughed uneasily. "I'll stay."

"Good. Come see Trevor and me tomorrow after work, okay?"

"Okay."

Marvin Edwards became a ghost. After the notes in the box and the attack on my daughter, and our possible sighting of him in the park that day, there was little evidence of his existence since Sabrina's disappearance.

And then, within two days of my family's leaving, they found her. Four fourth-graders playing Ninja Warriors in the undeveloped rough at the edge of Whitman Park did what the city and county police, two Explorer troops, Three Forks County Search and Rescue, and several hundred volunteer searchers had failed to do; they discovered what was left of Sabrina Parker. For the most part what they found were bones, along with pieces of the Tinker Bell nightgown she wore the night she was taken, and a couple of Smurf hair clips. Sabrina had been dragged to the far edge of the park and buried in a shallow grave. There was speculation that she had been molested and strangled, though the police were pretty close-mouthed regarding their evidence.

Sabrina might never have been discovered at all, but, to put it in the language of a low-budget nature documentary, she was unearthed when she became displaced in the food chain. The cops swarmed the place until they extricated the last of the scanty clues left untouched by time and the local animal population.

"Jerry's been having awful nightmares," Peggy Parker said in the waiting room a week and a half after the discovery of Sabrina's remains. "He wakes up screaming that someone's in the house. He acts like he thinks the man is coming to get *him*, but when I ask about it later, all he says is he's not scared of nothin'. It's scaring *me* to death, Wilson. I went into his room last night and he was convulsing so badly I thought he would quit breathing."

I looked down at Jerry beside her, standing defiantly, arms crossed. "Ain't scared of nothin', huh?"

He shook his head, and through clenched teeth said, "Nope," then crouched ninja style, stepped forward, and kicked the wall. "Gonna kill him."

Three days of exhausting play later, which resulted in the center calling in a local handyman to repair my office walls, Jerry stomped in and said, "I wanna go there."

"Where?"

"Where Sabrina was."

I hesitated. "You mean to the park?"

He nodded emphatically.

"How come?"

"TAKE ME!"

I handed him a plastic container of sponge blocks to

196

play with while I snuck quickly back down the hall to consult with Molly.

"I don't see any reason why not," she said. "If he wants to see then he wants to see. Maybe it'll knock something loose." She looked at me and smiled. *"Morbid* is different to Jerry than it is to you, Wilson. In fact, it doesn't exist for him. Don't worry about it."

Autumn around Three Forks can only be described as spectacular. The days are warm and balmy, the nights crisp. Whitman Park was beginning to resemble a drop cloth on the floor of the Sistine Chapel, bright reds and yellows and oranges splattered generously over a back-drop of deep green. Winters here can be gray and bitterly cold, summer days hot and breathless, but I will live in Three Forks, Washington, for the rest of my life just to experience fall.

Jerry and I jogged the two or three hundred yards across the freshly mowed expanse toward the rough, Jerry alternately running ahead, then turning back toward me, hands on hips, urging me to *hurry up.* I hung back a little, trying to decide what to expect Jerry to do when we got there. I had called Detective Palmer to be sure no significant clues had been left behind, and he assured me that apart from the loosened ground of the grave, and the fact that the media left the local plant life pan-cakelike, the place looked undisturbed. He was right. Were it not for his explicit instructions, I would never have known when we were there. We discovered the small site just as it was marked on Palmer's crude map. A shallow ditch next to a rotting fallen log and a few cigarette butts were all that set it apart from any other in the park. Jerry hesitated, then walked directly to the ditch and stood quietly, took two steps back, and sat on the log, resting his chin in his hands. It was not the re-action I expected. I hadn't seen Jerry Parker quiet and pensive for two minutes back to back in the entire year and a half I'd known him. In fact, I'm surprised he lies down to go to sleep.

I sat beside him and he sighed a deep sigh.

"What you thinkin', Big Man?" I asked quietly.

He said nothing, and we sat. When I looked over again, teardrops ran down his cheeks to his fists, then on down his tiny forearms. I put my arm around him and he leaned into me, convulsing into silent sobs.

"Pretty awful, isn't it?"

Jerry said, "Gonna get me."

"What?"

"Marv guy gonna get me."

"The hell he is."

"Said he would. Say he get me."

"Well, he's wrong."

"Comin' back," Jerry said. "Get me, too."

"Ain't gonna happen," I said, realizing this was the second kid I'd told I would protect from Marvin Edwards, thinking both times I'd never have to prove it.

We sat a while longer, Jerry unable to empower himself beyond his paralyzing fear, and me along for the ride. His eyes were dry before I finally said, "What say we blow this pop stand, my man? We can come back whenever you need to." He didn't resist, only stood up silently, turning to leave, and I saw his eyes go wide. Probably a full second passed before his shrill, truly bloodcurdling scream pierced the still air. I whirled to see a fearsome man approaching, two days' stubble dotting his creased face, clothes dirty and worn thin, gripping a fat stick probably four feet long. He stopped abruptly, staring. Jerry screamed on. I took the man for one of the transients who regularly call Whitman Park home in the summertime, and extended my arms, hands up, palms out, to calm him as I knelt beside Jerry. "It's

198

okay, it's okay," I said. "It's just a man. He probably sleeps here."

The man said not a word, only watched silently, gripping the huge stick. The intensity of Jerry's screams increased. "It's okay, Jerry. It's okay," I said again. "Come on. Let's go."

"IT'S HIM," he screamed. "IT'S HIM. HE GOTS ME."

When I looked again, the meat of the stick was screaming for my head, and I dropped like a shot put, barely under its orbit, shoving Jerry back into the dirt as I rolled. The stick drove down into the side of my ribs, and my stomach exploded in sickening heat. I rolled when it came again, escaping by inches, and scrambled to my feet. The man lunged for Jerry and I dove for his back, pulling him to the ground inches short of his prey. He brought the club back over his head, striking a glancing blow to my ear, but I held tight, yelling at Jerry to run. Jerry stood wide-eyed, paralyzed, and I screamed again. "Run! Jerry, run! Back to the car! RUN, JERRY!" but he wouldn't. He couldn't. The club came again, this time it missed by several inches, and I grabbed it, jerking it free of the man's grasp and rolling off. I scrambled to my feet again and leaped in front of Jerry, bumping his shoulder, hard, to bring him out of it. "Run, Jerry. I've got the stick now. I'll take care of him. You run for the car. There are big kids in the park. Tell them to call the police. Nine-one-one. You tell them to call 911. Tell them who you are. Tell them about Sabrina. They'll know you. They'll call. Then wait for the cops and bring them here. Be sure to tell the kids to tell the cops who you are. Now do it, Jerry. Run." And suddenly he was gone, the sound of his dusty footsteps disappearing down the path back the way we came.

I had no idea whether Jerry could pull it off, but at

least he was gone—safe. The man lay on the ground near my feet, then slowly brought himself to his knees.

I said, "Stay down. You make any funny moves I'll crack your fucking head like a melon."

He didn't speak, remaining on his knees.

"Just lay on the ground," I said, but he didn't move. I took a half-step closer, stomping my foot on his lower back, and he pitched forward into the dirt.

"I ain't who you think," he said.

"You don't know what I think. Just lay there." I tried to remember the mug shot I saw of Edwards at the police station, but couldn't see it clearly. Maybe yes, maybe no.

"Kid don't know me," he said. "Ain't never seen him. That's how I know I ain't who you think. I was just scared, that's all. Kids been comin' up here, messin' up my camp, takin' my shit."

"Well, I'm not a kid, and I didn't do anything to your camp. You could have killed me with this." I nodded toward the club in my hands.

"Come on, man. Lemme go. I can't be seein' no cops. They'll run me off, or throw me in jail. Got no place to stay." He starts to get up.

"Stay down," I warned. "Don't make me club you. If you didn't do anything, they'll let you go. If they run you off, you can always find another park."

"I don't wanna have to set up again," he said. "Please, mister, just let me go. I won't bother nobody no more. I shouldn't a jumped ya."

"Stay down," I said, though a part of me softened. It could be Jerry just *expected* to see Edwards and freaked out. But I said I'm a slow starter, I didn't say I'm brain dead.

"At least let me stand up," he said.

I *said* I was a slow starter. "Get up slow then." I gripped the club.

The man rose again to his knees, then fell back on his haunches, his back to me. I took a half-step forward, ready.

When something happens that quickly, it's hard to tell what is real and what seems real. I saw the flash as he whirled, and suddenly a piece of white meat dangled from my forearm as he lunged a second time. I leaped back, swinging. The club caught him flush on the side of the shoulder, knocking him off balance, but not down. I swung again, missing, and we circled, facing each other down.

"Come on," I said. "Come on, you cocksucker. Come on. A little closer. I'll knock your fuckin' head into the bleachers. Come on!"

He circled silently, eyes like an endangered animal.

I shot a quick glance to my arm. No blood yet, only muscle and tendon. My stomach jumped and I looked back quickly.

He smiled. "Gonna need stitches for that, fucker."

I forced the nausea down, breathing deep. The man swirled a bit in front of me, and I realized I didn't have much time to take him out before I dropped. My eyes rolled as my knees buckled, and he charged low, presenting me with a waist-high fast ball, and I swung from the ankles, hearing the sickening thud as the club connected with his left temple. The club splintered on impact, however, and what should have been a home run turned into a broken bat single, driving him to his knees instead of out of the park. The knife dropped harmlessly to the dirt, and I quickly knocked it away with what was left of the club, then scrambled to retrieve it. I whirled back to use it—and I'm convinced I would have—only to watch his back disappear into the trees.

I started after him, but got only twenty-five yards or so into the thick brush before feeling the warm flow of

201

blood running over my fingers. At the same time, I remembered Jerry. I removed my shirt, tearing it with my good hand, and wrapped it tightly around the slice in my arm, then sprinted for the park. On the freeway, sirens wailed. Jerry did it.

I didn't make it to the parking lot, where more than a dozen twelve- to fifteen-year-olds surrounded Jerry, ready to protect him from any monster man who might be foolish enough to stumble out of the woods. When I reached the edge of the open expanse, I simply sat on a park bench and fell forward, dropping my head between my knees to maintain consciousness. When I heard the police cars pull into the parking lot, I looked up, then yelled as loud as I could. Probably they wouldn't have heard me, but Jerry pointed toward the spot where we entered the rough and more than a dozen of Three Forks' finest came running.

When they actually got Edwards, I was lying on a cot at Holy Family Hospital while an ER intern with the sensibilities of a baseball seamstress stitched my arm shut. Edwards should have known the park better. He headed deeper into the rough, apparently unaware it ended abruptly at a two-hundred-foot cliff overlooking the freeway.

Sixteen

Detective Palmer called daily. "How's it looking today? The kid going to put this slimeball away?"

"Not today," was my usual reply. "He believes nothing can stop this guy. Doesn't even talk about him as human; Edwards is fucking *Kong*."

Palmer was tiring of Kong. "We're going to need something pretty soon," he said. "I don't want to push the little bugger any more than you do, Corder, but either I convince the prosecutor that we have something solid or Edwards will be charged only with your assault. This means he's got a chance for bail."

"Bail! What the hell are you talking about? They'd grant bail to some guy who almost cut my arm off?"

"He's got a good defender," Palmer said, unflapped. "Pricey guy named Keaton. Makes a name for himself defending the tough ones. Decent folks hate his guts until they need a good lawyer. Then he's the first one they call."

"Yeah, but *bail?*"

"Keaton can make a pretty good case for Edwards's assault on you being self-defense. Not that you attacked, but that he felt his little home away from home was threatened. He's got a half brother here in town who's willing to give him a place to stay. Says Marvin's kind of a turd, but that he'd never kill a kid. I don't know that they can get bail, but they have a lot better chance than I'd like. Edwards gets out long enough to take a shit and he's gone."

I was quiet. Thinking.

"Right now all we have on the kidnapping and murder is a witness at least forty-five yards from Parker's place in the middle of a moonless night."

"Shit," I said. "How long can you give us?"

"I don't know. The sooner the better."

I didn't know what it would do to Jerry if Edwards got out of jail. He'd seen him on television, hiding his face and ducking into cop cars, and he at least knew where Edwards was. If he discovered not even the cops were big enough to hold him, he'd never testify. I was also sure Edwards said more to him than "I'll kill her here" that night. From what Jerry said in the park, I guessed he told him he'd come back for *him*.

"Tell me what to do, Corder. Ball's in your court. Would it help for Jerry to see Edwards in jail? We can bring him over."

I said, "I'll bring it up. It's hard to get anything right now. When I talk about the real Marvin Edwards or what actually happened that night, he clams up completely. The kid is paralyzed."

"Well, do what you can, friend. We'll keep this sump dweller as long as we can. For once the media are our friends. If the court turns him loose, the viewing public will have a giant rectal discharge. Even a judge has to think about that."

For once in my life, I really felt that doing for the police was doing for my client. For once, my idea of therapy and the cops' idea of justice are one and the same. Jerry was helpless and terrified both times he

204

came up against Marvin Edwards. If he could have a part in putting that slimeball away, he could well start to feel powerful again, and begin to heal. He could also begin to work on the idea that his sister would still be alive if he'd done more. In all of his play, his victims pleaded and pleaded for help. That had to be Sabrina.

"One more thing, Corder," Palmer said. "In my business when we run up against coincidence, we automatically figure something's fishy. What do you do in your business when you run up against coincidence?"

"I automatically figure something's fishy," I said.

"So tell me this," he said. "What was Edwards doing out at the makeshift gravesite at the same time you and the kid were there?"

"I assumed he was camped out," I said.

"We haven't found a campsite yet, though we're going to take him out soon to show us. But he turned up *where* you were with the kid, *when* you were with the kid. You might think about who knew you were going out there."

"Shit . . ."

"Think about it," he said. "Let me know."

In treatment, Jerry Parker went nuts. He immediately regressed. He didn't get to see Marvin Edwards brought in, and his last memory was of him kicking my ass. He *did* get to see the eleven-inch cut on my forearm as I sat balanced on the edges of consciousness trying to tell the cops which way Edwards went. Jerry was more convinced than ever that the man who took his sister was indestructible. He became so predatory in group that we kept him away from the other children most of the time. He was particularly rough with the weaker kids. No more Prince Valiants found their way into his individual play, only Kong, raising hell. Often, toward the end of a session he'd collapse in exhaustion and sob. Once he even asked for a bottle.

Molly and I shared time with him in individual sessions, trying to walk him through his fear and grief while we gathered the goods on Marvin Edwards. We did not talk about the case anywhere but in team meetings, and even there, most of what we said was superficial. No more mysterious notes found their way to my mailbox.

The day before I escorted him to the courthouse with my brand-new revised treatment plan, I took Jerry into my office the moment he walked through the front door of the center, hoping for some straight talk before he could get cranked up. I said, "I need you to talk to me."

Jerry glanced around the room, avoiding my eyes.

"You think you know what I want to talk about?"

His eyes and his hunched shoulders said yes, but his voice said, "No."

"I want to talk about the guy who took your sister."

"Groooow!" and he swelled his chest, heading directly for the Kong inside.

I put an easy hand on his shoulder. "No, man. I mean about the *real* guy. The guy you've been seeing on television. The guy we saw in the park. The one who was in your house that night."

I thought I would lose him, but the angels were with me. "You mean the Marv guy."

"Yup."

"Don' wanna talk about him."

"I know you don't. But you know what?"

"What."

"You're the one that can make sure he stays in jail."

Jerry's eyes widened.

"That's right, buddy. You're the guy. You're the only one who ever saw him do anything wrong."

Jerry glanced around the room again and I guessed he

was looking inside his head at what he had seen Marvin Edwards do wrong.

"So, do you want him in jail?"

"My momma say he's already in jail."

"You wanna make sure he stays there?"

Jerry nodded emphatically, then stopped. "I don't gots no handcuffs."

"You won't need 'em," I said. "Cops got handcuffs. You only have to do one thing."

Jerry looked at me.

"You know what it is?"

He shook his head.

"You have to tell on him."

"I already told my mom. She say . . ."

"And that Marv guy went to jail, right?"

"Uh-huh," Jerry said, "They take him in this car where he gots to put on handcuffs an' he try to hide his face all the time, my momma say so the camera don't get no good pictures of him. He a scaredy." The last sentence was with conviction.

"Looks like it, doesn't it? All hidin' his face and everything." We played with Marvin Edwards the scaredy-cat for a few minutes, but Jerry danced away. It occurred to me I hadn't let him finish his sentence a moment ago. "What did your mom say?"

"Huh?"

"Your mom. What did she say after you told her about that Marv guy taking Sabrina?"

Jerry was quiet. I took a guess. "She say you shouldn't talk about it to anybody else?"

He started to nod, then stared away. "Okay," I said. "I just wondered what she said. So, anyway, do you want to keep the Marv guy in jail?"

Jerry said he did.

"Will you tell on him again?"

He nodded.

"You have to tell a man that you haven't ever seen. Someone you don't know. A stranger. Can you do that?"

He was feeling safe in my office, and didn't consider the commitment he was making. He said yes.

I offered to let him go into group if he would make a no-hitting contract, but he opted to play the rest of the session there in my office. For the most part we played quiet games, nothing that had to do with Sabrina or Marvin Edwards or anything ugly.

I dared to hope we'd get lucky and slide right through this. When the session was over, I called Detective Palmer to arrange a meeting for Jerry with the prosecutor and to take him on a tour of the courthouse—and particularly the courtroom in which Jerry would testify. If we did it right, there would be no strangers come the day.

But when Jerry arrived at the center the following day, he marched right down to my office, knocked once—loud—and pushed his way in.

"What's up, Big Guy?" I asked.

"I don't talk no court," he said, and started to leave.

"Wait," I said. "Why not?"

He was quiet, his hand on the door handle.

Softly I said, "Why not, Jerry?"

"He gonna get me."

At first I suspected this was his mother's doing. That she had pushed his "not getting involved," but no evidence of that arose. Jerry was simply convinced, when he remembered Edwards on the night of the kidnapping, and then in the park, that Marvin was simply too big and bad to be held. Nobody could stop him and nobody could keep him in jail.

"Did that Marv guy say he'd get you if you told?" I asked. "Did he say something like that?"

Jerry pursed his lips and I realized I was not helping.

"How about if I go with you?" I asked. "How about if I stay with you all the time you're telling?"

He considered a moment, but I was not nearly big or mean enough.

"We've got one shot," I said to Detective Palmer over coffee at Perkins's.

"Tell me."

"I think Jerry needs to see Edwards in real life," I said. "Somewhere away from the jail."

"It is not real likely Marvin Edwards will be anywhere away from jail unless we have to cut him loose," Palmer said. "And I thought you said Jerry needed to see him locked up—see the cops in control of him."

"Things change daily," I said. "I think Edwards is bigger than life to Jerry and as long as he's surrounded by cops all the time and in jail, Jerry can imagine him getting away—breaking bars, beating all the cops up. I think he needs to see him in a more normal setting—see he's not a giant or anything."

"This doesn't sound right, Corder. I know it's your job to know these things, but this doesn't sound right."

It isn't right, Palmer, just do what I want you to do and I'll make it right. "Doesn't he have to go to the courthouse for a hearing or something? All I need to do is have him walk through the halls."

"There's a preliminary hearing tomorrow," Palmer said. "On the assault charges. I think I can arrange a 'showing,' but it'll have to be quick. Edwards can't change cells without causing a media circus."

"And if you have your eyewitness by the time of the hearing, will that be enough?"

"That would do it."

I sat back in the booth. "I'll need one favor."

"Shoot."

"I need him *out* of handcuffs."

Palmer sat forward, gawking as if I'd grown a hairy wart in the middle of my forehead. "You want me to take the most hated man in this state to the courthouse without handcuffs? You're a funny guy, Corder, I've said that before. Shit. I'd be emptying parking meters for the next ten years."

"It's important. I understand it'd put your butt on the line, but it might be the only way to make Jerry Parker comfortable enough to talk."

"Is there more to this than you're saying?" Palmer asked. "Because if there is, you better let me in on it now."

I considered a moment. "There's more, but you're better off not knowing it. For your own protection and all that."

Palmer sat back, studying my face. "If I go along with you, if I put sixteen years on the force in jeopardy, can you guarantee me your boy will talk?"

"No guarantees in this life, friend," I said. "I can tell you it'll give us our best chance."

Molly and I stood with Jerry Parker near the fourth-floor railing early the following morning, watching the activity on the floor below. Jerry was nervous as a cat, pacing back and forth, peering down constantly to see if that Marv guy was coming yet.

"Remember," I said, "he won't be able to see you. Don't make any noise and he won't even look this direction. I'm going down closer, but Molly will stay right here with you."

Jerry didn't answer, but maintained the countenance of a hawk, eyes darting, radar on high. Below us, all three local TV stations began setting up equipment. Suffice it to say, I did not like the idea of preserving what I was about to do on tape. I tapped Molly lightly on the shoulder and slid away toward the stairway. In the chaos of the media setup, I worked my way to a spot directly under where Molly and Jerry stood above me, between the stairway entrance to the third floor and the courtroom where I knew they were taking Edwards, and waited. In less than fifteen minutes he appeared, surrounded by police, with Detective Palmer beside him. He wore no cuffs, and hid his head with his hands. Cameras rolled as the entourage moved slowly toward the courtroom.

When they were directly in front of me, I charged forward, shoving Edwards hard to free him of the police for a few seconds, then slammed a fist into the bridge of his nose. Before he could recover I grabbed the back of his head and jammed it against my upcoming knee, splattering his blood onto the marble wall. I hit him three more times as quick as possible, ignoring the excruciating pain in my stitched forearm, expecting to be dragged to the ground by the police, but to my surprise (I discovered later it was Palmer's doing) they were quite slow. Edwards screamed for help, but I bent him over and brought both hands down on his shoulder blades, forcing him to the ground in a heap. I stomped my foot on the back of his neck and looked up at Jerry, who, with Molly, stared down in amazement. I shoved a fist in the air, as one policeman clamped his hand onto my wrist, forcing it hard behind me. Another cop clamped down on the other. Then they led me away.

But the deed was done. The monster was down, beaten. Jerry Parker could now know that the man who took his sister wasn't indestructible.

And I'm in jail.

So is Marvin Edwards. As I walked out of the room

surrounded by men in blue, I glanced up again to see Jerry shadowboxing with Molly, performing his version of the Ali Shuffle and looking tougher than the day is long.

As they pushed my head forward into the backseat of the patrol car, I turned back to Palmer. "Tell the prosecutor to charge him with everything they've got. Jerry will be there."

Seventeen

In jail, before bail was posted, I received a message saying Sarah and the kids were coming back home. My attack on Mr. Edwards got brief play on CNN, and Trevor caught it on TV in Cannon Beach, Oregon. He raced out onto the beach after Sarah and Emily screaming, "Dad's gone crazy! Dad's gone crazy!" I understand that played to no one's particular surprise. Sarah called back to Three Forks for details, and she and Detective Palmer decided it was probably safe to come home. If I'd had my way, they'd have waited a bit, but the prosecutor's office had already brought charges against Edwards.

Within an hour of my attack on Edwards, Jerry sang like Pavarotti to the prosecutor, a career man named Beckett. Edwards's beating had the intended effect, and Molly escorted Jerry directly to Beckett's office to help him through the questioning while my foot on the back of Edwards's neck was still fresh in his mind. The charge was kidnapping and murder. Bail for Edwards was denied.

Not so for yours truly. My official line to the press was, I beat up Marvin Edwards because he beat up my daughter—an accusation, incidentally, that he denied vehemently from his cell—and when that hit the newsstands, funds began pouring in for my defense. It is in the nature of Americans, I think, to vigorously applaud revenge. I was careful never to mention that Jerry was anywhere in the courthouse that day, nor that he needed to see Edwards knocked off his fearsome pedestal in order to take him on. I would guess a good defense attorney would rip us to shreds with that, if he knew it. Luckily, if anyone did see Molly and Jerry up there through all the chaos, they made no mental connection.

So I'm out—for now at least—and back to work. This is our first team meeting since I made bail, and it's clear my recent behavior is playing to mixed reviews. Certainly there is little argument that I have displayed conduct unbecoming a therapist, that I've crossed some important professional lines, but there is also a certain amount of empathy in evidence. The team members believe what the rest of the public believes regarding my motives. Only Molly and Carla know differently. We don't want a slip of the tongue in the wrong place to weaken the case against Edwards. I haven't forgotten what Detective Palmer said about coincidences.

I have just told Carla my family is coming back, and we're discussing the ramifications of my continued active involvement at the center with felony charges pending, and John Sheldon, guardian angel for "the business" that he has come to be, is once again politely bucking to put me out of commission. His line of reasoning is sound, but as usual when John opens his mouth, something stinks that isn't necessarily his breath.

"While we can all appreciate the stress Wilson was under, I still think, for the image of the center, he should take himself out of the spotlight for now at least. I don't think we've felt the full impact of all this."

My capacity for patience has dwindled over the past weeks. "Jesus, John. What do you have? A fifty-five-gallon drum in your bedroom that fills up with words overnight and you got no place to dump them but on us?"

John looks directly at me. "I have the right to state my opinion." He turns to Carla. "And, I have the right to be heard."

Before Carla can answer, I interrupt again. "Yeah, John, but when you talk so much you use up too much oxygen. Next time just say, 'I think we should lay Wilson off for a while,' okay?"

Carla sighs and drops her pencil on her appointment book. "Okay, children. I don't care who started this, but if you can't get along you'll both have to go to your rooms."

The others laugh, as do I. Sheldon's face reddens like the upper reaches of a thermometer over a blowtorch. It does nothing for his self-image to be compared to a child. I sense I could ignite his fuse if I wanted to, but I have more than a passing interest in the outcome of this conversation. "I have too many other clients to just take off," I say. "This thing could take months to resolve and if I end up in the slammer I'm going to need to prepare my clients for that."

The meeting moves on to other agenda items and, for now, at least, the case is closed.

My last client before Men's Group is Craig Clark, and he brings me back to the reason I like working with children: my sense of wonder. Craig absolutely owns his time with me, and I can only follow him down the treacherous path toward resolution of his perception of the torture he has experienced with Daddy Jeff. The more sessions I have with him and the farther I get from my last conversation with Dr. Banner—in other words, the more I focus on the child alone—the more I find myself suspicious about what it is like to be a three-year-old stepkid in Banner's house. Due to the so-called delicate nature of the case, I am extremely careful not to lead Craig in any way, nor to interpret his play beyond what is appropriate. As long as Craig is safe and Dr. Banner doesn't try to pressure me, I'll be patient. Don Cavett keeps me in current status reports so we can be ready to land with both feet should Fred Cronk decide to whitewash all this and return Craig, which is something I worry about constantly because Fred has still to acknowledge a single report I've sent him. To some degree I feel a sense of betrayal toward Dr. Banner, because I have avoided his calls in the name of keeping my relationship with Craig clean. Normally that would be standard operating procedure, but somehow with Dr. Banner being so prominent—and seemingly up front—it feels dishonest. I'm not a believer in "taking care of our own," but something clear down at gut level wants to. I'm avoiding him because I don't want this focus blurred in any way, but I wonder sometimes if I'm being unfair in excluding his perspectives. Under normal circumstances I would have access to the alleged abuser as well as the victim, but the nature of this situation simply doesn't allow that. Several times after I've finished with Craig, I've seen Dr. Banner's rose-colored BMW parked on the street outside the center. There's no mistaking that crafty little piece of work; it probably cost him considerably more than my house cost me.

Craig's recent sessions have been a bit like Jerry's, though more agitated. He remains three in age only, and uses more toy figures than any other three kids on my client load. My office carpet is virtually buried under dinosaurs, sharks, superheroes, baskets, marbles, puppets, and stuffed animals. The casual observer would believe a hand grenade had exploded at Toys "Я" Us, such is the random distribution of pieces, but Craig knows exactly where everything is and, given time, includes it all. He remains in frantic control. At this point my job is only to validate his words and feed him starter lines when he needs them, which is darn seldom.

Craig seems to be adjusting to his grandparents' home, but still longs for his mother, Carrie, though he fears he can never win her away from Daddy Jeff, and clearly would rather sip hot lava through a flavor straw than go back with Daddy Jeff. Like Jerry with Marvin Edwards, Craig banishes Jeff to jail at the opening of each session, only to have him escape in particularly sneaky and treacherous ways. Unlike Jerry, Craig usually runs several subplots simultaneously, so while the saga of Jeff's continued Great Escape plays out about home, Craig indulges *all* the players he has strewn across the floor. Currently he has made scrambled eggs (from marbles) for all, has dished them into small bowls, and is feeding the flock. Some of the players won't eat while others want more than their share, and Craig moves constantly between them, cajoling, yelling, pleading with them to take nourishment. As he concentrates his efforts here, the Jeff character, placed earlier into a plastic basket prison, begins to escape. Without looking, Craig reaches back, moving Daddy Jeff closer and closer to the edge of freedom. When Daddy Jeff has worked his way out completely, Craig notices him with a shriek, initiating a madcap race to save all.

Today it works. All are saved—a new outcome—and when the last potential victim stands safely on higher ground, Craig turns back on Jeff—and shows me something I've never seen before, particularly with a three-year-old. He marches Daddy Jeff into the prison basket *backward*. I probably wouldn't notice, but when Daddy

Jeff struggles in Craig's hand to turn around, Craig screams at him, then turns him backward once again.

I ask the obvious. "Why do you want him to go in backward?"

He looks at me and shrugs, palms turned upward. "So when he turn around to sneak *out,*" he says, eyebrows raised, "he go *in.*" Then, with the gleam of discovery in his eye, he collects all the scrambled egg marbles into one bowl—and he is meticulous in retrieving every one—and pours them in on top of Daddy Jeff, who keeps turning around and going farther into prison.

I say, "You seem to have poured all the scrambled eggs into the prison on top of Jeff."

He smiles and nods, dusting his hands.

"Are they cold eggs or warm eggs?" I ask.

He smiles. "Warm." He smiles bigger. "Hot!"

Today, for the first time, Jeff does not get out. Craig is beginning to find resolution. I'm glad because if he had struggled with it much longer, I'd have had to introduce some possible resolutions myself to avoid hopelessness setting in, and resolutions are far more powerful coming from the child. I'm guessing he's starting to feel safe in his new home and that his grandparents, who are not impressed with Dr. Banner's credentials, have convinced him Jeff will not get another shot at him as long as one of them draws breath. It will be a while, but some healing has started. Toward the end of the session, he begins to eye the shark again, and I ask if the shark wants to tell me the secret, but I've got all I'm getting today.

Craig's hour is gone in a flash and as I open my office door to take him back, I realize he has transported me to a world completely apart from the one in which I am now struggling, and I almost stop to thank him for allowing me in, but refrain because Craig doesn't recognize the same boundaries I do and wouldn't know what the hell I was talking about. Instead I simply say, "It was very much fun playing with you today, Big Guy," and he nods his assent.

As we step into the hall, we nearly bowl John Sheldon over. John looks at Craig, and for a moment starts back into his office, then stops, seeming about to speak. Instead, he glances through my door at Craig's demolition handiwork and says, "Looks like you've got a wild one there."

Craig moves close to my leg, watching John warily.

"A little light redecorating," I say back, and John disappears on down the hall.

"You ever go inside John Sheldon?" I ask. Molly and I are sitting on her deck in the early evening heat, me in shorts, her in swimsuit bottom and a halter top. I want her.

She watches me warily, to be sure what I'm asking.

"Do you?" I ask again.

"Is this a trick?"

"No, I'm serious."

"I thought you didn't believe in that stuff."

I smile. "This is a test. Maybe I'll be a psychic convert." Molly and I don't talk much about her abilities in that area, nor about how she does or doesn't use them. They are a part of her life that has nothing to do with me—except that I benefit sometimes when we work with the same children—a separate part in which she deals only with people of like spirit. None of my personal experiences includes a connection to that world, but my experiences with this woman tell me *something's* going on that I can't see. She smiles. "No, I've never been inside John Sheldon. Why?"

"I don't know. Something's just strange about him."

"I don't need to go inside him to know something is strange."

"I mean stranger than usual," I say.

Molly gets up to make us another drink, and I close my eyes a second while she's gone, doing what my father taught me, turning down the sound.

"Tell me what you mean," she says, squatting on my knee, placing the drink on the table next to us.

I put my hands on the bare skin at the sides of her stomach and for a quick second nearly lose, my train of thought. She moves my hands. "Not till you tell me." She scoots back to her chair.

"For the past few months, John's been subtly trying to convince me it would be in everybody's best interest at the center for me to stop working."

"It's been a lot longer than that," Molly says. "John Sheldon has been trying to get you out of this business since he knew you were in it."

"Yeah, I know that. But for the last few months—I'm not sure when it started—he's been trying to get *me* to see it's in my best interest. Before, he just wanted everyone else to see it, like he might find a therapeutic quality control engineer somewhere. This is different. It doesn't make much sense, but I keep tracing it back to Sabrina Parker."

"If I were you, *everything* would trace back to Sabrina Parker right about now."

"I don't know," I say. "Maybe."

I drive by Sarah's house on my way home sometime after ten-thirty and see lights through the living room window, so I turn into the driveway, thinking I should ride to a phone booth and call in case Rob, Sarah's lover, is there. Our agreement is always to call first. But only

220

Sarah's car is out front, and I really want to see the kids, so I take a chance.

"Daddy!" Emily squeals at the door, and puts her arms around me. "I thought you were in jail." Trevor is immediately behind her.

"I was," I say, "And I might be again. But right now, I'm a free man."

Sarah appears in the kitchen doorway. "Sorry," I say. "I should have called, but I saw your light and there were no cars . . ."

"That's fine," she says, and crosses the room to hug me. Rob stands in the background.

I wave, a little embarrassed. "How you doin', man?"

He waves back. "Okay. Yourself?"

"Good. Didn't mean to interrupt. I'll only be a minute. Just wanted to see the kids . . ."

He raises his hand, says, "No sweat," and disappears back into the kitchen.

"I'm sorry," I say again.

"It's fine, Wilson. How are you?" Sarah says.

"Looks like you lost weight," Trevor says. "Food not too good in prison?"

"I wasn't in *prison*," I say. "I was in jail. For two days. The food was fine and I didn't lose any weight. I can still take you down before you know what hit you."

"Did you have to wear a striped suit?"

"Jeez. What have you been watching?"

The kids and I spend a little more time in the living room while Sarah goes back into the kitchen to be with Rob. "You were on the news and everything," Trevor says. "But I couldn't tell if they liked you or not. It was kind of like you were a hero but a jailbird, too. Were you really a 'mentally distressed therapist'? What is that?"

I look at Emily, who waits with me for Trevor to run down, then back to him.

"Did you really go crazy, Dad?" he asks.

"No, Trevor. I didn't go crazy. I did what I did for a reason that I can't tell you about right now, but I will later." I know I should maintain the fatherly revenge line, but I just can't stand to lie to the kids, to have them see their dad in a worse light than he belongs. "But for now, if any of your friends ask, you say I just got crazy mad because this guy beat up Emily and I beat him up back, okay?"

"What do you mean? What was the real reason? Wasn't that it?"

"Okay?" I say it emphatically.

"Okay," he says. "But tell me the real reason."

I notice Emily watching us quietly, which is unusual for her when Trevor is running off at the mouth like this. Normally she would have shoved her cast into his mouth. "Glad to be back?" I ask.

She nods.

"How you feeling?"

"Lots better," she says. "I started having some dreams, but they stopped."

"Well," I say, "I think things are under control. Edwards is in jail and I'm sure Jerry will testify against him now. The prosecutor thinks we have a good case and Jerry's been real clear talking about what he saw. I'm going to be in court with him, and as long as he knows that, he doesn't seem afraid."

"Is that why you beat him up?"

I snort a laugh and look away. "You're something, you know that?"

Emily crosses the short space between us and sits on my lap, adjusting her cast so she can lay her head on my shoulder.

222

At midnight the phone rings. The voice on the other end whispers, "Daddy?"

I have no trouble clearing my head. "Em?"

"Daddy," she whispers, "I have to tell you something. Rob taped all the news stories while we were gone and I got to see that Edwards man on two or three of them."

"Yeah?"

"Daddy, he's not the one."

"What?"

"He's not the man who beat me up that day. I couldn't tell from the picture at the police station, but he doesn't move like him or anything. And there's no way he's tall enough."

"Did you tell your mother?"

"No. I didn't want to scare her. I wanted to talk to you first."

My heart hammers so loudly I can barely hear my daughter talking, or myself think. "Listen," I say, grappling for time to think, "is Rob still there?"

"No, he went home. He has to work tomorrow."

Jesus. Whoever got Emily is still loose. "Listen," I say calmly, "just to be safe, go around and make sure all the doors and windows are locked. Then wake your mom up and tell her I'm coming over. And tell her why. Okay?"

"Okay, Daddy." There is a pause. "Daddy, do you think there's someone outside?"

"No. I don't. I don't think anyone even knows you're back. I just want to be safe, okay? Now, don't worry and just close everything up. I'll be there in twenty minutes. And don't wake your brother."

The bike is moving almost before I'm on it and I shoot across town on nearly deserted streets, hitting the lights perfectly, my mind racing almost as fast as the Honda.

So, who the hell is *this?* Does Marvin Edwards have a buddy? Rapists and kid killers usually work alone. They don't last long if anyone knows what they're up to. They're who the "good" bad guys always hurt. I guess the only thing I can be sure of is whatever I expect to happen, won't. Shit.

I pull the bike up in front of Sarah's house, giving the horn a short beep to let them know I'm here. At the door I ask Sarah for a flashlight and tell her I'll look around outside, on the off chance. I am relieved that she hasn't returned to the stance she took before Emily talked her into leaving on vacation.

Nothing is in the shrubbery alongside the house, or in the woodshed or the garage. Trevor has apparently pulled up the rope to his treehouse, which faces his upstairs bedroom window, but I shine the light between the slats just in case. I see nothing.

Inside, I get a blanket and pillow from the hall closet and settle on the couch. I want to talk about what Sarah and the kids should do next, but everyone is bone tired, and we decide to wait until morning. Trevor, who awoke despite Emily's efforts to avoid that, warns me that he may just be back in to sleep with me if there's any shadow action in his closet or under his bed.

Turns out the action is in his treehouse.

The shriek of the smoke alarm seconds after Trevor's scream brings me off the couch, hurtling toward his room on instinct. He calls to me from the other side of a wall of flames in his doorway. "Dad! Dad! I can't see! Come get me! It's hot, Dad! There's a fire!"

"I'm coming, Trev! Where are you?"

"I'm in the closet! It's by the door! The window's busted!"

"Is there fire there? By the window?"

He coughs. "No! Should I go there?"

It's too *fast*. I can't think whether or not the window is safe. Oxygen will fuel the fire there, but with the door open, the flames seem to be coming this way.

"There's a stick on the floor, Dad! It's on fire! Right by the door!"

A torch.

Sarah and Emily are beside me now, both amazingly calm, awaiting orders.

"Soak a blanket, Sarah. The one on the couch. Soak it in the laundry sink. Fast. If there's a break in these flames, I'll go . . ."

The picture window in the living room veritably explodes, and Sarah bolts down the staircase in time to see the couch burst into flame. The kitchen window is next. Sarah is back without the blanket and I grab her and Emily, shoving them down the stairs, where I kick out the lower hall window and we crawl through, Sarah screaming Trevor's name. I push them toward the tree, yelling to wait for me at the base, then scale the trunk and stand in the treehouse, looking straight across into Trevor's room. I see him there, on his hands and knees close to the window. There is no hand or foothold outside, but I see I can get three quick steps on a thick branch and dive. I *might* make it. I know I would rather fall to my death than watch my son burn.

The shattering pane cuts into my back as I crash through, rolling involuntarily toward the flames, searing my hand as I scramble back. Trevor has dropped to his stomach and, though conscious, appears completely disoriented as he screams my name.

"I'm right here, Trevor! We're outta here. Listen to me. We're going out the window. It might hurt, but it's only two stories! Just relax your body! Hear me? Relax your body!"

As I scoop him into my arms and scramble for the

window, flames licking at our heels, Emily screams from outside, and I know instantly *he* is there. At the window I see him, an enormous man, his thick hand on Emily's good wrist, slapping Sarah away.

The giant's gray coat flickers in the flames like a perfect target, and I remember with spectacular clarity, aerial photos of my father's World War II bombing strikes over Germany. We pored over those pictures for hours, he showing me the difference between pinpoint bombing and saturation bombing and telling tales of when they used each. The pictures with just a few puffs were pinpoint, those with dozens were saturation. Suddenly Trevor and I are a bomb. We're going for pinpoint.

Emily hears Trevor shriek as we jump and glances up to see us falling, jerking free in the nick of time as Trevor's and my combined near-three-hundred pounds crash onto the giant, crushing him into the ground. Sarah grabs Emily, and they rush quickly to the back of the yard. Trevor leaps up to follow, yelling all the way. In the distance sirens wail. If I can hold this animal a few minutes, my life can return to normal.

But the giant has a different idea. Somehow, three hundred pounds of free-falling Corder hasn't put him out. He struggles to his feet, barely dazed, his eyes dancing like a vicious animal's. I charge and he whirls, his fists locked as if throwing the hammer, and drives his knuckles into my nose. One quick, sickening crunch and my nasal passage is cut. I drop to the ground scarcely fast enough to avoid his next swing, and roll as I hit, but he is surprisingly quick and my next sensation is the burning pain of his steel-toed boot to my midsection, followed by a knee to the ribs. In the distance Sarah and Emily scream again, and I raise my head to see Trevor charging. I try to shout to him, but my wind is gone and the hysterical panic of suffocation fills me. Trevor's foot strikes inches from my hand, which whips out like a snake's tongue to trip him. Above me the giant bellows, and I don't know whether he's going after me or my son, and as traces of air seep back into my lungs I roll, convulsing, to my back, kicking wildly. His thick hand clamps onto my ankle and pain shoots clear past the hip. I don't see Trevor, and I can't tell if the giant has him or if he has run back to his mother.

Suddenly red and blue lights dance around us as shouting men's voices float from the front yard, and the giant is gone. I look up to see Trevor standing with my wife and daughter, and drop my forehead to the cool grass.

Eighteen

When I was young—really young, like three or four—I had what was probably the largest collection of children's puzzles in the Western Hemisphere. I was purely addicted to them, and every time Mom or Dad took me to the toy store we came out with a picture puzzle. I *loved* them. From as far back as I can remember, it was a source of tremendous joy to find the piece that fit. It remains in my memory as one of my first true feelings of accomplishment.

Dad never put one together for me, but he always helped by drawing my attention to matching colors or figures, or to the shapes of the pieces themselves. "You can't force it," he'd say. "If a piece won't quite fit, that's because it doesn't belong there. The one that does fit will go in smoothly." When I was six, he even took me to a factory where picture puzzles were produced, and we watched as they were stamped out. "The picture is there first, then the pieces are all cut at once," he said as I watched in amazement. "They *have* to fit." I realized much later that he took me there because he was sick to death of watching me cram pieces into the wrong places, ruining the puzzle.

I swear to God, right now I can't figure what this puzzle will look like put together. I mean, I am in no way a violent man. Generally speaking, I avoid physical confrontation like I avoid venereal disease, yet within the past few weeks, I've been involved in three near life-and-death struggles. Granted, I initiated one of them, but when *my* life gets this exciting, outside forces are at work.

Sarah and the kids are back in Cannon Beach, or maybe even farther south. We spent the remainder of the night before last in the hospital getting checked out physically. Though Trevor has some deep bruises and a couple of minor cuts from our fall, only I had to stay beyond that. Three sets of *serious* railroad tracks from the glass in Trevor's window run the length of my back, and oxygen takes major detours getting from my nose to my lungs. Nothing is broken, though my ankle's pretty tender from that monster trying to tear it off, and there's not a muscle in my body that doesn't scream out when I move, but that's all minor.

Yesterday morning, Sarah's insurance company wrote her an emergency check so fast I thought they must be taping a TV commercial. She and the kids shopped for clothes and necessities in the company of a police guard sometime before noon, then "hit the mattresses," as Trevor says. What a kid.

Then this evening, about an hour after the doctors told me I should be out by tomorrow at the latest, I lay resting, about half wigged out on codeine, floating above the pain, when I heard Jerry Parker's voice from that day we ran into John Sheldon in the hall, clear as day: *I know that guy.*

I popped awake and dialed Molly. "Hi. It's me, back from the dead. Listen . . ."

"Oh, hi, Wilson. I was just coming over to see you. I

229

was there earlier, but you weren't. Your body was, but you were gone."

"Yeah," I said. "I could get seriously addicted to this shit."

"Anyway," she said, "I just stopped here on the way home from work to see if anyone had torched *my* house. I could use some new stuff."

I started to tell her what was on my mind, then decided to wait until she got here.

So Molly sits next to my bed, massaging my temples and guiding me to my fantasy beach. Nothing has felt better in all my memory. Through the woods she walks me, then onto a narrow strip of sand that will disappear under the tide as soon as I have crossed it, to a sandy shore surrounded by sheer rock walls towering over blue-green water beneath deep blue skies dotted with marshmallow clouds. The temperature is seventy-eight, and I am protected by nature on all sides. Molly's voice is hypnotic and five minutes from when she walked through the door, I am stretched out on the sand, completely relaxed without a care in the world.

Her fingernails tickling my scalp seem distant, as does the pain from the deep slices in my back and my throbbing muscles. I would take Molly's beach to codeine any day.

"Are you going to see Jerry in group tomorrow?" I ask later over a particularly nasty cup of instant hospital coffee.

"Um-hmm. Why?"

"Well, I want you to try something. I want you to arrange for the two of you to run into Sheldon."

"You mean like with a car?"

I shake my head. "Don't get excited. Just in the hall.

230

Just stop and talk while Jerry is with you—do something to draw attention to him. Then check out Jerry's reaction. If you have to, ask him if he knows Sheldon."

"What's your idea, Wilson?"

I shift to find a more comfortable position. I've been lying on my stomach in order to keep off my stitches for almost twenty-four hours, and my lower back is killing me. The nurses have tried every position the bed has to offer and have yet to find one tolerable for long. "My idea is, that pompous asshole is mixed up in this some way."

"John Sheldon? Are you out of your mind? Your daughter would have ripped John Sheldon a new asshole. *Trevor* could take John Sheldon out."

I delight in the former vision. "No. I don't think he's doing any violence. I just think he's involved some way. After he bitched me out about making noise in the halls that day, Jerry said he knew him. I thought he just meant he'd run into him in the halls at the center, but he's never said that about anyone else, and he's been in treatment long enough to know every therapist in the place."

"Wilson, what are you saying? Do you think . . . ?"

"I don't know. All I know is every time something develops, John has something to say about it, or he just shows up." I shift again. "The other day Detective Palmer asked me what I do about coincidences and I told him. He thought it was a pretty big coincidence that Marvin Edwards would show up at the site of the killing at the same time Jerry and I did. I've been quiet, Molly. So have you. The only place any of this gets discussed is either with the cops or in team meetings. I'm with you. It's hard to imagine John Sheldon getting into anything remotely this dirty, but this son-of-a-bitch fits together *somehow*."

Molly shakes her head. "I don't know. It would sure

give criminals everywhere a bad name to add John Sheldon to their ranks."

"Look what it did for therapists."

The evening nurse enters to tend to my cuts and Molly takes the opportunity to duck out. "See you tomorrow. Call if you're getting out and I'll come get you, okay?"

I was released shortly after two in the afternoon but knew Molly would be up to her ears in work, and called a cab. The doctor gave me a special pad to cover the bandages on my back so I could sit. I thought about going to work, but glanced out into my backyard at the big old apricot tree throwing shade all over the cool grass, and remembered my insurance pays for down time. So I grabbed a book and a gin and tonic, and I've been out here medicating myself ever since.

I pick up the ringing phone to Molly's voice. "Boy, have I got something for you."

"Jerry say something about Sheldon?"

"No. John was at the dentist most of the morning, so Jerry was gone before he got to work. But he got here in time for the meeting."

"So?"

"Remember when you asked me if I'd ever been inside John Sheldon?"

I feel her shudder over the phone. I say I remember.

"Well, there's no reason to go inside John Sheldon. Most of our meeting time was spent talking about you, about how crazy this has gotten and about the fire."

"Uh-huh."

"And John was acting stranger than usual, which is hard to imagine if you weren't there. He was completely interested one minute, and *gone* the next."

"Yeah?"

"Yeah. And I started noticing. Every time Peggy Parker's name came up, he either spaced out or aimed the conversation elsewhere."

"And . . ."

"Not so fast," she says, and I hear mischief. "I think I want to make a deal."

"Tell me, Molly . . ."

"Now, I didn't go inside John Sheldon, but I *could* have. If this turns out to be right, there'll be no more calling me Broomhilda, agreed? No more 'Bubble bubble, toil and trouble.' No more asking me to get my broom from the parking lot so you can sweep out your office. Okay, Wilson? You *asked* for witchcraft. You can't ask for it, then make fun. Okay, Wilson?"

"Molly . . ."

"Okay, Wilson?"

"Okay," I say, "but this better be good."

"It's good. I'll bet you anything in the world John Sheldon has something going with Peggy Parker."

"What?"

"Da's right, honey," she says, slipping into her best Pearl Bailey. "You heard it here. Name your stakes. He avoided the subject of Peggy Parker like it was AIDS."

I think a moment. "I don't get it. What the hell would . . . Do I have to pay for an interpretation?"

"Indeed you do, baby, but I'll take it out in trade. To put it crudely," she says, returning to her own voice, "I think John Sheldon is fucking Peggy Parker. Or at least he was. Toward the end of the meeting, when Carla suggested she might call Peggy in to find out if she can shed any light on this, Sheldon turned into a complete squirrel. It's male-female, my friend. I'd know it anywhere."

"Jesus." I try to let it sink in, but my natural cynicism won't let it, so I say, "Speaking of male-female, why don't you come over here and talk about this one on one? I'm feeling much better."

"I'm on my way."

Molly is gone. She offered to stay, but I'm going to be tossing and turning all night with these wounds in my back, plus I don't know how safe this place is, so I sent her on her way. Probably I shouldn't stay here, either, but there's a loaded .357 Magnum in my headboard—which goes against all my stated political views—and I'm feeling more like fighting than running.

In the black of night I begin to drift, and the doorbell rings. My watch says eleven thirty-seven. I remove the pistol from the headboard, pull on my terry-cloth robe, and move silently down the stairs to the front door. At first glance through the window I see nothing, then the shadow of a head on the porch. I grip the handle of the gun beneath my robe, flipping on the porch light. A man there whirls and the light catches his face. Dr. Banner. I hustle to the kitchen and slide the gun into a drawer, hoping to avoid looking like a paranoid loon, then rush back to open the door.

"I'm sorry it's so late," Banner says as I open the door, "but I was hoping I'd catch you home."

I'm at a loss for words, and only stare.

"I know this is irregular, Wilson, but could I come in and talk?"

"Of course. I'm just surprised to see you. I was expecting someone else . . . actually, I was *expecting* no one, but if someone came I didn't expect it to be you . . ."

Banner sees I'm rattled. "I know. I read about your trouble in the paper. You must be in a bad way, and I really do apologize, but I need to talk with you."

"I take it this is about Craig."

He nods. "And I understand you want to keep your work with him separate from me. I appreciate that, but there are a few things I really need to say."

I step aside and motion him into the house, where he takes a seat on the edge of the couch. I sit across from him in an easy chair, and wait.

"I was angry," he starts, looking at his feet, "when I put Craig into the tub."

A short, uneasy silence follows, then, "Angrier than I said I was to CPS."

I nod.

"It's the classic story, and it goes largely the way I told it before. I'd been trying to potty-train him for several days, and told Carrie it'd be a cinch, and the little bugger would go *any*where but on the toilet." He shakes his head. "It was his third accident of the night, and this time I yelled at him, pretty loud, I think. I didn't want to go through another clean-up job and it was almost his bedtime, so I decided to just wash him off in the tub. I went into the bathroom, turned on the water, and went to get him ready."

"There was no phone call?"

Banner looks down again. "No. There was no phone call." He waits, then, "He flinched when I came into the room and I knew I'd scared him earlier, yelling, but I was still mad . . . and I'm afraid I *wanted* him to be scared."

"They can be a real pain," I say, thinking this explains why there were no splash burns on Craig. Banner actually put him in the tub.

Banner nods without commitment. "I just wasn't ready for it, I guess. We work with these people and their anger all the time, and I guess we think we know so much about it, we don't have to worry about our own."

I know what he means. It's a hazard of the trade and I say so. "What do you want from me, Dr. Banner?"

"Well," he says, "I know this is irregular and it's also quite unprofessional. But I guess I'm here with my hat in my hand. I'm aware Craig may well put my anger and his burning together—there's certainly no way he would know I didn't intend to scald him. I'd like you to take that into consideration in your interpretations of his work in play therapy." He looks directly across the room into my eyes. "You're a good therapist, Wilson. You're doing your job the way I'd want you to if you were working for me. But I need you to know I'm not a mean man. I'm not a child abuser, I'm really not. Everything I've ever worked for in my life is at stake here. This was a horrible accident, and I'm willing to work it out with Craig in sessions with you or whatever it takes. I just want you to know, however this works out, I'm not a monster."

Face to face, I have no choice but to believe him. There is no sense of slickness, or insincerity. I can't help but think what a horror show it would have been for me if I had ever been falsely accused. And the reality is, there are certainly times I could have been—times when Emily and Trevor were little that I lost my temper. Neither of them ever got hurt as a result, at least not physically, but there were certainly times when my behavior could have been taken out of context. I stand and extend my hand. "I believe you're not a monster, Dr. Banner. I've always had a lot of respect for you. I still have to go by the book with Craig, but that may very well include your coming in on some of his sessions. When the time comes, I'll let you know." I smile. "I don't have a completely clear interpretation of what he's doing yet."

Dr. Banner rises with me and takes my hand in a firm shake. "That's all I can ask for," he says and starts for the door, where he turns. "I realize," he says, "that it may look strange that I've taken up with Carrie. I mean she's certainly young enough to be my daughter. I've been a part-time teacher at the community college for a long time, and I have always followed the rigid practice of *never* becoming romantically involved with a student. But with Carrie I just couldn't help it. I don't know what happened, it just took me over. The moment I realized it I insisted that she transfer out of my class into another section so there'd be no conflict of interest of any kind."

I nod.

"I'm only saying that because if I were in your shoes I would include that in my evaluation of the situation." He steps out onto the porch and nods again. "Thanks again for your time, Wilson. I know it's late . . ."

I wave my hand. "I'm not sleeping that much these days anyway," I say.

"I'm sorry to hear that," he says and is gone.

I flip off the lights and sit in my robe in my overstuffed easy chair before a darkened television screen. Again, I wasn't totally honest with Dr. Banner. His anger at the time of the scalding would explain Craig's fear, and Craig certainly could have misinterpreted it for more than it was. But my sense of Craig is that his fear comes from more than one incident, that it comes from a way of life. And yet again, I want to believe Banner. I start to drift, and am slightly jarred when my digital watch beeps twice, marking the midnight hour. I see Don Cavett's face. *From now* (beep) . . . *to now, is six seconds* . . . That's it. If Banner put him in the water, he left him there six seconds. An eternity. If there was no phone call, then Banner never left the room.

* * *

I cancelled my last two afternoon clients to give me time to go down to the police station and look at mug shots. Again. Palmer brought some to my office earlier, but we had no luck. Looking at mug shots is not likely to turn into one of my favorite pastimes. This ain't like going through old yearbooks. Guys don't smile for these pictures. And if they get voted "Most Likely," it's to take a life.

"I didn't get a great look at him," I said as Palmer brought in two more stacks.

"Keep looking. Something in here might jar you."

After about an hour and a half and about eight cups of coffee—just when I was convinced that, black or white, every one of these assholes looks the same—a picture stopped me and I called for Palmer. "Could be this one," I said. "Something about him looks right."

Palmer looked quietly, nodding, more to himself than me.

I said, "Who is it?"

"Name's Charles Creech," he said. "Let me show you something." He hustled back to his office, returning with a computer composite. "Take a look." The composite was nearly identical to the picture.

"Where did this come from?"

Palmer's eyebrows raised. "Your daughter. Before she left with your ex. We just got it matched to a name a few minutes ago. That's why I brought in the extra books—see if you could pick him out independently."

I stared at the picture. "What do you know about him?"

"I'll tell you this much for now," Palmer said, gripping my shoulder with his huge hand. "He's dangerous. Best we get you some kind of protection. Or at least move you out of your house for a while. This guy's relentless."

I didn't argue.

* * *

"So, you've got your nose in our lives about as far as it goes, is it fair for us to stick our noses into yours?"

"Into my what?" I ask in jest.

"Into your life, asshole," Eric says back. Men's Group is due to start within minutes and we're seated in the group room, shooting the breeze, waiting for stragglers. My special cushion is tied to the back of my chair to keep from gouging my wounds.

"I don't know how I could stop you," I say, "unless I smash your television set." I've been on the six and eleven o'clock news so often for the past couple of weeks I'm thinking of asking for union scale.

"So who was it?" he asks. "Who torched your ex-old lady's place?"

"Yeah," Carl pipes in, "I might have a job for him."

I say I wish I knew.

"Is that right?" says Carl. "And what would you do? Ask him how he feels? Ask him if he wants to *talk* about his anger? I've always wondered what a mighty counselor does when somebody's pissing on *his* life."

"Why Carl," I say in mock surprise at his surly attitude, "I didn't know you cared."

"I don't fuckin' care. Except you been makin' the news pretty entertaining. I just wanna know how this soap opera ends."

Miles—Jockey Boy—is the last into the room, and he trips the door stop, letting the door close slowly against its hydraulic arm. He says, "Hi, you guys," sheepishly, and takes his customary seat. I'm ready to start, but Eric persists. "I'm serious, man. Do we get to know what's goin' on?"

I hold his gaze steadily, figuring his angle. Eric doesn't usually give me a hard time without reason, and I've

239

been hoping my situation wouldn't cause too much distraction. "How would it help to know anything more about what's going on with me?" I say finally. "What does that have to do with what you're here to get?"

"Anytime I go *anywhere,*" Eric says, "I want to know who's drivin'. Look, half of us in here got criminal records, right? An' if you'll remember right, that's been the source of considerable discussion, like whether we can be reasonable parents when we persist with certain kinds of behavior an' all that." Eric sits forward in his chair. "Now, I'm all for that. It's a good question. *My* question is whether you can do your job right while you persist with criminal behavior." There is a hint of a smile.

I know Eric is baiting me. He's been here a long time and we've been through a lot. This isn't really a question of trust. My beating up a child killer on national television would only serve to strengthen our bond. But anyone with half a brain who's seen me on TV knows I'm not telling all, and he merely wants the rest of the story. I raise one hand. "Hey, only *one* criminal behavior," I say. "One little old assault."

"Let's see," Miles says. "That would come under the heading of 'Anger Control.' " Miles is getting better, standing up for himself. I wish he'd do it with someone else.

I look at my watch. "Tell you what. I'll give this fifteen minutes. You guys tell me what you want to know, and if I can talk about it I will. If not, I won't; but *I'll* decide. I agree you need a certain amount of disclosure from me to maintain trust, but I also know that my job here is different than yours. So let's see what happens. But I get the same benefit of confidentiality you get. Nothing I say leaves this room, or whoever lets it out is a goner. Fair?"

They agree. Carl cuts to it. "Who's tryin' to get you? Is it Edwards?"

I decide not to talk about what went on at the police station earlier. "I don't know," I say. "I really don't. When I beat him up at the courthouse, I really did think he was the one who attacked my daughter. Turns out he's probably not. Turns out the guy who went after her originally is probably the same one who started the fire at my ex-wife's."

"You think Edwards has a buddy?" he asks.

"I don't know what else to think."

Eric shakes his head. "Tell you what, Counselor. It don't seem real likely. Guys like Edwards are low man in the joint. They don't have friends unless somebody needs 'em for somethin'. It's hard to picture the badass they described on TV doin' that pussy's dirty work."

That has nagged at me all along, but hearing Eric, a seven-year veteran of that system, confirm it, helps.

"If you *knew* it wasn't coming from Edwards," Eric says, "where would you guess?"

"You ask good questions. But I don't know. It's worth thinking about, though."

"It's worth more than thinkin' about," he says.

We go on to other things, though it's difficult to get them off the subject of me, largely, I suspect, because it gets them off the subject of *them*. When we do get to work, much of our time is spent on Miles and the fact that when he gets down on himself, he wrecks something he really cares about. Recently he has come very close to hurting the thing he cares about most: Miles, Jr. I am encouraged that he brings it up without coercion, and talks about the terror inside him when he thinks he can't stop himself. He's beginning to recognize the real danger inside, and recognition is the first step toward doing

241

something about it. He is near panic, however, because this is his worst nightmare: becoming his stepdad.

Walking toward my office at group's end, I am monumentally grateful that my father was the man he was. It is probably the biggest difference between Miles and me.

I feel a hand on my shoulder as I open my office door, and I whirl, surprised at my own jumpiness.

"Talk to you for a sec?" It's Eric.

"Sure." I motion him to a seat.

"I wasn't askin' all those questions to give you a hard time," he says and I smile. "Really."

"I believe you. I'm just laughing because I think Carl thought you guys had struck a gold mine."

"Carl's a tit," Eric says.

"So why *were* you asking all those questions?"

"You and I've been around the block a few times," he says. "You've stood by me through some tough shit, an' you never let me down. You never let me off the hook, either, an' that's what I needed. It got rough, but the bottom line is, you saved me."

"You saved yourself, Eric. All I did was help you splash around for the ring buoy."

"Whatever. I *wouldn't* 'a done it without you. I just want you to know that what you're messin' around with right now ain't therapy. It's street, and it's hardcore; maybe a little more down *my* line an', well, I want you to know if it comes down to the wire an' you need help, well, you call me."

Tears rim Eric's eyes, and I know he means what he's saying as much as he's ever meant anything. I am immensely and genuinely grateful. I say, "Thanks."

"There's one other thing," he says. "Different subject."

"Yeah?"

"It's Little E. Every time I approach him, if he's surprised, he flinches. I tell him over an' over it's okay, I'd

242

never hurt him. But he *flinches*. It kills me. It kills me every time. Will the little shit ever trust me?"

I take a deep breath and put my hand on Eric's shoulder. "That must hurt a lot," I say. "You've done a lot of work."

"You think it'll ever stop?"

"Yeah," I say. "I think it'll ever stop."

"When, for Christ's sake?"

"When it stops."

He smiles and starts to leave, when I remember something. Eric spent hard time with some of the roughest dudes in the state. I step inside the office and pull out a Polaroid picture and the copy of the police composite Palmer gave me. I say, "This is coming out in the paper tomorrow. Doesn't look familiar by any chance?"

Eric jerks both from my hand, eyes flaring. He says, "Jesus Christ."

"What?"

He's quiet a second, then looks at me and shakes his head. "If this is who it looks like, you're a dead man."

My stomach leaps. "Who is he?"

He looks closer. "Looks like a guy from the joint we called Poke. As in Cowpoke. I'm not sure I even know his real name. He's got a bronco tattooed onto his back— his whole back. Had it done in one sitting. He's a psycho, man. Kills for fun."

"Does the name Creech sound familiar?"

"Bingo. That's him. I'm sure. He a real big guy?"

"A *real* big guy."

"Gotta be him," he says. "I'll go down to the station tomorrow and talk to your detective. If it's Poke, he'll know him."

"Palmer already knows him."

"I'll go down anyway. This guy would break your arm over his knee just to hear the snap. Law don't know half what he's done. Word was he done a bunch of killin's he was never tagged with." Eric begins to leave again. "You keep an eye on your back, Counselor. This guy will do you in."

I thank him again for his offer and his information and see him to the door, then return to my office to sit in the dark, trying to quiet my heartbeat, and think. Molly left early and there's no one to talk to but myself. There's not much to say anyway, really, except that this just confirms already scary news.

Nineteen

"This is exciting," Molly says, pouring a cup of hot coffee from the thermos. "It's like real cops and robbers."

I take the cup. It's past midnight and we're in Molly's car, about a block from Peggy Parker's house, on the off chance John Sheldon will show and prove what we already know: that he's up to his earlobes in a relationship with Peggy that places his pitiful arrogant self very near the exact center of this mess. After nearly two hours, there has been no action, save for Jerry spilling out onto the front porch with Peggy in hot pursuit, grabbing his arm and jerking him back inside. Jerry is most likely hell on wheels at home these days, just as he is at the center. "If this is cops and robbers," I say, "I want to grow up to be something else. I'm bored." I don't really expect John to show, but he could, and sitting here is probably safer than staying home where a madman might show up to rip off my head and spit in my neck. Thoughts of my struggle with him the other night terrify me. Particularly after what Eric said. Eric got together with Detective Palmer today and they compared war stories about Creech. I'm sure the meeting didn't go down in Eric's book as his finest hour—whatever his level of rehabilitation, it doesn't include afternoon coffee with the police—but they came to the same conclusion: that the culprit is Creech and he's a twelve-on-a-scale-of-ten dangerous dude.

I finish my coffee and hand the empty cup to Molly. "More?" she asks. "We could be here a long time."

"More," I say.

"You think he'll really show up tonight?"

"Maybe not tonight," I say. "But John Sheldon is an impatient man. If he's worried at all about what Peggy might say, he'll have to check in once in a while. Old John's got a paranoid streak, I think."

Molly puts her hand on my leg. "What if he doesn't come? I say if he's not here by two, we crawl into the backseat and see if this car can do what it was really made for."

I smile and gently remove her hand. "Have to be later than that. I'm guessing he'll come really late. He's smart enough to know he can't afford to let Jerry see him."

Molly snaps her fingers in disappointment. "How many nights do we do this?"

"If he doesn't show by tomorrow, I'll bait him in the team meeting. Plant a little germ in his brain."

Molly scrunches back and stares at the ceiling. "Wilson, tell me one more time what you think is going on."

What the hell, it's a long wait. "Well, it really makes sense that Sheldon is screwing Peggy. When I started working with Jerry—after Sabrina disappeared—he was afraid I'd discover that. It *might* be—and I know this sounds crazy—that he hired someone to scare me because he thinks the only way to be sure I don't discover him is to get me as far away from Peggy Parker as possible, which would be completely away from the center."

"But how in the world would *John Sheldon* know who to get to do that?" she asks. "He's a worm, but he's a chicken worm. I can't imagine him having the guts even

246

to approach someone as vicious as this Poke character sounds."

"That's a part I don't get. But I know one thing. If a guy is desperate enough, he'll do anything.,'

"Jesus," she says. "Is John in that bad a shape?"

"He's in at least that bad a shape. Here's a guy with no family, no personal relationships at all that anyone knows about. John Sheldon has nothing real. He lives and dies on his reputation of propriety. He'd rather be gutted from throat to asshole than be humiliated. And if anyone finds out about Peggy, he'll be plenty humiliated."

Molly leans back more and puts her feet on the dashboard. "It's a curious world," she says. "A curious fucking world indeed."

We sit in silence awhile, staring down the block at Peggy's house, when I remember Jeffrey Banner's late night visit. "Listen," I say, "I need a favor."

"Name it, Big Boy. Just be prepared to pay in pounds of flesh."

"I need you to see Craig Clark a few times."

Molly shakes her head, teasing. "Craig Clark? God, can't you do *anything* on your own anymore?"

I tell her about Banner's visit, though I exclude my concerns about the amount of time Craig was in the scalding water. I want Molly's opinion strictly about Craig.

"He came to your house at midnight?" she asks incredulously. "Boy, some stuff is shaking loose there."

"It's the craziest one I've been involved with in a long time," I say. "I can't help believing Banner when I listen to him. I don't *feel* manipulated, I really don't. I look into his eyes and I can't imagine the person Craig sees. But I've seen Craig's work, and he's clear as a bell." I kiss Molly on the cheek, then longer on the mouth and up the side of her face toward her ear, tracing my tongue along the edge, then whisper, "So, if you'll see him for me . . ."

She squeezes the pressure point on the side of my knee so hard I jump back hard against the door. "You're a shameless man, Wilson Corder, taking advantage of my weakened state for personal gain. What do you want me to do with him?"

"I need a second opinion. I keep trying to stay away from Banner so I can do my job with Craig, but Banner keeps popping up. Just get a feel for what's going on and let him have one more person to trust. Let me know what you think of Banner through Craig's eyes."

"Okay," she says, "but I can tell you what I'll see already, just from what you've said. Kids don't lie about stuff like this, Wilson. Adults do. No coincidences, remember? That goes for Banner popping up, too."

"You're probably right, but I want you to just pay attention to Craig. Hey, you'll love him."

"It'll cost you big."

"Big it is," I say. "Tell you what. Do it and I'll give you five minutes with Sheldon in a locked room."

Molly nods hard. "Good enough." Then, "Do you think John makes a habit of making it with clients?"

"One thing I've learned is you never catch *anyone* doing something the first time. You don't catch a kid smoking dope the first time, you don't catch your husband or wife in bed with someone the first time, and you don't catch a therapist who preys on clients the first time. By the time you do catch them, it's a way of life. Guys who get into this line of work through the back door have radar for weaknesses. I'd be willing to bet if you traced Sheldon's history, you'd find him resigning positions for no good reason on several occasions. That means his employers covered for him, which is another ugly thing about this business: We're like cops or drug dealers or teenage shoplifters. We don't squeal on each other."

"So, you think John just moved on when hard times caught up with him."

"Right. Only this time things got out of hand. He knows he can't just walk away this time. Especially if I'm the one who catches him. I know it sounds *really* farfetched, but if he has anything to do with this Poke guy—like if he hired him to scare me or something—he's in deep. Eric says Poke gets a kick out of hurting people. By the time John figured that out, it had to be too late. I'd sure like to know how he got mixed up with him, though. He's not the kind of guy Sheldon meets at dinner parties. That's why I want to put pressure on Sheldon now. Big an asshole as he is, I doubt he wants anything to do with arson or assault."

Molly shakes her head. "I don't know, Wilson. It's hard to imagine all the little things that would have to happen to throw John Sheldon into cahoots with a psychopath. There has to be something we haven't seen yet to tie this together."

"I know. Believe me, I know. But every piece of a puzzle touches every other piece, either directly, or through contact with the other pieces. I don't know where Sheldon fits yet, but he touches Peggy Parker, and one way or another, she touches the rest. No coincidences."

Molly stares out the window. "This has really gotten out of hand, hasn't it?"

"Yup."

"Think the cops will be able to pick up Creech?"

"Hard to say. He may lie low until he gets another shot at me. I'm betting this is more fun than he's had in a long time."

It isn't my night—or early morning. John Sheldon doesn't show. At three-thirty I start the engine and head

249

back. After dropping Molly off, I drive back across town to my house, where I pack a suitcase and head for a motel. Man, I am flat scared. Police drive-bys just aren't enough to give me peace of mind.

In Wednesday's team meeting, I let it drop that Peggy Parker has contacted me to set up an individual session. She has something to say that no one else knows. I say she told me she couldn't talk on the phone because she believes hers has been bugged by the police for some reason.

That will get John Sheldon to her house. I'm tired of staying awake all night.

"Now what if he doesn't show?" Molly says as the clock again nears midnight.

"No chance. If he's involved with her, he's got to come now. The only way he can get to Peggy is in the dark of night if he believes her phone is bugged. Now that he thinks she's coming in to see me tomorrow, he has to figure he's got one chance."

"I don't know . . ."

"Wanna bet?"

"Sure," she says. "What?"

"Something sexual."

"Okay," Molly says. "If I win I get to cut off your . . ."

"Now, now. Hold on. I meant in the arena of sexual *favors.* You won't be doing either of us any favors dismembering me."

"I could put it in a jar," she teases. "Maybe have it pickled . . ."

A pair of headlights rounds the corner at the end of the block, and we scoot down in the seat. When the lights shut off I can barely make out the dark form of the car as it glides to a halt in front of Peggy's house.

"And if I win?" I say to Molly.

"If you win you get to do anything to me I want you to do," she says. "You think that's him?"

I squint into the darkness, nodding. "I think that's him. I can't quite make out the car but it looks enough like John's to get my heart beating pretty good. Who the hell else would come this time of night? I'll wait till he goes inside, then I'll take a closer look."

The car door opens and for a brief moment there is light on the driver's face, but he's too far away to identify. In seconds, Peggy's porch light snaps on to reveal the man standing facing her door. If it ain't John Sheldon it's his twin brother and since he's an only child—a fact he's constantly letting be known—the odds go up in my favor. The door opens and he disappears through.

"Wait here," I say. "I'm gonna be there when he comes out."

Molly opens the door on her side. "Fat chance, Lone Ranger. I didn't sit three celibate nights so I could let you have all the fun. I'm gonna see that little mole's face when he sees you."

Molly is not asking for my approval. It'd be a cold day in hell before she'd miss out on this. I snatch my camera from the backseat and we slide into the night.

The porch is dark, and I peer through the living room window, seeing only shadows of the furniture and knick-knacks on the mantle reflecting the light from another room where John and Peggy must have gone to talk. Carefully I try the door. No such luck.

"If that had opened," Molly whispers, "they'd have to change it when they make the movie."

I laugh quietly and hand her the camera. "I'm going around back to see if I can get in. If Sheldon comes out that door, empty the camera on him. It's got an automatic advance, so just fire away. Try to get the house address in at least one picture. This is illegal as hell, but let's make our best bluff. If he tries to grab the camera, run."

"If he tries to grab the camera," she says back, "I'll kick his ass."

"Or," I whisper, laughing, "you can kick his ass."

At the rear of the house I discover a window that, though locked, I can jimmy with my Swiss army knife. Though I've never been inside the house before tonight, Jerry has described it often enough that I know I'm entering Sabrina's old room. I marvel at my silent entry, thinking when they fire me from the center, probably tomorrow morning, I can begin a lucrative career as a cat burglar. Except that I'm scared shitless. If I weren't so fearful of Creech and what he'll likely do to me if I don't get to him, I'd turn around in a heartbeat, which I might add is pretty goddam loud right about now. I'm not afraid of John Sheldon, but I'm sure afraid of jail.

I crack open Sabrina's door and peer into the hall. The dull murmur of voices floats to me from a lighted room, most likely the kitchen. The door creaks as I push it open further. The voices stop. I wait. Peggy sticks her head around the kitchen doorway and peers in my direction, but apparently sees nothing in my darkened end of the hall. I wait for the voices to resume, then push the door quickly to avoid the creak, and step into the carpeted hall, moving silently and quickly to a spot only feet from the kitchen door.

"If you didn't call Corder," John is saying, "why would he have said that in the meeting?"

Peggy is contrite, obviously somewhat afraid. "I don't know, John. Really, I don't. He's tricky though, I know that. He can get Jerry talking about things I tell him to shut up about. He does it all the time."

"Yes," John says, "he does do it all the time . . ."

A moment of silence. Finally Peggy says, "What's going to happen?"

"I'm not certain. Corder may have said what he said merely to rattle me, but if that's so, he knows about us. I'm afraid you must have said something about me in front of the boy . . ."

"No," Peggy says. "I've never said one word. Honest I haven't. Jerry only saw you that first night you were here out on the lawn. That was more than a year and a half ago, and it was dark. He *couldn't* have seen you well. I've never said anything about you in front of him. Really, John, I haven't."

"God, I should have known better than to get involved with a woman who can't keep a confidence," John says, more to himself than to her. Then, "If I find out you're lying, I'll be very upset, Peggy. That's the kind of thing that can drive a man like me to violence."

Violence? Jesus, John. So he really is a big man with the ladies. Quick mood swings, too. I'll have to write that in his chart.

I start forward into the doorway, then stop, not satisfied I've gotten everything this conversation has to offer.

"John, I did everything you said. I even stayed out of individual counseling so I wouldn't let anything slip."

Let what slip? Say it, sweet Peggy. Say it.

"Maybe I spoke too soon," Sheldon says. "I apologize. I'm under a lot of pressure."

"It's all right," she says, and I hear her move to touch him. "There, does that feel better?"

I hear John moan; I guess she's rubbing his poor stress-tightened neck. In a minute when I get in there, I'll give him some stress for her to rub.

"It's just that, well, if people find out about you and me," John says, "it'll be the end of my career. And my

253

God, if they *ever* discover where you were when Sabrina—"

"I'm the one who'll get in trouble for that," Peggy interrupts. "I'm the one who left my children. I can't believe I did that again. I swore I would never take the chance after they were put in foster care the last time. But I couldn't resist you. I couldn't . . ."

"I know," he says. "It's partially my fault."

Jesus H. Christ! She was with Sheldon! That's why Jerry couldn't get her up.

"Will you tell them that, if it comes out? Will you tell them . . . ?"

A chair scrapes violently. "You listen to me! It's not going to come out and if it does *you'll* disavow any knowledge of me! Do you hear me? Do you hear me?"

Damn, that man is moody. Peggy emits a muffled choking sound, and I jump into their sight. "Sounds like *Mission Impossible*," I say. " 'Disavow any knowledge' and all that shit."

Peggy starts to scream, but Sheldon's hand is instantly over her mouth. "Corder!" he says. "How in blazes did you get in here?"

"Broke in through the back window. Why don't you call the police?"

"How long have you been there?"

I smile. "A long time, John. A long time."

"I don't know what to say."

"I'm not surprised. Why don't you take your hands off Peggy's neck? I might get the wrong idea. Excuse me a minute." I step into the living room, walking quickly to the front door, where I unlock the deadbolt and swing it open wide. Molly steps in.

She says, "Hi, John. How you doing?"

John's face is beet red, but he refuses to budge from his formal perch. He says, "This is quite irregular."

Molly takes a couple of quick shots with the camera. "Quite irregular is when you can't go to the bathroom on schedule," she says. "This is *amazingly* irregular. Is that the caption you want?" The camera's motor continues to whir.

John glances at the floor and for a moment I feel sorry for him; he looks ashamed.

Peggy sits in stunned silence, obviously with no clue how this all fits together. Finally she shoots a defiant look at me. "Wilson Corder, what are you doing in my house? I really could call the police, you know."

I nod. "I do know that, Peggy. And I'd go to jail. But probably not for very long and in the meantime, you'd have to explain to Child Protective Services where you were the night your daughter was kidnapped, and you'd risk losing your son. When they discovered—and I guarantee they would—that you've been blocking the therapeutic work Jerry needs to help recover from having watched a kidnapper steal his sister while threatening *his* life in the process, well, you'd have a pretty rough row to hoe. But call 'em if you want."

I catch movement out of the corner of my eye. Jerry stands in the doorway. "Wilson," he says sleepily. "How come you're here?"

"Hey, man," I say. "How you doing? I just dropped by to see your mom."

He looks around the room. "Hi, Molly. You here to see my mom, too?"

Molly nods. "Yup," she says. "Want me to take your picture?"

Jerry looks at her like she's crazy. He says, "It's kinda late at night."

I say, "Yeah, Jer, it is. We worked pretty late and it was important. Nothing you have to worry about, though. At least I don't think so. You know Mr. Sheldon?"

Jerry stares a moment at John, rubbing his eyes. "I think so. Out in our yard once at night." He turns to John. "Ain't you the guy Wilson made a Kong growl at? That was funny."

John looks at the floor again. "One and the same," I say. "So whaddaya think, Big Man. You've met everyone. No one's eating cookies without your knowing it. Want to go back to bed?"

"Is there cookies?" Jerry says, his eyes widening.

"No," Peggy says. "There's no cookies."

Jerry rubs his eyes again and nods. "To bed."

I look to Peggy. "You want to take him back or do you want Molly or me to do it?"

Jerry hesitates, then moves toward Molly, arms outstretched. Peggy looks hurt and Molly waits. "Go ahead," Peggy says, and looks away.

As Molly disappears with Jerry, I get comfortable in a seat at the kitchen table. John remains standing, leaning against the kitchen sink, desperately I think, maintaining his controlled posture. "Well," he says finally, "we have some work to do here."

"What do you mean, John?" I ask, subtly mimicking his air.

"Well, obviously some mistakes have been made."

I lean back. "You know, you use different terminology than I might choose. You call it a 'mistake' when you take advantage of a client's weaknesses and fears, or when you put a kid's emotional health on the line in order to keep some big secret. You say we have 'some work to do here' when you've been caught fucking up so bad your head ought to be swimming."

"What I meant was . . ."

"I wonder what you're going to call it when we're sitting in front of police investigators tomorrow, helping them sort through this shit."

"What do you mean?"

"I mean, some lunatic is out there coming after me and my kids. It ain't Marvin Edwards, he's in jail. You've got something to do with it, John, you're the only other person who wants me away from Jerry."

"Wilson, I swear . . ."

I raise my hands. "John, you unconscious asswipe, save it. I don't expect you to admit anything. What I do expect is your body at the police station tomorrow morning at nine o'clock."

Molly returns at the moment Peggy finds the courage to speak. "Wilson, am I going to lose Jerry?"

"I don't know, Peggy. I really don't. I have a piece of advice for you, though. Go in to CPS tomorrow morning first thing and tell them what's been going on. Tell them you were gone when Sabrina was taken and that you've been afraid and protecting yourself." I nod toward Sheldon. "Go ahead and tell them about Bozo. They'll know soon enough anyway."

"Wait just a minute, Wilson," Sheldon says, and *I* can feel his heart in his throat. "There must be some way we can preserve . . . I mean there must be another way to go about this."

Molly laughs. "You mean so you can keep on keeping on, Johnny? As my mother used to say in her delicate way, 'Fat fucking chance.' I hope no one else here wants to spill the beans, because I would consider it an honor and a privilege to be the first to break the news." Molly's eyes blaze, and I worry she might take a poke at him. "Let me tell you something, John Sheldon. Wilson had some advice for Peggy a minute ago, now I have some for you. Go over to Three Forks Community College tomorrow after you leave the police station and pick up a fall class schedule. Open it to 'Career Counseling,' because you're about to need a new one."

John looks to me. "Wilson, we've had some disagreements, but . . ."

I shrug. "Couldn't have said it better, John. I'm hoping next time I see you you'll be carrying boxes. And to tell you the truth, if I were you I'd get out of town. This has 'Channel Four news' written all over it."

John's eyes cloud. "I see. You want me to beg."

"John," I say, and feel myself soften, "I don't want you to beg. I really don't. This is a done deal, and begging wouldn't change a thing. All you can do at this point is try to salvage something you can live with. I'm going to be at the city police station tomorrow morning at nine. I want you to be there, too. I don't know what's been done that's illegal and what's been done that's just stupid, but we're gonna find out. And one more thing. I don't know for *sure* if you have anything to do with the guy who's been terrorizing me and my kids, but now that I know how bad you wanted me out of the way, I'd bet yes. And what I know about him is he's a dangerous, dangerous man, and I'd also bet you're no safer from him than I am."

He says, "Wilson, you have to believe me . . ."

"John, don't." What he doesn't know is, I don't want to hear that he knows *anything* about Creech at a time when no one is around capable of stopping me from beating him to death.

He removes his glasses, wiping his eyes, and I actually hurt for him. I hate it, but I do. I don't have to worry about caving in, though, because Molly would knock out my front teeth if I wobbled.

"You going to be there?" I ask.

No response.

"I won't be an asshole, John. I promise."

He looks up. "Very well. You can count on me. I'll be there."

Twenty

The exit hole was small and neat, leaving only a tiny spot of blood on the pillowcase. Molly is right. This has gotten out of hand.

When I arrived at the city police station this morning, John Sheldon wasn't there to meet me, and Detective Palmer and I waited more than a half hour before I called over to the center to determine whether he had come in to work. The receptionist said not, and that he hadn't called to cancel any of his appointments, which she considered unusual. There had been no answer when she called his home.

I hoped he had run.

Palmer knocked several times; no answer. A Strauss waltz floated to us from inside, and after checking all the doors, Palmer instructed the uniformed officer with us to break the glass in the kitchen window to gain entry.

John was upstairs in his bed, staring glassily at the ceiling, a .22 pistol clutched in his hand. Downstairs in the living room, his CD player was set on the REPEAT function and I thought, all things considered, there was a certain bit of grace to that.

Though disappointed we wouldn't get the information we needed on John's possible connection to Creech, I wasn't surprised, really. On the ride over in Palmer's car, a familiar feeling visited me, one I had experienced twice before upon hearing a client with nothing to lose had disappeared. You hope they've escaped some other way, by hiding out somewhere or getting drunk, but in your gut you know they haven't. I heard my last words to John Sheldon: *All you can do at this point is try to salvage something you can live with.* I was wrong.

I'm also not particularly sad. I suppose I could be, and I could feel guilty as hell, since it was I who laid things out so clearly last night, and not in a particularly sensitive way. But whether our lives are good or not, whether we're dealt a good or poor hand, at some point we have to play it as best we can, and I think John Sheldon could have played his hand a lot better. Probably he thought so too, at the end, and simply decided to fold.

It does leave us with the dilemma, as I said, of how Charles Creech fits in. When I saw John lying dead in his bed this morning, I kicked myself for not pushing the issue of Creech last night. If Sheldon actually hired him to harass me, it's possible Creech'll back off now that John is out of the picture. But at best that's a hunch. It certainly isn't a finely cut piece to this puzzle as yet. It is still very difficult for me to visualize John Sheldon negotiating with that prehistoric behemoth. I really don't even *know* Creech's part—only that he has one and that I won't feel safe having Sarah and the kids back until he's been dealt with. Detective Palmer agrees.

Molly enters my office during a rare mutual break, about midafternoon—my client canceled and the court case in which Molly was scheduled to testify was discontinued indefinitely—and plops into my chair. "Got a minute?"

"Want me to close the blinds?"

"Yes. But we better not. I need a couple of minutes to talk about Craig Clark."

"You saw him already?"

She nods. "I sure did. He came in gushing."

"Isn't he a piece of work? What'd you get?"

"For one thing," she says, leaning forward, "divorce the part of yourself that thinks Jeff Banner is such a wonderful guy. What he is, is insidious."

"Have you ever met him?"

Molly shakes her head. "I don't have to. I've met one of his victims."

"Say more."

"I'll say lots more. Craig spent about fifteen seconds getting to know me before starting in on everything you described: putting Bad Dad Jeff in jail, failing to rescue the other players from him, and generally storming around the room like a kid possessed. Then, from out of the blue, he started chanting what I thought was 'Penis and butt, penis and butt.'

"I didn't react because I was afraid he'd clam up. But then he came to me with the shark's secret, and instead of asking him to interpret it for me, which you said didn't work before, I simply nodded and said, 'When did that happen?' "

Immediately I wish I'd thought of that. "What did he say?"

"He said, 'You heard?' and I said, 'Yup, I talk shark. Can I ask him when it happened?' Craig nodded and stuck the shark back to my ear and for a second I thought I might have dug myself a real hole, because if I understood the first thing, I shouldn't have too much trouble understanding the rest. I was likely to get it in the *psst, psst, psst* of sharkbabble. But Craig came through like a U.N. interpreter. He said, 'Psst, psst, psst, always, psst.' "

Molly sat back in the chair, obviously proud of her work. "I looked the shark straight in the mouth and said, 'It always happens?' and Craig made the shark nod, so I said, 'It always happens to your friend Craig?' and the shark nodded again.

"So I asked the shark who all does it to him and all the shark said was 'Psst, psst, psst, psst,' but I could tell Craig was ready to explode because he was cramming the shark's nose into my eardrum. So I asked if anyone else did it and the shark shook his head and I took a chance and said, 'Just Jeff?' "

Now I'm leaning forward. "What'd he say?"

"He didn't say anything, but the shark nodded, so I held him by his dorsal fin, looked him straight in the eye, and asked if he were *sure* there was nobody else. Then to make completely certain, because I've been burned before by families that seem to name one person in every generation after a perpetrator, I said, 'Was it *Daddy* Jeff?' and he dropped the shark to the couch and screamed, 'Yes!' then ran around the room screaming, 'Yes! Yes! Yes!' He put his arms out as if he were an airplane, and started yelling, 'Penis and butt! Penis and butt! Penis and butt!'

"I let him fly awhile, mostly catching my own breath. I knew I needed to assure him no one would know except people he trusts to protect him. Then he crash-landed head first into my chest, breathing like he'd run a sub-four-minute mile. I let him lay there a few minutes, then asked him to tell me about 'Penis and butt,' and he jerked up and yelled, 'Penis *in* butt! In! In! Penis *in* butt!' So I said, 'Okay, penis *in* butt. Did he hurt you, Daddy Jeff?' Craig closed his mouth tight and nodded. Then, in a voice that sounded almost like a mimicking, he said, 'I always be here. You never tell. I no tell. Us secret. Mommy get hurt if we say. No tell. I be here always.'

262

"I wrote down his words verbatim onto a scrap of paper. Then he gathered up paper and markers and crayons and drew me a clear—if somewhat bizarre—scenario of physical and sexual abuse that seems to have started when Banner initially got with his mom."

Something's pretty out of whack here. Molly's almost never wrong interpreting a kid. Twice she's stood nearly alone against normal-looking—and powerful—adult abusers, and though both got off in court, both also reoffended, and Molly's initial interpretations turned out 99 percent correct. One of those guys was a partner in a *highly* regarded law firm, and the other was a Presbyterian minister. In my head I see Banner on my porch the other night.

Molly reads my mind. "Don't even think it, Wilson. I've told you a thousand times, stop working with adults. They lie."

I don't push it. "Do you think Carrie suspects?"

"Probably not. Craig always drew her out of the picture. And it fits, too. Craig was ambivalent as they get. Twice, he said he liked it, that it felt good. Banner's only nice words seemed to come when he preyed on him, so Craig's already been tricked into confusion about whether it was a good thing or a bad thing. Except for the final entry, which hurt like hell, he portrays most of Banner's touch as nurturing."

I have to go along with Molly. My number-one rule is to go with the kid, and I've been struggling with it only because of who Banner is and how he looks to me *apart from Craig.* Kids that young don't have the words and they have no reason to lie about sexual things unless adults give them reason. And the stakes are high. If Molly's right and if we don't keep Craig away from Banner, and do a lot of work with him about his confusion, people will have a very difficult time understanding his

263

behavior because of just this. His initial sexual information has been badly misnamed and he'll react to the world on the basis of that. He'll try to attach to people sexually because that's all he'll know, and folks will fear him and regard him as a pervert from a very young age simply because they won't understand how he got his information. And he will be hated and he will learn to be hateful. And that's the name of this game.

"Tell you what, Counselor," Molly says, "do us all a favor and have no further contact with Dr. Banner until this plays out. If he's innocent, what we don't know yet will show itself."

Molly's right, and I agree.

I'm on the phone with Detective Palmer, getting the lowdown on Creech, and it ain't pretty. Though he's only been *convicted* for assault and armed robbery, conventional wisdom on both sides of the law says he's a cold-blooded killer, too mean to leave tracks and too smart to get caught. Palmer is telling me to pack more things and move into my motel room indefinitely. After his descriptions of Creech's suspected actions—which include a night of unspeakable terror for a family of three, followed by murder, in a small town north of Seattle—I am convinced. The moment I hang up, I'll extend my reservations at the Sunset. It's just up the street from the center, and they have a parking lot in the rear that can't be seen from the street. Palmer agrees with that decision and, after offering many thanks for all the wonderful news, I hang up.

Within less than a minute the phone rings again.

"Wilson Corder."

"Hi, Corder. Palmer again. Listen, one of my people just brought me something."

"Yeah?"

"Yeah. It's a report from Probation and Parole. It seems when Creech was let out the last time, let's see, more than two years ago, he was referred to your center for some kind of medication. Seems they thought part of his problem was organic. Anyway, there are some entries here indicating he attended several appointment—or at least said he did. Would you have access to that information?"

"Sure. I can dig it out of Medical Records. Does it say who he saw? Is there a therapist's name—or a psych nurse?"

"Let me see . . ." Palmer is quiet a moment and I hear paper rattling. "Yeah," he says after a bit, "here it is. Looks like the name is Banner. Says he's a contract consultant, whatever that is. Anybody there by that name?"

Unbelievable. Un-goddam-believable. "Is there a first name?"

"Jeffery. There's a boatload of initials after the name. Looks like he's a full-fledged shrink."

"That he is, my man. That he is." My mind spins. "Listen, I'll see if I can get ahold of the file and take a look. If it looks like there's anything there you could use, I'll call you back. Then we'll have to deal with confidentiality."

"I'll wait breathlessly by the phone," he says, and I hear the click.

And what a file it was, boys and girls: Charles Creech, Charles Creech Returns, Son of Charles Creech, The Bride of Charles Creech, Charles Creech's Revenge. Five volumes, all but one filled prior to my days at the center. The fourth contained the information that would have made my life a whole lot easier if I'd known it from the

265

get-go. There were fifteen green sheets—that's fifteen therapy sessions—signed off by a consultant hired by the center, one Jeffery Banner, M.A., dated nearly ten years ago. It is clear, I discover from his notes, that Banner considered Creech untreatable, dangerous, and getting worse by the minute. He stopped short of calling him psychopathic, but for no reason I could discern. From what I read, the kid wouldn't kill an animal if it wasn't cute. What was fascinating about Banner's charting, however, wasn't so much the information as the tone. He seemed almost in awe of Creech, maybe admiring. After the final session, under "Therapist's Impressions," Banner wrote: "This guy will be famous someday. He's going to kill a lot of people."

I turned quickly to the fifth chart, opening to the back pages to confirm what I now believed. Bingo. A medical sheet and some charting, dated almost two and a half years ago, signed off by Dr. Jeffery Banner, M.D., Ph.D., Contracting Consultant.

So, the middle pieces to the puzzle suddenly lay before me, and I could see where they fit. A man who would benefit greatly from my being a hundred and fifty thousand therapeutic miles from Craig Clark is intimately acquainted with the darkest reaches of the soul of the man who is trying to do me and my kids in.

A great writer once said he allowed himself one good coincidence in each novel, no more. In the world of human deception, I allow myself none. This ain't John Sheldon's show. It never was. It's goddam Jeffery Banner's show. They're connected somehow—Sheldon was probably feeding Banner information from our meetings—but those are small pieces. The big piece is the one that connects Banner to Creech. I've been barking up the wrong goddam tree.

In an attempt to gain a leg up on Creech, I filtered

through his remaining four charts, and got a pretty good look—albeit with numerous long blank stretches—at his life. He initially came to our attention as an infant in 1964 after showing up at the hospital with a skull fracture and a broken femur. The nature of the child abuse prevention business was primitive then, and though the hospital social worker who wrote the report remained adamant something was wrong, Charlie's dad was able to convince both the police and the therapist involved that the injuries were the result of a horrible and unfortunate accident. Following a short period of little therapy and numerous meetings with Charlie's father, his attorney, and the caseworker, the therapist deemed it was safe for Charles to go home; nothing was seriously wrong in his household.

He showed up again at the age of five. His biological father was out of the picture at this point, having divorced his mother, but an anonymous babysitter reported a number of circular burns over little Charlie's face and arms and genitals. Charles was removed and placed in foster care, and his parents were ordered into treatment. It appeared as if they did better on this go-round. Mom admitted she burned the child once to keep him from playing with matches—that it had been a mistake but she was very frightened and frustrated. On two other occasions, she said, Charlie had carelessly backed into a burning cigarette. He was such a clumsy kid. She couldn't explain the burns on his genitals, but would supervise him very carefully in the future. She must have guessed who turned her in, because she tried to implicate the babysitter. Throughout therapy, Stepdad was quiet and supportive. Both attended all their sessions, showed proper remorse, dug into their own childhoods, and were pronounced cured after about six months. Meanwhile, Charlie bounced in and out of five foster homes, all un-

267

able to manage his wild and sometimes violent behavior. He never said a word that was charted in therapy, and it was interesting that the issue of the number of other reported burns went unattended. Everything in the charts pointed to the same thing: Charles Creech had been systematically tortured throughout most of his childhood. I'm guessing that only a very small fraction of his abuse ever came to light.

He showed up a number of times after that, referred by the foster care system, juvenile court, and finally the Department of Corrections.

In all the charting, through Charles Creech's years in and out of the center and in and out of incarceration, there was never a hint of remorse for anything he did, no accounts of tears, no indications he wanted anything in his life to change. My guess today about Charles Creech is that he thinks he can do anything he wants. Nothing the law can or will do, including putting him to death, can match his childhood. If I were to hear of him, or meet him for the first time tomorrow as a client, I'm sure I would find a connection and try to work with him. Certainly if I were to hear the full story of his burns for the first time from his lips, I would throw heroic efforts into helping him cope. But that would be for me, not for him. Charles Creech is a done deal. His life has turned him into a chilling madman. I read in a book once that when you see a rabid dog coming down the road, it doesn't do a lot of good to picture his puppyhood. Charles Creech is a rabid dog coming down my road.

Twenty-one

I cancelled the remainder of my afternoon clients, hopped onto my motorcycle, and whizzed over to Dr. Jeff Banner's private office for a powwow. I wanted answers and I was in a foul goddam mood at having been tricked into listening to his clever accounts of Craig's fate. I should have known if he was smart enough to look that good through all he'd been doing, he was a lot smarter than I was, and he wasn't going to roll over just because I stormed into his office demanding answers. In my anger, I ended up playing my pair of jacks—barely good enough for openers—before even mounting a decent bluff.

I walked past his receptionist's desk and banged twice on his door. "I'm sorry, sir," she said, "but Dr. Banner is with a client. You'll have to wait at least until he's finished. Do you have an appointment?"

"I have a standing appointment," I said. "Dr. Banner will see me whenever I deem it necessary."

She shuffled papers on her desk. "I'm sorry. He hasn't apprised me of any arrangement like that."

"We're about to make that arrangement," I said, banging again on his office door.

"Sir, this is highly irregular," she said, dialing his number.

But Dr. Banner appeared. "Yes? What is it? Can't you see I'm with someone?"

"Yes, I can see that," I said. "Reschedule them. Something more important has come up."

Banner met my eyes. "Yes. Very well. Give me a moment, Wilson, and I'll do just that. I'll reschedule."

Within moments, a woman appeared at the door dabbing at her eyes, walked to the receptionist's desk to reschedule, and disappeared through the swinging glass doors. Dr. Banner was behind her to usher me in. "I take it this is important, Corder. Is it about Craig?"

"It's about Charles Creech."

Banner stared blankly. "I'm afraid I don't know who that is."

"He's a man you treated at the mental health center. About ten years ago. You were a consultant."

"Creech," he said, almost under his breath, as if searching. Then, "Charles Creech! The man was a psychopath. My God, that *was* ten years ago." He leaned against his desktop. "What could that possibly have to do with anything going on now? And why, for God's sake, is this important enough to kick a client out of my office?"

"Because you saw him again about two years ago. And you're seeing him now," I said. "This is as current as the morning paper, friend. You know what I'm talking about, and you best talk to me, 'cause if you don't the next person you'll talk to wears a blue suit and a shiny badge."

"Wilson," Banner said, "I will talk to you, but I have to tell you, I truly don't know what to say. If you want to bring the police, be my guest, because quite frankly I'm lost. Or you can take the time to tell me what this is all about."

For a moment I struggled in the web of Dr. Banner's charm. *How stupid will I look if I'm wrong?* But once again, I turned down the sound. "I'll tell you what it's about," I said. "It's about me getting too close to what Craig's life with you was really like. It's about dead cats and psychopaths. It's about anonymous letters in my box. It's about Charles Creech hunting me and my family down."

Banner leaned back in his chair, eyeing me carefully, almost curiously. "I don't even know what most of that refers to," he said, "but if that's how you're putting this all together maybe it *would* be best for you to call the police. Get everything out in the open. What you're saying simply doesn't make sense. If you'd stop to think, you'd know that. I haven't seen Charles Creech in eight, maybe ten years, except to evaluate him for meds. I doubt I would even recognize him. And as I told you before—and I stand by it now—if you want me to come in and do therapeutic work with Craig about his perceptions of me, I am more than willing. In fact, I'd jump at the chance."

I decided to withhold the sexual information Craig disclosed to Molly. Anything I said to Banner at that point would receive a rational, calm rebuttal.

"A Detective Palmer will be in touch," I said.

"Have it your way, Wilson. I'm certainly willing to talk with anyone from the police department about anything. I've done quite a bit of work for them over the years, and know several of them personally. I've been cooperative with you from the start, and for the sake of my family I'll continue to be, but I have to say I'm a little put out with your accusations."

I backed to the office door.

"I'd be interested to know what you thought you'd get from me by coming here," he said.

I stopped, momentarily at a loss.

"If you're wrong," he said, "which you are, you'd get

just what you got, which is nothing. If you had been correct, well, all you'd have done was play your hand. I'd deny it and you'd still be in jeopardy, as would your family on the Oregon coast."

I charged, catching him completely off guard as I dove across his desk, intent on choking his life out. We tumbled to the floor, my hands locked around his throat. "How do you know where my family is?" I hissed. "How do you know?"

He smiled. Completely without oxygen, he smiled, and I knew he was far more dangerous than ever I had imagined. His receptionist appeared at the door and screamed. I whirled and Banner pushed me off, scrambling to his feet. He raised his hand and said, "It's all right, Mrs. Rush. Everything is under control."

"I'll call the police," she said.

"That won't be necessary," he answered. "It's *under control.*"

I was up, ready. "Go ahead and call," I said. "They'll be coming anyway." Then to Banner, "How did you know where my family is?"

"Get ahold of yourself, Corder. John Sheldon told me. We had dinner one night last week and he talked about the entire ordeal with the Parker boy. Actually, I think he was looking for therapy. He admitted his part with the boy's mother and I told him he needed to come clean."

I started to speak, but he continued.

"I know it was a breach of confidentiality," he said, "but I'm sure you know cases get discussed between professionals all the time."

"Which night?" I asked.

"What do you mean?"

"Which night did you have dinner with him?"

"I can't recall," Banner said. "Sometime early in the

272

week. I could look it up on my personal calendar if you'd like."

I said, "Never mind," and walked out.

It takes me fifteen minutes with Molly at lunchtime to understand what has taken place. "He knows where Sarah is?" she asks incredulously. "Do you know what that means?"

"I'm not sure," I say. "He said Sheldon told him, in a 'professional' conversation."

Molly holds my cheeks gently but firmly between her palms. "Tell me again about coincidences."

"There aren't any."

"And what am I supposed to do when I run into one?"

"Treat it like a lie."

"Right," and she holds my face tighter, forcing me to look at her. "You're still actually a teeny bit worried that Banner will get a raw deal, aren't you?"

"I'm acting like it, aren't I?"

"Yeah, you are. And you better can it. If Jeff Banner knows where your family is, Charles Creech knows where your family is. Listen to me, Wilson. I've seen Craig twice now, for about two and a half to three hours total. There is *no* doubt that his stepfather purposely scalded him and sexually abused him over a long period of time. If Banner is able to persuade you he might be an upstanding citizen, there's only one *possible* reason. Jeffery Banner is Charles Creech with brains. He's sick, Wilson. Really sick. And if Banner hired Creech to do his dirty work, he did it partly because he knows Creech will get off on it. Jesus, Wilson, it's gone way past scaring you out of the business to protect John Sheldon's secret or Banner's reputation. What's going to happen in that regard is going to happen, and that asshole knows it. He's

273

just fucking with you now. This is fun for him. Can you get ahold of Sarah?"

I say no. I don't know for certain if she's even in Cannon Beach. I only assume it because that's where they had gone before.

"Do you know where they usually stay?"

"There's a house on the beach just south of town. A friend of Sarah's spends winters there, but leaves in the summer and fall."

"Do you know the number?"

"No phone."

Molly takes a deep breath. "Are they supposed to call or anything? Do you have any way of keeping in touch?"

"Sarah calls whenever," I say. "She may have called already, but I had no way of letting her know I moved into the motel. She'll probably try to contact me at the center within the next few days."

"Well, I'd call Detective Palmer and ask him what to do," Molly says. "He must have some way of getting in touch with the authorities in Oregon. Maybe get them to put a guard on your family."

It finally dawns on me loud and clear that Charles Creech is probably headed for Cannon Beach to get my kids and my ex-wife. In fact, he may already be there. Panic blocks my thinking. I close my eyes and try to focus, hyperventilating as Molly holds my hand. Creech will have to hunt for them. Cannon Beach isn't a big town, but Sarah and Emily and Trevor aren't regulars, and it will take him a while to track them down. I have to get there.

I leave Molly with instructions to warn Sarah in the event she calls the center, ask her to advise Palmer of my destination, and head for my bike.

* * *

274

On my way out of town, I stop one more time at Banner's office, a white-hot fire burning inside my head. Molly told me to stay away, but something in me thinks I can make that son-of-a-bitch talk, give me some advantage when I get to Cannon Beach. She told me Palmer advised that I stay away from *there,* too, that he could get the Oregon authorities to give my family protection, but shit tends to happen when I'm not around, and that's my family.

I sprint up the sidewalk in front of the professional building housing Banner's office, and storm once again into the waiting room. The receptionist takes one look and moves her chair back from the desk. "He's not in," she says, but I push my way through. The office is empty, the blinds pulled.

Within seconds I'm back on the street, cranking up the Honda and heading out of town.

The eastern Washington scabland shoots past in a blur as my speedometer needle hovers just over ninety and the hot wind whistles through my hair. Cannon Beach is a six-hour drive by car; I plan to be there in four and a half. God, I hope Sarah and the kids aren't there. I pray they went farther south in the first place.

But Jesus, if they're not at the house, how will I know *where* they are, or how to get to them?

As I shoot into the Columbia Gorge, my mind races even ahead of the bike. If Creech is there, I'll have one chance at best. When I fought with him the night he set Sarah's house on fire, he handled me like a toy, would certainly have killed me had the fire department not shown up. I'm hauling ass at speeds up to a hundred miles an hour toward something I better not find, but my terror rides below my rage and only my mind's picture

275

of Emily and Trevor in that madman's clutches keeps it that way. As I inch the throttle up, I search inside myself for the focus and courage that will allow me to make the right choices first.

While rummaging around in the attic during summer vacation of my sophomore year in college, I found an old newspaper clipping, dated sometime in 1943: LOCAL FLYBOY PILOTS CRIPPLED BOMBER HOME. What followed was a detailed account of my father bringing his B-17 back from a bombing mission deep behind German lines, on two—and sometimes only one—engines. Normally Dad didn't talk much about the war, but I caught him a couple of beers into a warm summer evening and struck storyland paydirt.

He told me of a twenty-one-year-old man-child, at once terrified of death and passionately drawn to the romance of fighting the Hun. Gazing across the porch at me in the late summer sun, he said, "I had no idea such fear existed."

I knew Dad flew thirty-five missions. I couldn't understand how he did it.

"I'm not sure," he said. "You surprise yourself sometimes, I guess."

"The clipping says you were only a few miles from the Swiss border when the third engine went. Switzerland was neutral. What stopped you from just going there?"

"And sit out the war in some Swiss village?" he said, smiling, "surrounded by innocent blond beauties and drinking fine, cold, northern beer?"

That sounded good with or without a war raging. "Yeah."

"To tell the truth several of my crew asked me the same thing," he said. "But you know, Wilson, things were different then. There was a madman loose and if he were allowed to do his dirty deed there, we knew he'd be headed this way, and though we didn't have a clear picture of what was happening to the Jews then, there were plenty of horror stories we had no trouble believing."

"So tell me about this flight," I said, nodding toward the clipping in his hand.

"Well, we were going after a German wartime factory that everybody knew was heavily defended. It was hot, and I stuffed an extra flak suit between my ass and the seat back and took my place in formation. I had no more than five or six missions under my belt, so I was still pretty green and this was the first time they had told us even before we took off how much shit we'd be getting into. We figured a one-third casualty rate.

"And buddy boy, they weren't kidding. We flew at least twenty miles through an exploding sky. My rig rocked like a punching bag. I lost two engines before we got over the target, but we dumped our load and went into serious evasive action. Just as the last bomb cleared the bomb bay, a crashing, ripping noise filled the plane from below me, and the next thing I knew the back of my chair and one flak suit disappeared through the top of the cockpit. If that shell hadn't been a dud, your mom and your brother would be living alone on army air corps money. Then the third engine started racing and I had to shut her down."

"Jesus," I said, "you were flying a four-engine plane on one?"

Dad smiled. "That B-17 was a *flying* machine," he said. "Sometimes she felt like if you just rolled her out of the hangar she'd pop into the air. I knew we'd lose altitude, and finally go down, but one good engine gave us time with the others." He smiled again. "My copilot looked up and saw Switzerland just beyond the moun-

277

tains and said he thought we could clear them. I *knew* we could, but I turned her around."

"Jesus," I said incredulously, "what did he say?"

"He said, 'Yessir.' I had a pretty good idea if the third engine got some cooling time, she'd crank up again, and by now we had moved quite a ways from enemy fire. When she'd had a chance to cool down, we gave her a go, and by God, she answered us. Then all we had to do was ride her on in. A seventeen could fly by itself on two engines."

"And if you'd gone to Switzerland?"

"We'd have sat out the war. Those were the rules."

"God, Dad, if you were that scared of dying, why didn't you just do it? No one would have blamed you."

"No, Wilson," he said. "No one would have blamed me. But you need to remember, in my head it got real personal. If we didn't beat this guy, he'd be coming after your mom and brother next. Sometimes all courage is, really, is having nothing to lose."

Dad flew that B-17 at the same age I was when he told me the story. I'd have given anything to have erased that bridge of time and known him young buck to young buck.

Shooting through the Columbia Gorge and south toward Portland and beyond, I'm hoping courage doesn't skip a generation. My daughter has it—exactly like my dad. I hope I do.

The sun drops lower in the sky, reflecting directly in both rearview mirrors, and it's hard to see behind me as I rocket from lane to lane, weaving through the light traffic, though at this speed I don't worry much about someone coming up behind me. If I pick up a cop, I'll drag him with me as far as I can. My mind is made up;

I'm stopping for nothing. I'd only get arrested if they didn't believe my story, and I can't afford to take the chance.

Suddenly a shadow slips across my right rearview mirror. I glance into it, but the sun blocks my view. *Something* there is moving at my speed. Again it crosses my mirrors like a strobe, but again I stare into a fifty-million-watt bulb. I back off the throttle and whip my head around for a better look.

Banner.

It's that fucking BMW. This bike can flat move, but over a long stretch of open road, that hummer's got me hands down. At least, I'm sure now he's in this up to his lying teeth. Fuck it, he may get there ahead of me, but it won't be by much. And I have the advantage of knowing where to look.

Banner pulls beside me in the left lane and as I glance over, I see only my own reflection in his dark tinted side window. I open my throttle, moving a bit ahead, but he pulls next to me again and the window glides down. As I look into his sunglasses, he smiles, gives a little wave, and jerks his wheel to the right. I swerve hard, only to find myself on the gravel shoulder. A wide left turn looms ahead that I simply won't make if I can't get my tires back on pavement. The gravel slows my speed some, but too much brake will send me end over end, and all my strength goes to holding the bike upright. Banner is in my lane now, slowing with me, edging me over. The slope is steep and rocky to the right, falling twenty to thirty feet directly into the Columbia River, and if I can't hold it around the turn, I'm a goner. A second strobe blinks in my rearview mirror, giving me the flashing image of a motorcycle, though that must be a hallucination. Banner's right side tires are in the gravel now. I know I'm going over, and with only seconds to take off, I lean hard right, aiming the bike directly at the drop-off, and gun it, hoping to clear the rocks. In midair I tuck my legs to the seat and push away hard; I don't want to land with the bike. I have always believed if I ever got into an airplane that just fell out of the air, or was pushed from a tall building, I'd die from fright long before I hit. That doesn't happen. My flight seems endless, and I close my eyes, waiting for the crash. My life does not flash before my eyes, only my children.

I hear the bike splash a few yards from me, and am immediately immersed in the river. I'm going to live. One place I have never been hurt is in the water. I kick to the surface, looking instantly toward the road. The Beemer backs around the wide corner on the highway above me, and I take a deep breath and dive, hoping Banner didn't see me surface. If I can stay under long enough, he may think I've drowned and go on. Under these conditions, I'm not good for much more than thirty seconds, though I can stretch it with some breath-control tricks I learned as a kid, letting out little bits of air at a time. When I surface again, gasping, the Beemer has disappeared, and I hear the roar of a Harley directly above me. I'm close in to shore now, and swim hard toward the rocks. Dragging myself out, I lie against the warm rocks for a second, trying to catch my breath, and think. I don't know where Banner is, but I have to think he's not finished with me.

A sharp *pop!* of metal against glass in the distance, followed by a loud crash, sends me scrambling over the rocks toward the highway. About three hundred yards away, a man leans a Harley on its kickstand and sprints down the bank.

I dash toward the action as fast as my water-soaked Levi's will allow, and pull up gasping next to the idling bike. Over the edge I see the biker—a huge hairy man in a sleeveless leather jacket scrambling toward Banner's Beemer, which has come to rest—wheels spinning harmlessly in the air—on its roof. The biker bellows all the way, to no response. I *think* I'd know that roar anywhere.

I have to see this up close, and start back down over the rocks, hearing the shattering of glass followed by a second roar. Now I'm almost sure. When I reach them, the biker is dragging Banner through the side window, shouting at him, and slapping his face from side to side. Banner has survived the crash, and he moans and grunts with each blow.

I yell to Eric to stop, still hoping to get information from Banner, and he whirls toward me.

"Eric!"

He stops, lets Banner's head fall hard against a rock, and stumbles over the rocks toward me. "Jesus motherfuckin' Christ, Corder. I saw you go over. How'd you get out of that shit alive?"

"Where the hell did *you* come from? How did you know?"

"I was with your cop friend when your ex-old lady called to check in with Palmer again. They told me you were headed this way."

"She call from Cannon Beach?"

Eric nods. "After what Molly said you'd found out, I figured this asshole would have to come after you, so I hauled ass. Haven't had a shot at this kind of action since I quit kickin' the shit out of guys in bars."

"You think Creech is there?"

"I'd bet my hairy ass on it. I'll tell you on the bike," he says. "We gotta get to Cannon Beach."

"What do we do with him?" I ask, pointing to Banner who lies bleeding from the forehead, half in and half out of his mangled BMW.

"I'll just break his neck," Eric says. "Nobody saw this

shit happen or the place would be crawling with souvenir seekers. They'll just think his neck broke in the wreck." Eric starts back for him.

"Eric, wait!" I don't want to watch Eric snap somebody's neck, even if it is Banner's. "I need information from him."

Eric nods. "Let's get it."

He grabs Banner, who is only semiconscious, by the hair and jerks him close. When Banner's eyes roll, Eric slaps him three times, hard. "Wake up, motherfucker. You got one chance to stay alive. Get ready to sing." He slaps him again, and Banner's eyes pop open. Eric folds his forearms around Banner's neck in an unbreakable stranglehold, then motions to me with his head. "Tell 'im what you want to know, Counselor. Make it quick, we need to get on the road."

I drop my face toward Banner's. He says, "If you're going to kill me, do it."

"I'm not going to kill you," I say. "Eric is."

He closes his eyes.

"Listen to me carefully, Dr. Jeff, because you're either believable or you're dead. My friend can pop your head right off your neck, and don't doubt for a second that he'd do it."

Banner grimaces as Eric tightens his grip.

"You've been real slick, telling me what I already know for the past few months, but you got no room for slips now. I know you're up to your scummy neck with Creech, or you wouldn't be here. Tell me everything, starting with where's Creech?"

"You should have let me go, Corder," Banner says, and Eric tightens the grip. Banner's eyes bulge and I tap Eric's arm. He relaxes a bit.

"Where's Creech?" I ask again.

"He's in Cannon Beach looking for your kids. I was

going down to try to stop him. He's out of control, just like everything else. A classic psycho. You should have let me go. I could have gotten close enough to kill him. You won't have a chance. All he wants now is the thrill. Once you stopped him at your ex-wife's place, it got real personal. I believe he's killed other families. Now it's you he wants. And your kids."

Close enough to kill him. Banner never stops throwing curves. "What do you mean 'close enough to kill him'? If you wanted to kill him, why did you try to kill me?"

"Because I couldn't pass up the chance when I saw you on the road. You wouldn't give it up with Craig. When you didn't back off in the face of the threatening notes, the stakes went up. I tried to kill you to save my reputation."

No coincidences. I stand. "Go ahead and break his neck, Eric."

"Wait!" he screams.

I drop back into a squat and grab his face in my hands. "Listen to me, you worthless cocksucker, you've got one more chance," I say, Molly's description of Craig's sexual abuse banging at my brain. "You didn't make a fucking *mistake* with Craig. You tortured him. The mistake you're making is now. All along you've told me what you think I might already know, and made it look good. Only now I know a lot more than you think. You didn't just happen to run into me on the one stretch in four hundred miles with no cars on it. You've been back there all along, waiting for your shot. And you don't give a shit that Creech is out of hand. Now, tell me everything you know, and don't make any more mistakes. Eric's arms are getting tired."

"What guarantee do I have that he won't kill me once I've talked?"

"None," Eric says. "Only guarantee you get is that I will if you don't."

I raise my eyebrows at Banner and shrug.

Banner hesitates.

Eric looks at me in disgust. "Shit, Corder. You boys just gonna sit here an' chitchat all afternoon, or what?"

"I need to know the truth," I say. "I need to know what the danger is."

"The danger's high and you don't need to know shit," Eric says back. "An' you can tell if this asshole's lyin' by whether his mouth is movin'."

"Just one more thing," I say, turning back to Banner. "What about it, Doc? What was supposed to happen in Cannon Beach?"

"I don't know for sure," he says. "Creech is completely out of my control. I came to get rid of you. For a while I thought I had a hold on him, but it's long gone. I think he just wants to get at your ex-wife and your kids. He'll want you there, too. The man has committed some *monstrous* crimes and he's still loose only because he leaves no clues. Once I took care of you, I would have tried to kill him, only because I'm one of the clues he couldn't afford to leave behind. The day I hired him to scare you, I was marked."

"How the fuck crazy are you, Banner? I know what you did to Craig. How crazy are you?"

Eric sighs. He says, "Fifteen seconds."

Banner smiles and I get an *idea* how crazy he is. "I killed John Sheldon."

"You killed Sheldon? Bullshit. I saw John in bed. He killed himself."

"I put the gun in his hand. He talked to me after you caught him at the Parker woman's house. He was terrified and wanted to know what I was going to do to stop you. John's been feeding me information for some time;

I convinced him a while back that scaring you was in both our interests. It was John that left the notes. He wasn't all that bright—pretty easy to convince. When he said he had to come to the police station with you in the morning if I didn't come up with something, I came up with something." Banner smiles again. "I never liked that whiny little coward. You have to admit, the music was a nice touch."

I remember John's CD was playing when we went in.

"That good enough?" he asks. "Need anymore *truth,* Corder?"

"Yeah, Corder," Eric says. "Need any more truth? Or can we get the fuck out of here?"

"One more question. Do you know what Creech has in mind? Do you know how he wants to do it?"

Banner snorts. "Creech doesn't have a mind. If he gets to them before you do, he'll kill them. And you can bet it'll be slow. And remember this: No matter what you and your friend do to me here, my revenge comes when Creech gets to your family. You've made my life hell. At least I have some satisfaction now that the tables are turned." He smiles. "Whatever Creech does, think of it as a card from me."

"Fuck you, Banner," I say, and tap Eric on the arm. "Let's go, man."

"I'm gonna do him first," Eric says. "This guy's scum. He set you up. I'm gonna finish him; it'll look like part of the wreck."

I tighten my fingers on his arm. "Don't do it, Eric. Don't do it. He can't hurt us. We can get the law on him later."

Eric shakes his head. "Guys like this don't get what they have comin'," he says. "Fuckin' law'll let him off. This asshole deserves *way* worse than he'll get. Besides, we don't know how bad he's hurt. He can get up to the highway and get a ride. You may be convinced he's tellin' the truth, but I ain't. He could be plannin' to meet Poke."

"Eric, we can't kill him. Right now, I feel like you do, but if we get through all this and back to Three Forks, I'll have all kinds of ethical and legal considerations. Don't do something that will risk your life with Little E."

He stares at me and his jaw tightens.

"We've been through a lot, Eric. Don't fuck it up now."

"Okay, Counselor, but I ain't havin' this asshole get in my way once we get to Cannon Beach. If we have to take on Poke there, we'll have our hands full."

"He won't get out of here for a while," I say. "He's . . ."

"Goddam right he won't," Eric says, releasing Banner's neck at the same time he clamps his right arm in both enormous hands. With a quick, sickening crunch he brings the arm over his knee, visibly exposing the splintered bone, as Banner's screams echo across the gorge. "Now, let's get goin'."

I crawl over the rocks back up to the highway as fast as I can. At the top, I begin to hyperventilate involuntarily, certain I'll gag. Eric slaps my back, hard. "No time for it, Counselor. Don't dump your cookies here, you're going to need your strength. This was the easy part."

Twenty-two

"That a Jap bike you dumped in the drink?" Eric yells back through hundred-mile-per-hour wind.

I smile. I know what *real* bikers think of Hondas. "Yup," I shout back.

"Hope the warranty's good. Hard to get parts at a reasonable price for them quick little Nipponese mothers."

"And even harder to put 'em in at the bottom of the river." The wind is freezing against my wet skin as we fly through the gorge, soon to cut south for Portland.

"I'd give anything if that bastard wasn't there," I say.

Eric nods. "He's there. That's the most *focused* crazy motherfucker I've ever run into. He *loves* other people's fear. If he's supposed to scare somebody, he scares 'em. If he's supposed to kill somebody, he kills 'em." He pauses and nods again. "In fact, if he's supposed to scare somebody, he usually kills 'em."

We ride a ways further in silence, my clothes dripping dry at fast-forward speed, and my body temperature rising again toward normal. Eric turns partially around on his seat. "I've seen Poke go after guys in the joint," he says. *"Nothin'* stops him."

A shiver shoots through me as I remember him on the night of the fire.

"What's the plan," Eric yells, "when we get there?"

"We'll just go to the house where they usually stay. It's a cabin, really. If they're there, I'll get them packed into Sarah's car and put you up in a motel. Then we'll head south, and I'll call Palmer. He must have the law on the lookout."

"That he does. What if they ain't there?"

Then I'll have to decide whether he's got 'em or not, I think. "I don't know."

As we cross over the Cannon Beach city limit, my heart races, escalating to jackhammer intensity as we glide through town, riding the main street along the edge of the coast toward the house in which I hope to find my innocent and unsuspecting family untouched, or to find the local authorities standing guard. It's dark, well after nine, and I consider directing Eric to the police station first, but the monsters of anxiety in my stomach won't allow it.

The cabin stands nearly half a mile past the southern edge of town, wedged behind several massive breadloaf-style rocks on the beach side and hidden from the main road by tall evergreens.

Eric shuts down the Harley nearly fifty yards from the path leading to the front porch, and we walk through the weeds in the ditch along the side of the road to avoid being caught in the light from the streetlamps. Sarah's car sits in the darkened, tree-covered driveway. I point it out, whispering, "They're here."

Eric nods and pushes forward. The path to the back porch is hidden beneath the trees, and we feel our way silently onto the hardwood walkway running alongside the cabin to the expansive front deck facing the rocks and the ocean. All the windows are dark and as we work our way toward the front, I worry there won't be enough light for us to see inside.

Now we stand silently at the edge of the deck, afraid to move out onto it, should Creech be waiting in the dark of the house. Sparse, glittery reflections from town bounce off the water, splattering hints of light onto the deck, and I poke my head around the corner, peering into the full glass front. Straining to focus, I let my eyes adjust, but at best I see only shadows.

Then, movement. Behind the pine bar dividing the kitchen from the living room, I extend a forearm to stop Eric, who has started to move beside me, squat to my knees and focus. Nothing.

Then a second movement. A giant shadow, sliding cat-like across the back of the kitchen, toward the bedrooms. A smaller shadow moves ahead of it, and I bolt for the side door, but Eric's hand clamps my arm like a vise. "One chance," he whispers. "Don't fuck it up."

I choke back my pounding heart and breathe deep. "He's in there. The fucker's in there with Sarah and the kids."

"You don't know that," Eric whispers. "We don't know who all's in there for sure. If it's them, we sure as hell don't want to spook him." He stops a moment to think and I flash on how the tables have turned. Eric has been dependent on me for close to two years to guide him through tough and unfamiliar emotional terrain, but now he's in charge and we both know it. "Listen, you're not gonna like this," he whispers, his face inches from my ear, "but do it anyway. The key's in the Harley. Push it at least fifty yards, then ride into town and get the cops. I'll stay here. If things get out of hand, I'll take him."

"No," I whisper. "You go. I'll stay."

In a flash Eric grips my collar, pulling me close enough to smell his sweat and tobacco breath. "You listen to me, Counselor, and listen good. We're doin' this my way. You don't have a *clue* how crazy this motherfucker is. I've got a good fifty pounds on you an' you're a pussy. Now, I'm way out on a limb here an' either we do it my way or I throw you through that fuckin' window."

I nod. "Okay, I'll get the cops. We'll come quiet. Tell me where you'll be."

"I'll be right fuckin' here," Eric says, "unless I have reason to move. Now go. If he leaves, I'll follow him. I'll try to leave a trail."

I hate to go but know I have to. "Listen," I say, "if something happens, you know, if something happens to you, is Little E someplace okay?"

Eric grabs my collar again and jerks me to his face. "Shut the fuck up! What the fuck is the matter with you? I don't need to think about that. Just get out of here."

Eric is right and I feel foolish. I wish I could take it back. "Sorry, I . . ."

"Go."

I tiptoe across the walkway and dive into the ditch, crawling twenty-five yards or so through the weeds, then stand and run like the wind for the bike, kicking the transmission into neutral, so I can push it around the first corner before stomping the kick start and flying toward the police station.

Three state patrol cars and two from the county mounties stand in front of the station, and I ease the Harley onto the sidewalk, drop the kickstand, and take the five wooden stairs in two steps.

A city cop stands behind the front desk. "You must be Wilson Corder. Better come on in."

If he knows me, I'm already way behind. He ushers me to a small backroom filled with six state patrolmen, two county sheriffs, and another city cop, all staring at a speaker telephone in the middle of a long wooden table.

The group glances up in unison as I come through the door, and the state patrolman in charge repeats the desk jockey's line: "You must be Wilson Corder."

I nod. "What's going on? Why does everybody know that?"

He motions me to a seat. "I'm afraid we have some bad news," he says. "It seems this Creech fellow is holding your children and your ex-wife."

Oh, Jesus. "Where?"

"We're not sure. As near as we can piece it together, he's hijacked a fishing boat from a charter place here in town. A couple of witnesses saw him take the owner at knifepoint, though no one has actually seen any of your family. He phoned once, and told us to stand by. That was a few hours ago."

I tell them quickly what I saw at the cabin. "I don't think it could be anyone but Creech. My friend Eric is down there alone, and we better get him some help quick. He knows Creech from prison and he says he's off-the-charts dangerous."

The state patrolmen immediately move out, assigning one city cop to wait by the phone. I agree to accompany two state cops and one county cop back to the cabin, and within minutes we are rolling slowly, lights out, to a spot within a hundred yards of the place. Officer Cox, the patrolman in charge, kills the engine and we silently pile out, slide into the ditch, and hurry toward the cabin. In the driveway Sarah's car is missing, and I know instantly we've missed a huge chance to get Creech, unless Eric used it to escape. We split up, surrounding the house, Cox and myself moving to the front deck where I left Eric.

The air explodes out of me. Parked against the inside of the window, inches from my nose, his motorcycle chain tight around his neck and blood running from his

291

nose and ears, is my friend. I gasp and convulse, and Cox pushes me back, looking once, then storming the glass door next to the window. The officers from the other side crash through the back door, and short, loud bursts of instructions fill the room as the lights flash on. Within seconds they are through the empty bedrooms and up into the loft. Nothing. Cox stands beside me as I feel for Eric's pulse.

There is none. I remove the chain and Eric's head falls sickeningly, limply to the side. Dazed, I lay him down as Cox's hand grips firmly under my arm. "Nothing you can do," he says, lifting me. "We need to move fast."

In seconds we are sprinting again toward the car. Cox jerks his door open to the sound of his police radio. ". . . to 2150. Base to 2150. We have phone contact with Creech. Better get back here. Base to 2150 . . ."

"Roger," Cox says into his mouthpiece. "We are on our way," and our tires spin on the pavement.

"Had him on the box," says Peterson, the county cop, as we walk through the door. "Says he won't talk on the radio because of the Coast Guard monitor. He's got one of those cellular phones on board. Claims to have Mrs. Corder and both kids and says he'll call us later to let the captain confirm that. Says nobody's been hurt yet, that he'll be back in touch. Not to call him, he'll call us." Peterson nods to the phone. "We've got Detective Palmer from Three Forks on the other line if you want to talk to him."

Cox hits the button muting the speaker and lifts the handset, introducing himself to Palmer, then listens to what I assume is the rundown on Creech. Cox is short with his responses, thanks Palmer, and hands me the phone. "Hi, Detective. This is Wilson."

"You holding up okay?" His concern travels over the line as if he were in the room with me.

"No. I'm not. Creech killed Eric. Strangled him."

Silence. Then, "I'm sorry. I wish I were there. . . . We could have done better coordinating efforts. . . ."

Twin beeps indicate another call coming in. "Gotta cut you," I say. "I'll put you on hold." Before he can respond I switch lines and access the speaker.

"This is Ed Carsey," a voice says. "This here's my ship. Got a fellow here name of Creech. Says folks call him Poke. He's got a woman and two kids with him that he took from a house in town. Says he means to kill 'em and to tell the truth, I believe him. Says I got nothin' to worry about, but . . ." There is a slight commotion, then, "Says I got nothin' to worry about. I'm here to tell you that so far, everyone's still okay—at least nobody's hurt. The man's a goddam giant, and he's got a long huntin' knife. From here on you'll be talkin' to him."

I drop my head to the table, face down on my arms. Creech is telling them they're going to die, I know he is. Trevor must be so scared he's frozen. I'd do anything to stop this.

My thoughts are blasted back to reality by Creech's voice, deep and almost amiable. "How y'all folks doin'? This here's Charlie Creech. My friends call me Charlie. You can call me Poke." I gaze around the table, but no one will return my stare, all remaining transfixed by the box in the center of the table. "I don't usually do my dirty work this public," the voice drawls on, "but then usually I don't get sniffed out, either. Y'all caught me this time though, ain't it hell. This'll be a new experience for all of us."

Officer Cox leans toward the speaker. "Look, Creech, what do you want? Maybe we can work something out."

"What makes y'all think I want anything? Hell, I got most of what I want right here."

"If you didn't want anything," Cox says, "you wouldn't be talking to us."

"You're right smart, for an officer of the law," Creech says. "Right smart. Must be state. Ain't no local."

"I'm state," Cox replies. He looks like the state patrol poster boy, six feet, a hundred ninety pounds. Rock hard.

There is a short pause. "What I want is these children's daddy down here."

I start to answer, but Cox's hand shoots up as he shakes his head violently.

"Kids shouldn't be out this late at night without their daddy," Creech continues. "Now I know you're probably hooked up with the law in Three Forks, so you tell them to go over to ole Wilson Corder's bitch's house an' tell him to crawl on off her an' get down here fast as he can. I figure about an hour by plane to Portland, then another hour down here, depending on what you guys can rig up. So in two hours I want to hear that sweet-talkin' counselor's voice floatin' over the telephone waves to my cruise ship. How's that for starters?"

"That sounds doable," Cox says. "Might need a *little* more time than that, though. Got to get him to a plane. Can you give us two and a half?"

"Feelin' right charitable on this end," Creech says. "Two and a half hours it is. Now I'm gonna sign off for a while, but I got a few conditions to lay down, you know, so if I decide to take a little nap, I can sleep good."

Cox says, "Go."

"Well, first off, if any y'all decide to come out here for a closer look, there'll be some serious bloodshed, starting with the ex-Mrs. here. I don't wanna see no motorboats, no canoes, no rowboats. Hell, I don't care if it's

294

a fuckin' ark, anything comes close an' June Cleaver gets it. Right in front of the Beav and Nancy Drew."

"Poke," Cox says, "we can keep most anything away from there tonight, but when the sun comes up . . ."

"When the sun comes up, this'll all be history," Creech says.

Cox doesn't answer.

"Furthermore," Creech continues, "along the lines of conditions. I don't wanna see no low-flyin' planes or whirlybirds, an' I don't wanna see no funny bubbles comin' up under me. When Father Knows Best gets down here, you ring me up, and we'll go from there. He'll have to try somethin'. I seen him jump into that fire to get his kid. Shouldn'ta fucked with me. 'Fore this is over, he'll wish he'da let him burn. Now I'm gonna hang up for a while, 'cause I'm startin' to feel like somebody's secretary or somethin'."

"Okay," Cox says, "we'll play it by your book. No tricks."

"That's bullshit, Officer. We both know that. You got to try somethin'. You already did. You think I didn't see you bozos lookin' all over town for these people all day— back an' forth like a buncha decapitated chickens? You couldn't find 'em 'cause I already had 'em tucked away, nice and safe. You'll try somethin' because you know there'll be a big ol' red spot right here on the ocean come sunrise. I'm just tellin' you what I'm gonna do when you try. This ain't some two-bit psycho talkin' to ya. This here's a million-dollar psycho." He laughs. "Oh, yeah, and by the way, if you mosey on over to these nice folks' place, you'll see I left you a present."

"We'll go look," Cox says.

There is a click, and we're left staring at the phone. The door from the front office opens and the Cannon Beach night cop sticks his head in. "Detective Palmer says he's got some psychologist with him who wants to talk."

Cox pushes the button and the speakerphone crackles. "Go ahead, Palmer," he says. "This is Officer Cox. We're all right here."

"I have Dr. Frazier here with me," Palmer says. "He's our resident psycho specialist and he wants to tell you a few things about dealing with Creech."

Cox says, "Shoot."

"Officer Cox, Dr. Frazier here. I know you people are real busy, so I'll make this short. I won't go into any history, but there are a couple of important things you need to know about this Creech."

"Okay."

"One, don't *ever* show weakness. You beg, or show terror, he's like a man about to climax and he'll push it all the way."

"Got it," Cox says.

"Don't lie to him about intentions, or facts you aren't ninety-nine percent sure he *can't* already know about. And don't patronize him. If he gets the idea you think you can outsmart him, he'll likely as not go into a rage. These guys have radar." Frazier is quiet a moment. "Do you have any questions of me?"

Cox shakes his head and looks around the table. "Anybody got any questions?"

"Dr. Frazier," I say, "this is Wilson Corder. Detective Palmer probably told you that's my family out there."

"Yes, Mr. Corder, I'm sorry . . ."

"Yeah, so am I. Listen. Creech seems to think I'm still up in Three Forks. He gave us a few hours to get me down here. There was another guy with me, and Creech killed him over at the house. Do you think we need to tell Creech I'm already here? Will he make the connection between Eric and me?"

"Is there any way he'd know the two of you are connected?"

"Well, this guy spent some time in prison with him, and it's possible, though not probable, that Creech could have seen him at the mental health center. I don't think he could know Eric was seeing me, but he knows I work at the center. I also don't know if he recognized Eric when he killed him. It was pretty dark."

Frazier is quiet, and for a moment the line sounds dead. Then, "It's a guess, but I think if he made that connection he wouldn't have given you the time. Most likely he wants you down there to be part of the terror, and if he thought you were there already, he'd have said so. I'd let it ride. But I'll tell you this, he'll be thinking about why Eric showed up so it may come up."

"If it does?"

"It's a judgment call, but try to determine how certain Creech sounds. If he's guessing, stay with your original story. That's the kind of lie he can't be certain about. He's seeing all the terror here as a feast and he won't want to cheat himself out of any of it. I know it sounds cruel for me to say that, Corder, but—"

"Forget it." *Jesus. A feast.* If I let half the truth into my brain right now, my head will explode. God, what must these people be thinking as they stare across the table at me?

"One more thing for any of you who have to deal directly with Creech," Frazier says. "He's as good at telling lies as he is at sniffing out yours. Take *nothing* at face value. If there were Ph.D.s in deception, this man would be passing them out." There is another short silence. "If no one has any further questions of me, I'll turn this over to Detective Palmer."

Cox peers around the table. "No questions," he says. "But I'd appreciate it if you'd stay on board."

297

"Will do," Frazier says.

Detective Palmer is back on the line. "Anything else we can do from this end?"

"Nothing I can think of," Cox answers. "We've got the Coast Guard on alert and I think they'll be able to keep any craft out of the area. I'm in contact with a S.W.A.T. team out of Portland, though I don't know what they can do. Creech can see all four directions. We have sight of him; looks to be a little less than two miles out. He hasn't bothered to black himself out. There's a bit of a moon, enough that he could make out anything we could send."

Palmer hesitates. "Has there been any contact with the hostages? Either Sarah or the kids?"

"Negative," Cox says. "The captain told us about a half hour ago everyone was okay. That's the last we've heard." He glances uneasily at me. "Do you make anything of that?"

Palmer hesitates again. "No. I'd believe that until I heard otherwise. Wilson, are you there?"

"Yeah, I'm here."

"I'm really sorry, man. I know how you must be feeling . . ."

I can't imagine that he does, but I say thanks.

Helplessness covers the table like a wet wool shroud. I ask what's next.

"The Coast Guard is trying to figure a way to get close, maybe send some divers," Cox says. "I'm waiting for a plan from headquarters, or possibly Portland. There's not much we can do but wait to see if he'll deal."

I rise and walk out of the building onto the nearly deserted street, staring up at the open sky. The moon is slightly less than a quarter on the horizon. It will be gone soon and the sky will explode with stars. I ask them for an answer, and my mind flashes involuntarily back to my lifeguard days.

The only drowning happened when I wasn't there.

I walk back inside to the sound of Creech's chilling voice. "This here'll more'n likely be my last family," he is saying, "so I wanna do 'er right. You tell Corder when he comes I'm savin' the boy for last." He waits. "You there, Cox? You listenin'?"

Cox says, "We're listening."

"You tell him, hear?"

"When he gets here," Cox says evenly, "we'll tell him everything that's been said."

"Yeah, well, tell him I'm savin' the boy till last," he says again. "He's a scared little shit, oughta be able to work him up into a gen-u-ine frenzy, time I'm done with his momma and his big sister. Hey, she's a morsel, huh? Might hafta go *real* slow with her."

Cox punches the button, muting the speaker, and picks up the handset, waving me out of the room. I motion him to cover the mouthpiece, staring directly into his eyes. "I'm going out there."

He shakes his head, and in a few sentences finishes up with Creech. Then, "I'm sorry, Mr. Corder. I can't allow you to do that. He'd see any craft before it got within four hundred yards. That boat has a floodlight that's good up to several hundred yards anyway."

"I'm not going in a boat. I'm going to swim."

Cox stares.

"Look," I say. "The boat is lighted—we can see it from here, for Christ's sake. It's less than two miles . . ."

"You can swim two miles? And what are you going to do when you get there?"

"I'm going to kill the son-of-a-bitch. Look, I was a distance swimmer, a good one. Two miles isn't even a good midseason workout. I've swum open water before. Not much, but some. I can get there."

"I can't let you go out there. Do you know what the temperature of that water is?"

"It's cold. But I've been in colder."

"For how long?" Cox asks. "This hasn't been a warm summer along the coast, and the water doesn't warm up much anyway. It's bite-ass cold. You'd more than likely get hypothermia and die. Then what good are you to your family?"

I lean across the table. "What the fuck good am I to my family sitting in this room listening to that bastard get ready to murder them?"

Cox sets his jaw. "I'm sorry, Corder, I can't authorize it. We have people working on this at several levels. A plan could come in at any time."

I stand. "I'm not asking you to authorize it, Cox. I'm telling you what I'm going to do. The reality is my ex-wife and kids have about a one-in-a-hundred chance of getting out of this alive. You're not going to come up with a better plan. He can see anything that comes close."

"I'm sorry, Mr. Corder. I'll have to stop you if you try. You're a civilian and I can't allow you to get in the way of a police operation. There's too much at stake. If you insist, I'll have to arrest you. I know you're distraught . . ."

I close my eyes, pinching my nose, then move slowly around the table, near another of the officers, who places a friendly hand on my shoulder. As he does, my hand whips to his hammer strap and I unsnap his holster, pulling his revolver and pushing him away. "You'll have to shoot me," I say quietly to Cox. "Now, you guys go ahead and plan whatever you're planning. Pretend you don't even know I'm out there. I won't tell your superiors, if I'm alive to tell anyone anything. I'd appreciate you keep-

ing it off the airwaves, though. Creech's gotta be moni-
toring the Coast Guard."

"Corder, you can get in a lot of trouble for this . . ."

"There is no more trouble than I'm already in," I say.
"That's the beauty of it. Neither Creech or I have anything to lose now. That cocksucker has brought me to
his level."

"There are people who can help us," Cox pleads.
"Don't do this. You could be ruining the only chance
your family has."

But I'm already backing out of the room. In two hours
or so, Creech will be a lot harder to appease. He'll be
hollering for my head. I need to get my head out there
before that. "I think you know this plan is the only one
that has a chance. I understand you have to try to stop
me, but do me a favor and don't try too hard. I have one
request. If Creech starts telling you to deliver me to
watch his stage show before I get out there, tell him I'm
here and on my way. Keep him occupied as long as you
can. If I can find a way to keep this gun dry, I'll shoot
him when I get there."

Cox visibly softens. "Look," he says, "if I can't stop
you, at least let *me* find something to keep it dry. If
you're going anyway . . ."

But I can't trust him. "I'll find something." I back out
of the building. Outside I jump onto Eric's Harley and
roar out of town in the opposite direction of the cabin,
heading north long enough to be certain the cops are not
going to follow, then cut over to a back road toward the
cabin.

I leave the cabin lights out and feel my way frantically
through the kitchen, looking for something waterproof
to wrap the revolver in. Finding nothing, I scout the remainder of the rooms, carefully avoiding that corner of
the living room by the window, where Eric's body still

lies, staring blankly out onto the ocean. I believe for a moment I've struck paydirt on the back porch when I find the bottom portion of a dry wetsuit, thinking I can wear it—keeping myself warm and the gun dry—but upon closer inspection, discover it is a children's size. With scissors from the bathroom, I cut out a large rectangular piece from the leg and wrap the gun in it, tying it off with heavy twine from the kitchen junk drawer. Then I empty a garbage can and remove the Hefty bag, place the gun inside it, wrapping it around several times before tying it off. It's the best I can do.

On the beach I step out of my clothes and tie the packaged gun to my belt with the twine, then slip it over my head. In open water, with nothing to guide me but the pinpoint light of the boat, which I'll have to stop swimming to see each time, it will likely take me the better part of an hour and a half to get to them. By then, Creech will be getting restless.

My ankles immediately throb as I step into the water, reminding me of cold water swims past, and I try not to think about what will soon happen to my nuts. As I dive forward, my head screams in pain and I begin to stroke, placing Trevor's face in front of my eyes; a face filled with terror at what he will be forced to watch if I don't get there. If I can get past the first few minutes, my body will begin to numb and the swimming will be easier.

I develop a cadence of fifty strokes between orientation stops. My stroke feels strong. Winds are down and the water is fairly calm, and after about fifteen minutes, though distance over water is nearly impossible to gauge, I'm sure the lights of the boat are getting closer. I cling to my pictures of the horror Creech wants to create, and the strength of my stroke increases with my resolve. Things are different now; we're *both* in a killing mood. The stakes are up; we are all swimming in the deep end.

The wetsuit material buoys the gun, and though it bangs against my shoulder blades, it rides fairly comfortably.

At what seems like the halfway point, my arms begin to lose power. The numbing sinks deeper into my shoulders and upper arms, and my stroke is harder to hold. I pick up the pace, hoping to warm myself from inside, but feel myself slowing. I have never experienced hypothermia, but it gets *bad* press, and I hope to God I won't experience it now.

I see lights. Not of the fishing boat, but inside my head, the kind that normally flash from a blow to the head. I focus on the kids, on Emily driving to the hoop, and Trevor sneaking into my bed on a scary night. *Please* don't let them exist only in history. When those things begin to run together and I can't tell whether I'm thinking or dreaming, I switch to songs. I start with popular songs, Paul Simon and Tom Petty, then slip into the old rock 'n' roll of Del Shannon singing "Runaway" and Roy Orbison doing "Oh Pretty Woman," but what I finally settle on is "Little Ducky Duddle" from kindergarten. If it works . . .

I'm close now. It seems quicker than I had anticipated, though that could be part of my disorientation. I see the outline of the boat now, rather than merely the lights, and I stop to tread water, and think. I'm almost close enough to see into the cabin and imagine three heads there, but I'm pretty sure it's just that: imagination. There is no room for mistakes. I breast-stroke closer, my eyes glued to the boat, remembering what Cox said about the searchlight, ready to dive at any time should Creech decide to scan the waters. Moving even closer, I see motion inside the cabin. My eyes burn from the salt, and huge fuzzy rainbows circle each light, but I can definitely make out more than one person there. Creech hasn't yet gone completely mad.

I'm only twenty yards away when the searchlight starts its first sweep. I bring my hands up over my head, pushing down, holding myself under, staring up as the diffused light passes over me—I hope to God I'm deep enough—and kick slowly to the surface when it has passed. The beam doesn't sweep back my way, so I'm pretty sure he didn't see me, and I breast-stroke to a position at the back of the boat, where a fixed metal ladder hangs to the water.

From here on, every decision has to be the right one. Silently I slip the belt over my head and untie the garbage bag, reaching in to extract the wetsuit material, and hoping to God I wrapped the gun tightly enough to keep it dry. The wetsuit material seems damp throughout, but I can't be certain because my hands are wet, and too goddam cold to feel. *Cops go out in the rain,* I reason. I have to believe it'll shoot.

I need the best possible shot at Creech; I'm not a marksman. I'll wait until he's away from them, maybe takes another sweep with the searchlight. My breathing slows, and I listen. There are voices, but I can't make them out, though twice I believe I hear Trevor pleading, "Please, mister!" and I remember what Frazier, the psychologist, said about Creech smelling out fear.

Don't crank this guy up, Trevor, I think *Please don't.*

Now that I'm not moving, the aching returns to my shoulders and head, which are out of the water. I want to move up the ladder, but I don't know the layout of the boat. I *have* to have some advantage when the action starts.

A subtle shivering starts deep in me, and I know if I don't act, it will become uncontrollable; it won't matter whether or not the gun will fire. I float away from the ladder, holding the gun in the air, and kick eggbeater style to keep myself afloat, hoping the output of energy will warm me, listening for any indication that Creech has come out of the cabin. I need him far enough from my family for one clean shot.

Something bumps against my back and I gasp, whirling. A dark form floats beside me and I instinctively drop my mouth underwater to stifle my cry. The form doesn't move, only bounces gently against me, and I reach to touch it, still holding the gun aloft, kicking hard. I touch what feels like hair, and when I lift it a face appears, eyes rolled back. The body below doesn't move with the head. Panicky convulsions grip my stomach, and a rolling flood of nausea courses through me. I drop the head, slit at the throat, forcing my face back into the water to silently gag. For fifteen to twenty seconds I vomit, bobbing my head to take in air, forcing it down again to release in silence.

I know this must be the ship's captain, and that I must act quickly because I don't know what else Creech has done. I kick back toward the boat, aware the pistol was fully immersed for some time in that exchange. I'm suddenly in a rage at Cox and the rest of the lawmen back in Cannon Beach. Those fuckers could have helped me. This *was* the best plan, the only plan.

Back at the ladder, I take several deep silent breaths and pull myself up, careful not to rock the boat any more than necessary. I picture myself again and again, squeezing the trigger. Drawing the bead . . . squeezing the trigger. I can do it. All I need is a good shot.

I peer carefully over the back of the boat. The windows all face forward and light reflects out onto the deck at an angle. I move carefully toward it, stopping suddenly when I hear voices, clear this time: "Please mister. *Please.* Let me stay with my mom. I don't want to go out there. You'll hurt me."

"Aaah, whaddaya 'fraid of, Buckaroo? I just wanna

take a look-see if they're sendin' the cavalry yet. Kinda like to have an audience when the show starts."

"Please," Trevor pleads. "Just let me stay with my mom." His voice trails to sobs.

"Git up, you little chickenshit baby," Creech yells and in the next second is out the side door, a handful of Trevor's hair in one hand, the searchlight in the other. He drags Trevor, sobbing, to the bow of the boat and flashes the light onto the water.

I draw my bead. Creech is partially obscured by the cabin. Doubts of the gun firing, and of my marksmanship, crowd into my brain, nearly paralyzing me, but Trevor's continued sobbing holds me steady. I step out from the cabin, finally catching Creech's full form, backlighted by the searchlight. In front of him, Trevor is totally obscured. *What if the bullet goes through Creech?* Creech guides the searchlight slowly, sweeping a full hundred and eighty degrees in front of him. He'll be coming to the back soon. It's now or never.

I cock the hammer slowly, aiming directly at the back of his head, and squeeze the trigger.

Click!

Creech whirls, bellowing. I storm him as he drops the light, smashing into him at the same moment I see the flash of a blade. I crash into him chest high, forcing him off balance against the rail, then grasp for a handful of hair, catapulting myself over the edge. Creech's head snaps back and his huge body follows me, dragging Trevor with him.

The water boils in chaos; Creech releases everything, flailing like a drowning man, while Trevor erupts with a high, continuous, piercing screech. Creech sucks deep, uneven breaths as the cold water assaults him. For a brief second, he grips my arm, but I relax, then jerk back hard, pulling it free. I kick away, swimming toward Trevor's voice, realize suddenly he probably doesn't know it's me. I find him, grip his shoulders, and shake him hard. "Trevor, stop it! Stop it! It's me. It's your dad."

"Dad!" he screams. "Dad!"

I glance behind us to see Creech's head still above water. "Swim to the boat!" I yell to Trevor. "The ladder is at the back. If your mom knows how to start it, tell her to move away from us. I can swim to you. Tell her I want her to get far enough away that Creech can't get back. I'll be there in a minute." I'm kicking us away from Creech as I talk, aware he's lunging toward us, like any drowning man would. Trevor's a good swimmer, I know he can do it; it isn't fifteen yards to the boat. I grip his shoulders- tighter. "Trevor, the captain's body is in the water. If you run into it, just keep swimming. Don't look."

"Okay, Dad."

I feel a vise on my shoulder, and I push Trevor toward the boat. "Swim! Tell Mom to get the boat away!"

My head is forced underwater and I feel a sharp hot pain in my left shoulder blade, but I push myself even farther down, knowing from years of lifeguard training that a drowning man will always fight for the surface.

I kick down and away, trying to use my arms to power me, but my left arm is useless. I surface and Creech is on me, flailing, and once again I glimpse the knife, realizing instantly what the pain in my shoulder blade is. I kick harder, distancing us from the boat. If he's panicked or enraged enough, he has to keep coming after me. He continues lunging as I kick out of reach, dragging my left arm, compensating with my right. I am vaguely aware of voices yelling from the boat, and turn to scream to Sarah to get away from us, when suddenly Creech's splashing stops and the shadow of his head disappears below the surface. I wait. I must be absolutely certain he's drowned.

Shit, if I could only *see*. Kicking slowly backward, I have no bearings and have to scan for the boat, at the same time squinting about me for signs of movement in the dark water. Then I hear Sarah kick over the engine, helping to orient me. Viselike fingers clamp onto my ankle, dragging me down, then Creech's face is in mine, then the knife. I roll and tuck, kicking hard into his stomach. His grip loosens as I frantically kick away.

I hear him laugh. *Take nothing at face value . . . a Ph.D. in deception*. His drowning was a lie.

I kick back, holding my distance. So the fucker can swim. But no way can he match me—too much of his life has been spent far from swimming pools, *that* I can be sure of. Now, hearing the engine turn over again, I kick farther from the boat. Let Creech keep coming after me, but keep him away from them. He lunges twice more, but the water is a great equalizer and even with the loss of my left arm, I can stay free of him. *As long as I know where he is*.

But as I think it, he is gone. Knowing I can kick faster than he can swim underwater, I work my legs hard. He can't have great breath control; he'll have to surface quickly. I can keep him at bay all night if I have to.

Creech surfaces more than ten yards away, and it takes me only a split second to know he's headed back for the boat. I change direction and sprint back for him, using a one-armed version of the crawl. If I can't keep him in the water, we're all dead. He hears my splash and spins as I pull back, treading with my legs. His voice is deep and gravelly—all cowboy affectation gone. "You'll watch their heads bob," he says, and clamps the knife between his teeth, resuming his grotesque dog paddle toward the boat. I lunge for his foot, taking a hard kick to my jaw, and lights explode in my head.

Surfacing, I scream to Sarah. "He's coming! Sarah, he's coming! He has to get up the ladder! Get something big! Sarah! Hit him! Emily!" But I hear only the sound of the starter grinding the engine.

Creech reaches the ladder a split second ahead of me, and grips the bottom rung, pulling himself up. He has to be tired. Some of that monstrous strength *has* to be gone. If I can *just keep him in the water. . .* I catch the back of his belt and pull myself hard toward him as he starts up the ladder. He swings back to knock me off, hammering my temple once, then again, but I hold my grip. He stops swinging to renew his grip on the rung, and I lock my forearm around his throat, plant my feet on the side of the boat, and push with all my remaining strength. His fingers give way, and we tumble back into the water.

The engine still grinds, but above it I hear Emily. "Daddy! Daddy! Is that you? Is that you?" All my strength is locked in this death struggle. If I were to yell back, I'd drown on the spot. "Daddy! Daddy!" she yells into the night.

A bright light flashes across us, which must be Emily with the searchlight, but I can't think whether the dark is to my advantage or Creech's. I hold my one-arm lock on his throat as he flails back at me with that enormous hunting knife. He has missed me twice, but my luck can't last. Suddenly my grip is gone, my hand falling limp as the blade sinks into my forearm. He whirls and is on me. I hear three loud *cracks!* and see the flash of his blade. I wait to die. I blew it. My family is dead.

But Creech falls away. His blade does not find me. Three more *cracks!* ring out and Creech flounders like a harpooned seal.

"Hang on, Corder! Hang on! Don't move!" *Cox.*

Though my arms are useless, my legs whip to keep my head above water, and within seconds Creech sinks from sight and men are in the water beside me, easing me up the ladder and into the boat. I lie helpless while two men work frantically on my wounds and Sarah rushes to cover my naked body with a blanket. My eyes begin to close and I feel myself drift, but the blurry sight of Trevor and Emily snaps me back.

"Dad!" Trevor screams. "Dad! Look, Em! He's okay! Dad!"

I gaze into their faces as they kneel toward me, reaching, and almost manage a smile as one of the paramedics lifts Trevor gently back by the shoulders, telling him he needs a little room, that I'll be fine.

Epilogue

Molly's long leg drapes over mine as she props her head on one elbow, lightly tracing her fingernail over the numerous scars zigzagging across my body from what she calls the time I was "up with Creech without a paddle." Molly's a real wordsmith. "No wonder he called himself Poke," she is saying. "Look at all what he did to you." She follows a long scar down my back.

"Can't count that one," I say. "That's from the glass in Trevor's window."

"Well, you sure wouldn't have jumped through Trevor's window if it weren't for Creech."

I nod. "That's true. You can count on it."

"Jesus," she says. "If they hadn't shot him dead in the water, I'd have clawed his eyes out with my bare hands. This is the first time in eight weeks I've been able to fuck you without worrying which wound I'm going to rake. I *hate* staying conscious when we make love. From now on, if someone's going to be making slashes in you, it better be me."

I agree with Molly completely and start to roll over on my side.

"Oh no you don't, Mr. I-Can-Bag-My-Limit-of-Salt-

311

Water-Psychos-but-Die-After-One-Roll-in-the-Hay. You owe me."

"Only fooling," I say, and roll back with a smile. Molly's rock-hard body glistens with sweat, her dark hair plastered to her forehead, her eyes fiery. With my tongue I trace a shallow stream of perspiration from her neck between her breasts to her belly, and lightly run my fingers up her thigh.

A loud *bang* sends me flying back, sitting straight up.

In the bedroom doorway, his blanket clutched in one hand and a soft yellow Ducky Duddle in the other, stands a nearly three-year-old boy. He looks at Molly, uncovered to the waist, then back at me.

I shrug. "Parenthood."

It's over, and the psychological wounds are going the way of my physical scars, hardening over from the healing effects of time and care. Life goes on.

Emily called into Cannon Beach on the cellular phone the second Creech and Trevor and I hit the water, and in one act saved us that night, that was it. Both my kids still have horrific nightmares, but they are waning after more than two months, and Sarah and I have vowed to shitcan any and all petty conflicts; we are so incredibly grateful to have our lives and the lives of our children. Maybe every good divorce needs a psychopathic madman to cement perspectives.

The rest of the puzzle pieces have fallen together, mostly with the help of Dr. Banner, who lay on the rock beside the river until late the next morning, when the Highway Patrol picked him up, nearly dead. He did kill John Sheldon, and he did set Creech on my trail. He's been in this since an accidental conversation with John Sheldon at their health club shortly after my first session with Craig Clark, where he understood that both could benefit from my being gone. To John's credit, big a jerk as he was, he had no idea of the gravity of things until it was far, far too late. Once Banner knew of John's affair with Peggy Parker, he had him by the short ones. I don't think John ever knew Banner had intentionally scalded his stepson, and certainly not that he had been molesting him.

I'm not sure who killed my cat—timing says it had to be Sheldon, but I can't picture that—so I'll just have to live with it, and I still don't know who Jerry saw in Whitman Park that day, but I'm guessing it was Creech. No wonder Jerry ran like hell.

Under any circumstances, Banner's away for a long time.

And Marvin Edwards is away for even longer. Jerry was articulate and fearless in court, and that, combined with the mountain of evidence his play therapy produced, convinced the jury that Marvin Edwards indeed killed Sabrina Parker. They didn't get him on Cindy Miller's death, but, given his sentence, the judge must have taken her into consideration.

That is happy news for court cases to come. Evidence coming out of play therapy has consistently been considered hearsay in Superior Court and therefore disallowed, and four-year-old witnesses have traditionally been discounted as unreliable, or have fallen apart in the face of their tormentors. Maybe the country is ready to get serious about protecting the helpless.

"What's the matter, Little E? My one-night stand making too much noise?"

313

"Nosy," he says.

"Noisy it is," I say. "It is very noisy. Molly is a very noisy lady."

"Scared."

I look over at Molly, who is smiling. "Me, too," I say. "Wanna hop in here?"

Little E nods big. "Yup."

He's mine now, though I'll never change his name. His dad went through far too much to have his son gobbled up again by the foster care system, only to be spit out into juvenile justice twelve years later and state prison four years after that. It doesn't always happen that way, but I'm cutting Little E's risk to a minimum. It won't be easy; Little E was all Eric's. But his dad took the ultimate risk for me, and I'll give his son a life or die trying.

I'll tell Little E about Eric as he gets older. I'll tell him how his dad nearly shook him senseless when E was a baby because he couldn't control his rage and because no one ever taught him anything different. And I'll tell him of his father's tremendous courage, attending groups three nights a week, heroically facing up to his heinous crime against his baby each and every time a new member joined us. I'll tell Little E how his father turned his back on his own history to make a different history for his son, how in the toughest of times, Eric stood strong and tall. I'll tell him about his dad's Harley, which is in the garage waiting for him, and I'll tell him about his dad's tattoos. I'll tell Little E how his father loved his son.

And sure, I'll tell him about his father's lesser heroics, too. How he helped save my life on a dark night on the Oregon coast, faced down a man he knew to be too monstrous for words, simply to help a friend he thought had

314

helped him. I'll raise Little E to be a fine, strong man, hugely proud of every gene in his bloodstream; and I will gaze into his eyes each and every day of my life in search of his father.